Katie *of* Malheur Oregon Country

'Lewis, Amanda, and Arthur Rinehart, circa 1890

Katie of Malheur Oregon Country

Stone House, 1872

A Historical Inspirational Fiction

Marjorie Vaughn Eldred

A Historical Inspirational
Fiction

Golden Valley Gems
6403 241st Avenue East
Buckley, WA 98321

ISBN: 978-0-9849859-6-8

Printed in the United States of America

Table of Contents

Acknowledgments

First of all I want to thank Linda Boulanger of Tell-Tale Books who created the expressive cover of *Katie of Malheur Oregon Country.* I shared with her only that I wanted Katie, Midnight, Stone House and Rinehart Buttes pictured on the cover.

Linda demonstrated great patience and grace during the whole process. I My husband Clio and I viewed her original wonderful concept and fell in love with it. We suggested minor changes, she worked her magic, and what you see is the result.

The second person I want to thank is my husband. Writer's block is a very real phenomenon, and about half way through this book I experienced the granddaddy of all those unwelcome aberrations. Clio shared ideas and constantly encouraged, wanting to hear every word I wrote. I couldn't have finished the book without him. I also thank him for his patience during the many hours I spent in the creation of Katie's story.

Stone House gave Vale, Malheur County Oregon its first name. When I learned that fact and began to research the house's history I discovered the Rineharts who built it. Sometime during all this research I became inspired. Katie of Malheur Oregon Country is the result.

My curiosity about the Indian Wars and Indian customs in Malheur County and Oregon State led me to many sites on the Internet, as did my search for the facts about the Malheur Indian Reservation and the agents who served there. My thanks to the gatherers of the information which proved so helpful to me..

Much of the knowledge I used in *Katie of Malheur Oregon Country* came from the wonderful book by Jacob Ray Gregg, *Pioneer Days in Malheur*

County published in 1950. I was in the 7th or 8th grade that year in Vale.

I found the book on Amazon, and, because of the price, expected it to be a huge book such as those published by historical societies all over the country. I paid over $85.00 for it, and when it arrived in my mailbox I was shocked by its small 6x9 inch size. My disappointment disappeared when I started reading. I found the book loaded with all kinds of early first-hand information, and also maps which I studied and used over and over. Thank you, Jacob Ray Gregg for filling my mind with so much inspiration.

Gary Fugate, director of Stone House Museum answered many of my questions and graciously sent me maps which helped me to envision the location of the Malheur Reservation.

Ed Bryant of Advanced Digital Solutions willingly rescued me from many stubborn computer occasions which slowed my work. His patience and competence amaze me.

My Facebook friends helped and encouraged me in so many ways.

Thank you, Dear Reader, for your patience while I completed my manuscript and for following through with your desire to read Katie of Malheur Oregon Country.

Chapter 1: Home at Tule Lake

1872

Eleven year old Katie Erickson loved her home, the lake nearby, and the wildlife she saw daily. In early spring she looked forward to watching the arrival of the birds that called Tule Lake in Northern California their summer home; Canada Geese, primarily. Moments they shared expanded her well-being and love of life.

All spring and summer Katie enjoyed the warm blanket of brown feathers that covered the usual blue of Tule Lake. Spring was Katie's favorite time of year; the geese raised their young then. They built nests in the marshy wetlands along the lake; the mothers roosted patiently on their nests keeping the eggs warm. The fathers guarded from their places nearby.

Katie loved roaming the swamps and looking for the nests with the white eggs, sometimes as many as twenty. The nest often rested on a small mound of dirt near the water. Once she found it, she haunted the location and watched the parents in their nesting mode. She delighted in the first-hatched goslings, yellow-brown and fluffy. Sometimes she spied on the goose parents as they led the goslings in their first trip to the water; mother up front, chicks following, and father guarding from behind. It's a train of love, Katie thought, like my parents protect me.

Katie's favorite memory of her father formed several years ago in June. Katie and he rode across the homestead, and ahead on the range they saw a herd of pronghorn antelope.

Katie knew the sight of them wouldn't usually detract Daddy from his business, but this time was different.

"The herd is frightened. Look at the white hair on their backs, how it's standing straight up. I'd better check it out," he said, and pulled his reins to the right, guiding his horse to approach the herd. "Katie, you stay here. They're wild animals; you can't be sure what they'll do."

Katie watched as her dad walked toward the herd, stopping occasionally to pull a plant from the ground. The wary animals moved away, except for a male protector and a fawn lying on the ground. Katie watched her father creep toward them, holding both hands toward the animals. The fawn appeared to be hurt. Maybe it's stepped into a badger hole and broken its leg, Katie thought.

She watched her dad inch nearer to the male antelope and extend his hand, holding the plants toward its nose. The antelope tossed his antlers and pawed the ground. Her dad stopped and stood for several minutes, murmuring to the animal until it quieted and nuzzled the plants he offered. He laid them on the ground and. moved toward the fawn, bent over it and inspected its legs. She saw her dad lift the fawn in his arms and retrace his steps. The male antelope followed him.

They put a splint on the fawn's leg, nursed it for several weeks in the barn at home, fed it grass and plants from the field, and even sagebrush. Katie, amazed at the fondness the fawn had for the pungent brush, covered her nose when she fed it to the animal.

The baby grew into a youngster; horns began to form above its huge eyes, and its coat changed color until her dad told them he knew it was a male. They named the pronghorn fawn Stumble.

One day when Katie was playing with Stumble in the yard, he gazed at her for a long moment, turned back toward the field, and trotted away.

Katie felt both sad and happy. *He must be well now. Our family helped Stumble get well enough to go home. I'll miss him.*

Katie's father, Clifton Erickson, had purchased this acreage not too far from the Lava Beds to the south several years ago. The rich volcanic soil, black and red, grew bountiful crops of grain and wild grasses he could harvest and dry for hay. He had horses in the barn he had built, and cows which provided milk, cheese, and meat the family could cool in Lost Creek nearby.

Their house had a large main room which served as kitchen, dining room, library and sitting room, and two bedrooms; one for her parents, another for children. Katie was the only child. "Curious, careful Katie;" Daddy called her; both a descriptive and warning phrase, Katie thought.

Her parents were concerned, Katie knew from their conversations, about the Modoc Indians that had frequented the Lava Beds lately. Daddy said that President Grant had forced them to leave their native lands and move to the Klamath Reservation in Oregon—onto the same lands shared by their enemies, the Klamath tribes. The Modocs were angry. They had petitioned the government for permission to move back to their country in Northern California, but without success; so they left the reservation illegally and slipped back into their ancestral homeland.

"President Grant ordered the army to chase them down and make them move back to the reservation, and the army is following the order," Katie heard her father tell her mother. "General Canby will teach them to respect authority."

"Do you really think we'll be safe?" Her mother's worried face searched Daddy's as she spoke. "We're so close to those Lava Beds where they're hiding in caves and behind rocks. I can't help worrying."

"Let me worry about that, My Dearest. Don't trouble your pretty head about those Indians. The army can take care of them. Trust me."

Chapter 2: The Road to Tomorrow

November 1872

Katie could remember it all: the morning sun bathed the beauty of the lake as she looked through the red and white checked gingham-framed cabin window and saw the Indians in their war-paint and canoes rowing across Tule Lake. Her mother's screams pierced her memory yet.

"Katie! Hide where no one can find you, Don't talk!"

The last time she saw her father he cocked his rifle, getting ready to fire. "Get out of the house, Katie! Run!"

Katie ran out the back door away from the lake and buried herself in a haystack behind the barn. She heard her mother's screaming, several gun-shots, and then deathly silence. She waited in the stuffy hay, itching and struggling to breathe, while two chattering Indians walked past. She hoped they didn't have scalps on their belt. Terrified by her own thoughts Katie struggled to stay motionless the rest of the day, afraid of what she would find if she crept from her hiding place. After what seemed like an endless time of misery, she heard voices, voices speaking a language she could understand. She pushed up through the hay, terrified to hear what they might say to her.

"You're alive." The soldier speaking seemed surprised. "We followed the Modoc Indians here, he said. "They killed fourteen families this side of the lake. I'm sorry but your parents are among them. We buried your dad and mom."

"I'm so sorry," one soldier said. He put his arm around the trembling girl. "We hate what happened. We'll take you with us and find someone who can take care of you. My name is Brad; Corporal Brad Jennings. I think I know a family in Eastern Oregon who'll love you. They lost their little girl several years ago."

Katie listened, still remembering her mother's last words. *I want mama and daddy.* Tears escaped and trailed down her cheeks. *I don't want to be that woman's little girl.*

The soldiers led her past the burned ruins of their cabin. She saw the scattered bits and pieces of her life, and bent to pick up her rag doll with both its legs missing. Katie hugged it to her body, refusing to let go when one of the soldiers tried to take it from her.

"It would be better if you left it here," he said.

The travel north with the soldiers continued day after day. Katie rode on a horse that had belonged to a soldier whom the Indians had killed, a man without a family. The horse was beautiful, with a shiny black coat, flowing mane, and a friendly disposition. Katie liked the animal, and thought she'd really like to have her own horse for a friend.

"That horse likes you," Brad said. "He belongs to you now. He needs you as much as you need him."

Katie, still clinging to her mangled doll, stroked the horse's mane, but said nothing. *I'll call him Midnight,* she told herself. *He'll be my family now.*

Brad looked at her, wishing she would speak. She did not reply but her sad smile expressed the first bit of hope since her loss.

They followed endless trails through timber and desert, crossing Northern California into Oregon, sometimes riding ten hours per day. As they passed into Southern Oregon she began to see Canada Geese flying south for the winter.

Memories rushed into her mind: Katie could hear her mother laugh as they stumbled through the pastureland and up a hillside near their home at Tule Lake, hurrying to see the geese. She could see the two of them on the hillside; hear her mother call out long before they could see the V formation. *Can you hear them, Katie? See the leader, there at the point of the V.* Love for her mother rushed into her heart, bringing pain as its companion. *I'll never see her again, her red hair and smiling face. I'll never get another of her hugs.* Scalding tears escaped and made their way down her cheeks. She turned her head away and stared into the distance so no one would see.

Tall, lanky, smiling, Brad stayed close by every day, teaching her how to take care of the horse, helping make her comfortable in the outdoor life they lived. One evening he led her and Midnight out of camp and said, "Your horse needs a brand to show he'll always belong to you. We'll put your initials, KE on him. It will hurt him, and he will cry, but just for a little while you must be brave, and then he can always stay with you."

They built a fire and roasted a little beef for their supper. Brad branded Midnight and Katie screamed with the suffering horse. Those moments of shared pain made Midnight hers. They rode back to camp together on Brad's horse, leading Midnight slowly along the trail.

That night Brad told her they were taking her to a place called Stone House in the Malheur River Valley. "The Rineharts started building the house you'll live in about a year ago and finished it lately," he said. "You'll love the Rineharts. They welcome people from all over the country; wagon trains and individuals on the Oregon Trail cross the Malheur River near there. Mrs. Rinehart's name is Amanda. Mr. Rinehart's is Lewis. Stone House is the only house within twenty miles of the juncture of the Malheur and the Snake Rivers."

Brad's words made Katie feel lonely. She needed a friend, a friend besides Midnight. Where would she find a friend in that empty country? Wishing for a friend reminded her of how she and her father had shared such special times, how she'd loved the stories about his and Mom's trip west in the covered wagon; he'd told the stories every night after supper. The precious memory brought renewed tears.

"The Rineharts own a lot of land around the Stone House and the river. Two peaks southeast of the Malheur River are named after the family." Brad looked at Katie and smiled. "Those buttes have hot springs flowing from them and are near the fork of the Malheur with Willow Creek. You'll be close enough to have a great time swimming there." Seeing Katie's lonely, disinterested look, he continued. "Don't worry, Katie. I'll come to see you every time I come near Stone House."

Katie thought about the family in Oregon and wondered what they would do together. Would she like Mrs. Rinehart or would Mrs. Rinehart make her a handy servant to do all the things she didn't want to do herself? What would Mrs. Rinehart think about a girl who couldn't talk anymore? The heartbroken girl bowed her head and sobbed.

Chapter 3: Stone House:Vale, Oregon

November 1872

"Stone House is just ahead," Brad told Katie about a week later. "Remember everything I told you. Mrs. Rinehart is a lovely lady who cares about everyone. All the wagon trains and travelers through the area will be stopping. You'll meet lots of interesting people, hear all the news, and have the time of your life. They will have a stall for your horse, too. You'll be able to explore the river banks, the hot springs, the hills and the country around." Brad paused as if he had second thoughts. "Just remember to take someone with you. There will always be Indians."

Katie suddenly felt her aloneness. Brad would be going on without her. Entering a stranger's house and asking them to keep her didn't sound like anything she wanted to do. She didn't like the country through which they traveled. It felt like a desert, even in November. The house looked more like a fort. Blocky and tall, built of large stones, it stood two stories high. No grass or trees offered welcome, no inviting path to the door. One thing she saw gave her comfort. A barn stood in the back. Midnight could live there.

Mrs. Rinehart stood in the doorway welcoming the soldiers. When she saw Katie, she smiled warmly and said, “My name’s Amanda. What’s yours? I’ll find *you* a special place to sleep.”

Katie saw with surprise that Mrs. Rinehart looked very young, maybe twenty, and she thought her beautiful. She smiled her acceptance of Mrs. Rinehart’s help.

Brad noticed the hostess talking to Katie and moved to stand beside them. “Ma’am, when you get everyone taken care of, there’s something I’d like to talk to you about.”

“Sure, Brad. Want to help me get these men settled so they can rest? Supper will be at six on the dot.”

Mrs. Rinehart guided Katie to a small room with two single beds. Katie saw Rinehart Buttes through billowing curtains on windows looking out toward the high hills. *Beautiful.* She suddenly realized how tired and cold she’d been during the traveling just past and looked longingly at the bed.

“Why don’t you rest for an hour, Katie? There’s time before we eat. You can wash up here.” Mrs. Rinehart indicated a wash bowl and pitcher on a stand. “See you later.” She left the room wondering why such a young girl stayed so quiet and why she was traveling with the army.

Brad joined Amanda Rinehart in the kitchen. “May I speak with you in private, Amanda?”

“Of course you may, if you don’t mind my dinner preparations while we talk.”

“Thanks, Ma’am. It’s about Katie. We found her hiding in a haystack at a farm near Tule Lake in Northern California Territory. A group of angry Modoc Indians murdered her parents. We found several other families they killed that day We were following them after a battle. I've never heard the girl speak a word. She communicates with facial expression; she's very good at that."

"How sad. Does she have anyone to take care of her?"

"Well, Ma'am, that's what we're wondering. Could you please take her? You should know that we gave her a volunteer's horse after a guy with no family lost his life. The girl has really bonded with the animal. I know it's a lot to ask, you being as busy as you are."

Amanda stood quietly for several minutes, so long that Brad feared she would say no. "She can have Carolyn's room," she said when she finally spoke. "What a blessing it is God would send me another daughter."

"She may never speak again," Brad reminded her.

"We'll hug a lot, and she speaks eloquently with her eyes. We'll get by." Amanda paused. "Maybe her silence has everything to do with what happened at their farm. Maybe she'll speak again. I'll tell her we want her after supper."

"What about Lewis? Will he be okay with your decision?"

"I can't do anything to displease Lewis. He thinks I'm wonderful. Just don't tell him anything different."

"I give you my word, Ma'am. Thank you."

"

Chapter 4: Beginning Again

"We need another girl." Amanda pushed back her plate, looking at Katie. "We lost our Carolyn to measles when she was only four. You need a home. I know I can never take the place of your mother, and Lewis can't replace your dad, but everybody needs friends, and if you'll let us, we'll be yours. We want you to stay here with us; be a member of our family."

Katie stood mutely looking at the floor. She willed herself not to cry or scream. Scenes of the last day she saw her parents ran roughshod through her mind. She remembered the smell of smoke from the burned cabin, and felt sick at her stomach. She saw the terror on her mother's face and heard her screaming.

Why did everything have to change? Her home at Tule Lake was prettier. Amanda didn't look like a mother, she looked like a schoolgirl. This house looked more like a hotel than a home. She wanted to run out of the room. Instead, she nodded.

"You're tired," Amanda said. "Why don't you go to your room and rest? Come with me, I'll tuck you in. We'll talk in the morning at breakfast."

Amanda put her arm around Katie and they walked to Katie's room. She turned down the covers and gently tucked them around Katie. “Sleep tight,” she said.

When Katie was alone, scalding tears sought to diminish the pain in her heart. After a long hour of weeping, she fell asleep.

***

When Katie opened her eyes the next morning, she felt rested. Either the crying or the comfortable sleep had helped. She walked into the kitchen and saw a man—much older than she’d expected—sitting at the long table where they’d eaten supper the night before.

“Good morning, Katie. Welcome! I’m Lewis. We’re glad to have a girl around here. We think they’re pretty special. Sit down and eat some breakfast. Amanda’s fixed steak and eggs, and muffins, too, or you can eat oatmeal if you’d rather.”

Katie felt hungry. She sat down and reached for a muffin.

“We’ll wait for Amanda. She’s getting my coffee. Then we’ll take time to say thank you to the One who gives us everything we need.”

He sounds just like Dad. Katie relaxed a bit and waited. She remembered the large group of soldiers at supper last night. Her face questioned *where are they?*

As if reading her mind, Lewis spoke again. “The soldiers left. They always get up with the sun. Brad asked me to say good bye to you and give you this.” He pulled a currying brush from a big pocket in his jacket. “He said you’d know what to do with it.” Lewis paused, and seeing Katie’s questioning expression, continued, “The soldiers go through here every so often. They’ll be back.”

Amanda entered the room, poured coffee for Lewis, and sat down. Lewis took her hand, reached out for Katie’s and bowed his head. “Dear Lord, You give us everything we have and we're grateful. Help us always be willing to share. In Jesus Name, Amen."

"We don't have neighbors very close," Lewis turned his eyes toward Katie. "Last year we bought the land with the first log house in the territory on it. It was being used as a way-station by Jonathan Keeney and his wife. When we built this house we wanted to continue to offer overnight and refuge services to those who need them. We completed the living areas in August. We're still working on a ballroom upstairs. Hopefully it will be finished by New Year's Eve when we plan to give a ball. People should come from miles around."

Lewis waited for Katie's response. She appeared to be listening with interest, but remained quiet. "We have eleven hundred acres in all, including the buttes you can see from your room and the hot springs. You'll have lots of room to enjoy your horse. However, you're not to go out riding alone. Hostile Indians roam through every once in a while. I hear the government is opening a large piece of land for them near here, so we hope they'll pretty much stay on that land after the reservation opens. Maybe things will be better then."

"Want to go riding with me today, Katie?" Amanda smiled and looked at Katie. "I love to ride. My horse's name is Biscuit, for his favorite food. We'll ride to the river. I love the scenery there. Emigrants on the trail usually stop their trains at the juncture of Willow Creek with the Malheur River and rest for awhile. The women do their washing in the springs, and they all take baths. It's a well-known place. We'll at least take off our shoes and socks and wade if the day stays warm. The water's always perfect."

Katie nodded her reply and smiled. *I'm glad we'll be doing something besides talking.* She looked forward to the ride and being with Midnight. She'd brush him with the new brush and feed him whatever food she could find. She anticipated the sunshine and the new country scenery. *I hope we'll see something besides sage brush.*

Chapter 5: The Horseback Ride

After Katie helped clean the kitchen they changed into riding clothes and fixed sandwiches for a picnic lunch. While she brushed Midnight Katie thought of the gift Brad had left for her. *He didn't have to give me the curry brush or Midnight. He must like me. I'm glad.* She missed Brad.

When they were ready at last and on their horses, Amanda turned her horse toward the Southwest, and Katie followed cross-country toward the North Fork.

"When we reach the river Katie, we'll come back along it to the crossing, and then continue on to Willow Creek before we head home. We won't go up the mountain today." The two rode silently till they reached the North Fork of the Malheur.

After the gray sage brush and grey-green greasewood so much in evidence everywhere, the tall flowing grass and willow clumps along the river seemed to beckon, and wave to them in welcome.

"See that grass, Katie? Look how tall it is." Amanda gestured toward the waving verdure. "Lewis says it's like gold to him. He makes wild hay from it for his cattle. In some places down the Malheur toward the

Snake River it's tall enough that a man can ride through it almost unseen."

Amanda guided her horse into a north-easterly direction. "We'll continue along the river now, toward the hot springs and The Crossing. We'll stop for our picnic when we get hungry."

For another hour Katie enjoyed the sunshine on her face and the soft breezes that played with her hair while they rode along the river bank. She noticed the river widening and shallowing. And then, towering above them across the river they saw Rinehart Buttes. Katie enjoyed the shadowed path the buttes provided while she listened to Amanda.

"The hot springs flow from the buttes a mile or so ahead," Amanda said, and then as an after-thought she added, "I'll bet you're ready for some lunch."

Katie rubbed her stomach. *You bet I'm ready. I'm about starved to death!*

"Do you want something now?" Amanda asked, pulling on the bridle and retrieving a half sandwich from her saddlebag. She held it toward the pre-teen who smiled gratefully and without hesitation stuffed most of it into her mouth.

"We'll be there soon." Amanda tapped Biscuit's side with her heel, and they were on their way again.

When they reached the crossing, a peaceful landscape greeted them. Waving grass and willows along the river banks comprised the scenery, and cool breezes rustled the willow branches. Amanda guided Biscuit to the shade of a willow and stopped. "We'll eat here in the shade and rest."

Katie dismounted Midnight and patted his neck. She stretched her tired muscles and leaned against a large rock to wait while Amanda pulled their lunch from her bag. "Will you get the quilt from behind the saddle, Katie? That would help a lot. Spread it on the grass so we can sit."

Katie unfolded and spread the quilt. Amanda set the beef sandwiches, carrot sticks and apples down on the quilt. They made themselves comfortable, offered thanks and began to eat. The peace of the river's murmur as it slid over smooth rocks and the susurrus of breezes sifting through the willow leaves settled into their spirits.

"Katie, I want to ask you a question. I know you want your parents back, but since that's not possible, what one thing do you want more than anything else?"

The girl's face showed surprise and then longing. She wrapped her arms around her body in a hug.

"I can give you plenty of hugs, Katie. Is that what you want?"

Katie shook her head and pointed first to Midnight, then to Amanda, and then off into the distance.

"I think you might mean you want friends. Is that it?"

Katie's screams pierced the quiet of their surroundings. "Amanda, Look!!"

"Sweetheart, what is it?"

The girl sat frozen, sheer panic on her face. Pictures of the last day she had seen her parents, etched permanently into her memory, filled her mind with images of the Indians walking by the haystack holding their bloody knives. Katie pointed. Amanda turned to look toward the river. Striding toward them she saw the Indian in his paint. He walked boldly till he stood above them.

Oh no! Amanda's mind screamed at her, *it's going to happen!* Her panic matched Katie's until she saw the Indian rub his stomach and reach out for her sandwich.

"Here! You can have it." She shoved the food toward the Paiute. "Katie, give him your sandwich." Katie's shaking fingers gave him what was left of hers. Amanda reached into her bag and pulled out the remaining food. "Take it all," she said, trembling as she held it. She turned the empty bag over and dumped it. The Indian stood staring and stuffing the food into his mouth. Katie hadn't moved. Amanda thought the girl might scream again. *Oh, what shall I do?*

The Indian persisted, looking them over as a fox surveys a flock of geese. He reached down and pulled on Amanda's blonde hair, petrifying her, shook his head and then walked away, leaving the two picnickers terrified, yet weak with relief.

Feeling they'd had quite enough adventure for one day the womenfolk hastily gathered their belongings, mounted their horses, spurred them into a gallop and raced toward Stone House, imagining the Indian followed right behind.

Chapter 6: Sequel to Terror

"It's okay now, Katie. He's gone." Amanda moved toward the girl and hugged her. Katie threw her arms around Amanda, clinging and sobbing.

Since they'd returned from their horseback ride, the girl, caught up in unreasoning fear, pale-faced, insisted on staying near the window and watching for the Indian.

"He didn't follow us, Honey. He got what he wanted, something to eat. He doesn't know where we are. We're safe here in the Stone House."

Gradually, when no Indian appeared, Katie relaxed, and a tiny seed of thanksgiving for the safety of the huge stone house sprouted in her heart. Amanda made more beef sandwiches and they ate.

As Amanda began to unwind, she sorted through the details of the day. *The Indian approached behind me. Katie screamed. Katie spoke my name. Katie-spoke-my-name! Katie-can-speak! She just needs encouragement, or maybe permission.*

"Thank you, Katie, for warning me the Indian was coming. You said my name. It was so wonderful to hear your voice." Amanda gathered her into another hug.

Katie bowed her red head as if conscience stricken. “Mama told me not to talk.”

“Oh Katie! She didn’t mean you should never speak again. She wanted you to be quiet while the Indians were there. She wanted to protect you.”

Katie, again caught up in the terror of the unforgettable day, wept out her tears in Amanda’s arms. When the tears ceased Amanda walked the frightened girl to her bedroom and tenderly tucked her into bed. “Remember, Katie. You have a Father in Heaven,” she said. “Snuggle in His arms, and sleep, my child.”

***

“Remember we said we were going to give a ball for New Years Eve, Katie?” Amanda bustled around the kitchen getting breakfast. “Today’s December 15. I hope the weather will stay nice like it’s been lately. It would make everything so much easier for our guests who have to travel.”

“How do they travel, Amanda?” Katie asked. “Do they ride their horses?”

“The men usually ride horse-back, and, if it’s not snowing, some of the women will ride too. If it snows enough they could bring a sleigh. Sleighs are warmer since the women can bundle into quilts and tuck in hot bricks to keep their feet warm. People figure out all kinds of conveyances. What’s important to them is that they get here for the fun.”

“Do I get to dance, Amanda?”

“Of course you get to dance. Everybody dances.”

“What if I don’t know how? I’ve never been to a ball before.”

“Then we’ll teach you. Everybody else will help you, too, but Lewis and I will get you started. Maybe we can get one of the Keeney brothers to bring his fiddle over some night and provide the music. That’s the hardest part, getting the music. Oh, Katie. I miss music so much! Back East someone always played the piano or sang, or played violin. Out here music is a luxury for special occasions."

"Who's doing the music for the ball?"

"The Keeney brothers and their fiddles will have to do. They can keep a crowd moving all right!"

"How many people will be coming?"

"My darling, you're so full of questions. We started inviting people and spreading the word about the ball when we began building the house. We plan to have forty one couples, so we sold forty one tickets for $5.00 each. We'll have about eighty two guests. The house will be full."

"Where did you find all those people?" Katie's eyes widened. She pictured the empty acres around them, the sage brush prairies devoid of people.

"Lewis travels all over the valley. People will come from the Weiser River Valley, the Boise Valley, over around the fork of the Snake and Payette Rivers. They'll come from Canyon City, Jordan Valley and Harney County. We have several army fellows coming."

Katie immediately thought of Brad. Would he be one of the guests? She couldn't help thinking how kind he'd been to her, and she hoped he'd be here. She would always be glad to see Brad.

Amanda paused. "It's always a wonder to me how far people will come to get together with neighbors. These balls are special occasions when we can meet and get acquainted and at the same time enjoy a lot of fun dancing."

"I won't know anyone." Katie looked discouraged.

"Don't you worry about that, Honey. Lewis will want to dance with you and I'll bet you'll have a line of eager young men waiting. Till then we've got a lot to get done. Are you willing to help me?"

She sounds like a mother. I'm glad. "Tell me what to do," Katie said.

Chapter 7: Surprise Company

Lewis was home from his constant travels for a change. His involvement in the affairs of Malheur County, his cattle business, and occasional trips back to Union County where he and Amanda had lived previously kept him busy. They had guests tonight. Several of the army's officers had stopped by on their way to Southeastern Oregon, the Modoc country. Excitement filled Katie's heart when she saw Brad among the men.

"What's the army up to this trip?" Lewis asked when everyone was seated at the table and they'd offered thanks.

The lieutenant in charge spoke. "Captain Crook is down south in Oregon trying to keep the Modoc Indians on their reservation. They've grown restless. They're wandering around causing all kinds of trouble. We're on our way to help out." Katie felt sick with remembrance and ran for the chamber pot and stood heaving over it.

"From what I hear," Lewis said, "the way the government keeps breaking treaties with them is the chief cause of their restlessness."

"I can't much blame the Indians either, Mr. Rinehart," the lieutenant said. "Our government isn't coming through with the food allotments they promised to the Indians when they were persuading them to accept reservation life. The Indians are hungry."

Brad spoke up. "Did you folks know President Grant has authorized a reservation right here in Oregon? I hear it's going to cover over a million acres. Its boundaries aren't far from here. Southern Oregon's problems may soon be ours."

"Their restlessness isn't all the government's fault," Lewis said. "Settlers need to take responsibility to make sure they're not on reservation land before they turn their cattle onto it or build their houses. If settlers won't act sensibly we'll never have peace with the Indians."

Katie listened with interested anger to the men's conversation. It made her realize the Indians had needs that weren't being met, but she could never forget what the Modocs did to her parents and her home. Being hungry certainly didn't justify murdering her parents, but she'd never look at the Indians' actions quite the same way again, perhaps she'd have to look at things from their side, if only a little.

Brad's voice interrupted her conflicted thoughts. "Take me out to see Midnight, young lady."

Deep in her thoughts, Katie jumped. She hadn't expected attention, but welcomed it anytime as long as it came from Brad. She arose and headed out the back door toward the barn. The sweet smell of hay greeted them as they entered. Brad followed her past Biscuit's stall in the shadowed light. Several other horses whinnied. Midnight neighed and tossed his head in greeting.

"How are you and Midnight getting along?" Brad asked. "Has he dumped you on the ground yet?"

The young man turned and stroked the eager horse's neck and mane.

"No way. Midnight likes me. I'm nice to him." She changed the subject. "Thank you so much for leaving the curry brush for me and Midnight. He loves it when I brush him. When we're through I give him a carrot or apple, so he really thinks he's had a wonderful treat when we finish."

"My, my, Katie. Such a lot of words for a little gal who wouldn't say even one last time I saw her. You must be feeling a lot better and liking it here."

"Amanda and I went riding and while we were eating lunch I saw an Indian and yelled at Amanda to make her see him. Then I felt guilty that I'd talked until she helped me understand what my mother meant when she said; 'Don't talk.' Now I know it's okay for me to talk when Indians aren't around. I really like Amanda."

"What happened when you saw the Indian?" Brad's voice reflected his concern.

"All he wanted was our lunch. We gave it to him and he went away. I was really, really scared, especially when he pulled on Amanda's hair. I wanted to scream."

"I'm scared, too, Katie. You never know what an Indian might do. I guess it depends on what mood he's in. I'm glad you're safe."

"Me too. Did you know Amanda and Lewis are giving a big dance? It's called a ball. Amanda said I could go, but I don't know how to dance."

"Shall I show you a little bit?" Brad took her hands in his and sang a waltz-like tune. "Down in the Valley, Valley so low, Hang your head over, Hear the Wind blow. Count one-two-three, one-two-three, one-two-three. See how easy that was? I'll be coming to the ball and we can practice."

"I'm so glad to see you," Katie rushed on. "I missed you when you were gone. I'm glad you're coming. It'll be nice to have you here again so soon."

"I miss you, too, Katie."

Brad turned and headed for the house.

"Lewis is leaving tomorrow to go to Boise Valley for the food we'll need for all those people on New Year's Eve. We'll have beef, of course, pot roast, I think. It'll take a lot of food for eighty five people. Amanda and I are making dozens and dozens of sugar and gingerbread cookies. We're going to eat a midnight supper at the dance. I'm really glad you're coming, Brad."

As Brad looked at the young girl he saw the admiration shining in her eyes.

Chapter 8: Growing Family

A week later Lewis told Katie, "Dance lessons tonight. I'll be home and I've asked Jonathan Keeney to come by and have dinner with us. So get on your dancing shoes."

"I don't have any dancing shoes, Mr. Rinehart." Katie looked ready to cry.

"That's just an expression that means to get ready." You won't need any special shoes. Are you ready to learn to dance?"

"Is it hard? Will I look funny?"

"It's not hard, Katie. Dancing is fun. Do you like music?"

"I haven't heard much music, but when I do it makes me tap my feet."

"See, you already know a lot about how to dance. The most important part is that you feel the beat. The dancing is just keeping time with the music and knowing what to do with your feet. We're going to teach you a few of the steps. The dances usually begin with a grand march, but we're leaving that out and starting with square dancing. Ladies around here don't have much finery to parade in a grand march."

Lewis put his arm around Katie. “Square dancing can seem hard, but if you tell the other dancers in the square you don’t know what to do, they’ll help you. The caller is usually responsive to the skills of the dancers, too. You’ll have fun if you don’t worry about your mistakes. You may need to sit out on the round dancing, but there’ll be plenty of times you can take part.”

“I’m so excited I can’t sit still,” Katie said. “I wish it were happening tomorrow.”

“Don’t wish it any sooner, Katie.” Amanda clasped her head between her hands. “We’ve less than a week before people will be parking their rigs all around the house. Don’t worry about what to wear,” Amanda added. “People come in everyday clothes. The ones who have dress clothes are so few that they’re the ones who really look out of place. I’m wearing my print house dress. Remember, our frontier dress is the reason we’re not having the grand march. Now, do you feel better?”

“Yes, Amanda,” I really do. I can look forward to New Years Eve now.” Katie’s eyes lit up. “Brad said he’ll be coming. He’ll help me learn too.”

***

Katie looked out the window and saw two cowboys ride up and tie their horses at the hitching post. “Amanda, two guys are coming in on their horses. The tall guy has a guitar on his back. Do you want me to put extra plates on the table?”

“Yes,” Amanda said on her way to the door. “They’ll be hungry.”

Two tired wranglers stood, obviously hoping for an invitation into the pleasant room they saw. “Won’t you come in,” she said. “Supper’s almost ready.”

Lewis came into the room. "Welcome to Stone House," he said. "You can wash up in the front hallway here. What are you guys doing in this area?"

The tallest man, tanned and curly-headed, the one with a guitar on his back, answered. "We've been checking out the gold up around Canyon City and Willow Creek. We didn't have much luck. Actually, we're looking to hire on as ranch hands. We heard you run a lot of beef. My name is Les Vaughne. This is my brother Al."

"Your timing is good," Lewis said. "I've begun to realize I need help with my cattle. You'd be out on the range a lot, herding and feeding, usually, but I can put you to work here immediately. Our New Year's Eve ball is scheduled for Monday night. All day more horses and wagons than you can imagine will be showing up. I'd like you to supervise the parking and horse stabling and keep everything orderly. The horses will need to be fed and watered, too. How does that sound? We have several horses in the barn right now you can help with, too. Think about it while we have supper."

"Sounds really good to me," Al said, "I don't need to think," and Les agreed.

***

Katie helped Amanda get supper on the table and they sat down to a supper of pancakes, bacon, and eggs.

"This is Jonathan Keeney and his wife," Lewis said, introducing the men. "Jonathan, meet Les and Al Vaughne. They're going to work for me."

Turning to Les and pointing to the guitar sitting in the corner, he said, "Do you play that guitar?"

"Yes, as a matter of fact, I do a lot of entertaining. Mostly I do solo work, but occasionally Al sings harmony with me—we sing a close harmony only family can achieve."

"You don't say! We'd like to hear some of your music, and this is the perfect occasion. We've promised our Katie some dancing lessons after supper. Jonathan is playing fiddle for us. We'd love to have you join in, or take your turn. Music is such a luxury out here in the wilderness you'd be doing us a favor. Of course, you'll be staying the night. We have lots of room for guests."

It was a night Katie would never forget. Mr. Keeney and the Vaughnes played and sang together while Lewis taught Katie her dance steps and some of the simpler square dance calls. They laughed and sang and played together for hours. When Lewis decided it was time for bed, he addressed Les who stood nearby. "You guys sound good. We'd like to have you help with the music for our ball coming up in a few days."

"Our pleasure," said Les. "You won't be sorry."

***

Two days later, on the 30th, the army contingent arrived bringing a Christmas tree and another surprise guest. Mrs. McNeill looked about fifty years old, but her eyes reflected an older age, and recent pain resided there. Her husband had died trying to defend their home from Modoc Indians who had scalped him and left his body for her to find, she said. She found him out by the lake one evening after he didn't return to the house. Mrs. McNeill had tried to face living without her husband but found living alone on the property where the Modocs had killed him terrified her, and she chose to leave; for where she did not know. She managed to bring with her a team of horses with a wagon containing those things she couldn't bear to leave behind.

"Well Brad," Lewis said, this is the second time you've come to our rescue." To Mrs. McNeill he said,

"We're happy to have you here with us." Lewis laid his hand on the older woman's shoulder. "Amanda needs help with all the beds, cooking, and preparations for the ball. If you'd be willing to help her we'd be much obliged. In return we'll give you food and shelter and a small wage until you figure out what you'd like to do. If you like we could talk about a more permanent position for you."

Mrs. McNeill's eyes filled with tears. "You're so kind. How can I ever thank you? You're so very kind."

"Don't mention it, Ma'am. It's what neighbors do for one another."

Katie approached Mrs. McNeill. "You can help us put up the tree. Can we do it tonight, Amanda?"

"Yes, Dear, It'll be a nice decoration for the ball, even though Christmas is past. We'll all do it together."

Chapter 9: The Day is Finally Here

On Monday, the 31st of December, the weather turned crisp and cold; the sagebrush wore a dress of icy frost. People traveling to the ball felt frost nipping their noses and needed to bundle in warm clothing and blankets; many added hot bricks to warm their feet. Wagons pulled by teams of horses—bits in their mouths and wearing rattling harness—would be the choice transportation of most guests. Usually some started their journey a day earlier, so wagons would soon be pulling into the areas around Stone House. Inside Amanda and Lewis bustled, putting last minute arrangements into place.

Katie stood in her room before Mrs. McNeill wearing a soft blue puff-sleeved dress. The woman's fingers were busy adjusting it to fit Katie. "I made the dress for my twelve year old daughter, Sally," said Mrs. McNeill. "I want you to wear it for the ball tonight. You'll feel very beautiful, won't you?"

"Oh yes." Katie swirled and watched the soft folds of the skirt fall around her. "Thank you, Mrs. McNeill I feel almost like Cinderella. I can hardly wait for the ball!"

Les and Al Vaughne busied themselves in the barn, feeding and watering the resident horses and making things ready for the arrival of the many guests.

During the afternoon, early and late, eighty two guests arrived, ready to indulge themselves in dance and discussion.

Lewis and Amanda made sure everyone knew that Katie was now their daughter, "We claim her as our own," Lewis said, and introduced Katie, Les and Al Vaughne, and Mrs. McNeill to their guests. "Our family has really grown," Amanda said. "It's wonderful."

The guests ate in shifts—a hearty beef and vegetable stew cooked on the coal-black wood stove. Cheese and biscuits would finish the meal. The women helped Amanda and Mrs. McNeill tidy the kitchen and then retreated, a few at a time, to share the bedrooms and primp for the ball.

Jonathan Keeney and his brother carried their fiddles to the upstairs ballroom where the Christmas tree glowed with candlelight, and chairs waited for the ladies. Les and Al joined the fiddlers as they warmed up. *Yellow Rose of Texas, Home on the Range, Red River Valley, Clementine, and Cattle Call* warmed the room and their voices for the evening of singing. Katie, ready and waiting, sat and savored the music.

When Brad joined her, saying, "It's time to practice. How lovely you look," she blushed and stood.

"I'm going to show you some of the easiest square dance calls and what they mean," he said. "You'll understand some of them without my help. Your partner is always on your left. The man on your right is your Corner. The first call you'll hear is '*circle to the left.*' Join hands and keep circling until you hear the next call. Hold hands with your partner, and generally with anyone you are next to." Brad continued his explanations until Katie's head felt like a bomb ticking away the time.

"*Alamande Left* means to extend your left hand, hold your Corner's forearm, and circle around him, like this." Brad demonstrated, turning Katie through the move. Katie followed in a daze. She'd never imagined so much detail in a dance. Brad went on, "*Dosado* means to walk toward the other person passing right shoulders and without turning move around him and back to your original position. Let's do it now."

Too much, too fast, Katie wanted to say, but wanting to impress Brad, bit her tongue and followed through the move.

Brad, having square danced many times and oblivious to Katie's mounting despair, continued. "To *Swing*, while facing the person, feet side by side, join right hands with the man. He will put his left hand on your back near the waistline; you put your left hand on his shoulder, like this." Just when Katie was ready to scream Stop!! Brad said, "Let's get Al to come over here and be your Corner. We'll do a little practice. Al, could we borrow you for a minute?"

Al came immediately, smiling broadly. "Do I get to dance with you, Katie?" The three practiced the moves till Katie relaxed, seeing much more of the picture after her second practice.

More and more people moved into the ballroom.

Brad gave last minute directions to Katie. "Lewis asked the caller to do a very simple combination of moves for the first dance of each tip (set of two dances). Each tip is two songs. You dance the first half-tip and trade with Amanda or Mrs. McNeill. Let them do the second half which will be a higher level set including a lot more moves than you will know. How does that sound, Katie?"

"I'm scared." Katie looked as if she'd like to run.

"May I have the first dance?" Brad asked.

Katie, trembling, but thrilled, said "Yes."

Chapter 10: I Wanta Dance with You

The caller moved to the front of the ballroom. Jonathan Keeney drew the bow across his fiddle strings. "Square up," the caller said. "Get ready for some fun."

Squares of four couples grouped around the room.

Brad led Katie to the floor. "Our backs are to the caller," he told her. "That means we're the number one couple in this square. We're 'heads' so when you hear the term it means we'll be following the call. The couple across from us is also a 'head' couple."

Katie tensed with the added instructions.

"The other two couples, numbered two and four, are called 'side' couples." Brad noticed Katie's discomfort, and thinking it might help her relax added, "After we start dancing, if you don't know what to do, just hold out your hand. Someone will take it and guide you through the move. Here we go, Katie."

The opening measures of *Little Liza Jane* filled the room. "Circle left" the caller said, and the dance flowed. Katie felt caught up in it all, surprising herself, moving faster than she'd ever expected, in time to the music. She felt energized, taking one hand after another, dancing with and being assisted by everyone in the square. When the music stopped, she remembered to ask Amanda to take her place as Brad's partner and then relaxed on a chair by Mrs. McNeill. "That was fun," she said.

"You look so nice, Katie. Seeing you having fun is almost like having my daughter back. I miss her so much."

"Where is your daughter, Mrs. McNeill?"

"Modoc Indians carried her off several years ago. The army's never been able to find her. I thought I'd go mad when they took her. I struggled with God over it a long time before I finally put everything in His hands. Now I know He can and will take care of her. I can't."

Sympathy welled in Katie's heart. *Mrs. McNeill must feel awful.* Katie reached over and squeezed the grieving mother's hand. *What would happen to a girl carried off by Indians?* She couldn't imagine, but she knew it wouldn't be good.

"I'm glad I remind you of her, Mrs. McNeill. Maybe we can pretend I'm *your* girl, too. *Amanda wouldn't mind. I know she wouldn't."*

After numerous tips of square dance, Les and Al moved to the front and broke into the opening measures of *Home on the Range*.

Brad took Katie's hand and led her to the floor. He arranged her in the waltz position and whispered, "Remember how we practiced in the barn? Count one-two-three, one-two-three and move to the rhythm of the music. Let me guide you."

Katie delighted in the feel of Brad's strong arms guiding her around the floor. *I wonder, is he as **happy** to be with me as I am to be with him?* She felt as if the waltz picked her up and carried her on clouds of tickle-pink. The music ended far too soon. Brad brought her back to her chair and sat down beside her.

"Well Miss Katie, do you like dancing?"

"Oh yes! I hope it never ends."

It did end, all too soon. Before she knew it Lewis was asking everyone to go down stairs while the tables for the midnight banquet were set up. Les, Al, Jonathan and Brad stayed to help prepare the ballroom for the feast. The women waited for the tables to be set up and then headed for the kitchen to bring the overflowing platters and containers of food upstairs to the tables. Meanwhile the men carefully carried stacks of plates—borrowed from nearly everyone there—to the ballroom. The younger people carried the eating utensils.

Everyone contributed food. With all Amanda had cooked, food supply exceeded all possibility of being eaten, even with so many empty plates and empty stomachs.

Men and women lined up and filled their plates with delightful foods. Brad waited in line with Katie. She began to feel truly beautiful and attractive. She indulged herself in dreams of romance. *I'm going to marry him someday and take care of him like Mom did Dad and Amanda does Lewis.* The ten-year difference in their ages didn't seem important. They were so comfortable with each other.

Tables taken down, they tackled the dishes, each woman in turn washing a stack. When the task ended, the music and dancing began.

Katie danced almost every dance; if she wasn't dancing with Brad, another partner reached out his hand. By two o'clock in the morning she felt almost like she imagined Midnight felt after he ran a mile. Amanda awakened her where she'd fallen asleep, walked her to her bedroom and tucked her in. "There'll be another time, Katie. Sleep tight."

When Katie awoke the next afternoon, guests were already pulling out, ready for the long trip home. She couldn't see army uniforms anywhere. *He's gone again, before I said goodbye.* Disappointed with the realization, she walked, head bowed, shoulders slumped, to the table and sat. Those who preceded her were engaged in serious conversation. The subject they discussed hardly raised her spirits.

"Is anyone else concerned about what the Modocs are doing, showing up anywhere they please, stealing horses and cattle, killing heads of families?" one settler asked.

"It keeps me awake at night, wondering when they'll show up and burn the house down around us," another said.

"If I lived closer to their territory, my family and I would sleep along the creeks among the willows," a tall wiry-looking man commented ruefully.

"Travelers aren't safe anymore," the first man replied. "They'll approach you and stare, mutter to one another, and take your provisions if they're in a good mood, or your life if they're not. I'm nervous every time I have to leave my wife alone while I'm freighting."

Nearly everyone told a story about a recent frightening event. All expressed their thankfulness for the army's presence—intended to discourage the Indians' intrusions into their lives.

Lewis approached the table. "You're all welcome to shelter here if things get too scary. Remember that."

Around the table people mouthed the words, "Thank you."

Chapter 11: The Stroups

March 1873

Word spread rapidly to the settlements: The Stroup family, moving through the area, had pulled off the trail and into a valley for lunch and was trying to get some rest. A group of eighteen to twenty war-painted and armed Indians moving down the trail followed them into the meadow, surrounded them, and stared at them with surly, angry looking faces. The Indians talked among themselves for what seemed an eternity to the pale-faced travelers, and then moved on down the trail.

"It's a miracle they're alive," the settlers opined, and prayed they would be spared that kind of intrusion.

"We were scared out of our wits," Mr. Stroup reportedly said. "We knew too much to be complacent and waited in terror for whatever the Indians would do. We suspected the Indians were Bannocks from Idaho, angry over that botched treaty with the government about five years ago. It failed to award them the Camas Prairie near the mouth of the Snake River. The government promised the prairie to them verbally as terms of the treaty. Disappointed because they'd lost an important food source, the Indians felt betrayed and unsettled. Their peace-loving chief had died in1871."

The listeners riveted their attention to every word. The settler continued, "When they heard the Indians were roving around again, it scared them to death. Sure enough they came their way as they traveled through the country. You can imagine how terrified the family was when they followed and surrounded them."

Like a spark in dry grass, the Stroup's fear spread.

***

The Macomb Smiths lived on the Malheur River over at the Butte, probably ten miles away. They ran a dairy and sold butter to the mining camps in Idaho for seventy-five cents to a dollar a pound; The Brinnons lived near the mouth of the Malheur where it joined the Snake, the same area where Lewis had turned loose his first cattle. This settlement was known Washoe. When the Stroups moved into the area, Lewis invited them to Stone House for a visit. They came in late March.

Mr. Stroup seemed to be a quiet man; at least he allowed his wife to answer most of Lewis and Amanda's questions.

When they sat down to the table, Lewis took the lead. "My wife here is Amanda" He looked at Mrs. Stroup. "You two women appear to be close to the same age. I'm sure you'll be friends."

"I'm eighteen, and my name's Susan. My husband is Jacob," Mrs. Stroup replied. "Mr. Stroup and I got married in Missouri and got on the train to come west within the same week. I've been in a state of shock ever since." She shrugged half-heartedly.

"I hope things will get easier for you," Amanda replied. "I'm twenty-one now. Lewis and I got married when I was in my mid-teens. We lived in Union County then, and Indians plagued us daily during those years. It's been easier since we've been in Malheur County."

"From the first day we got off the train it started." Mrs. Stroup gazed intently at Amanda. "We bought mules, a wagon, and a camping outfit and followed the old Kelton Trail in Utah to the Boise stage road. The miles stretched endlessly through miles and miles of desolate, uninhabited country. The Goose Creek Mountains, deep in snow and slush terrified me. I could imagine the wagon stuck and us freezing to death." Mrs. Stroup crossed her arms and hugged herself.

Katie, all ears, asked, "I heard about the eighteen Indians that interrupted your lunch. Were you scared then?"

"We were scared spit-less," Mr. Stroup replied.

Susan chimed in, "I was so full of dread I hid on the wagon tongue, pulled my bonnet way down over my face and didn't look at them or move the whole time they were there." Her faced paled with the memory. "Mr. Stroup said they looked so angry. To say we were relieved when they went on up the trail would be a gross understatement." She brushed tears from her eyes. "It seems I'm scared all the time, out here."

"Did you have any fun at all on the way?" Katie couldn't imagine being scared all the time.

"We stopped at Glenn's Ferry when we crossed the Snake River. The Indians were fishing for salmon. We watched for most of a day while they pulled fish from the water with their nets. I wasn't scared then because the Glenns and Mr. Stroup were there, and the Indians were so busy they didn't seem to pay any attention to us."

"Oh," Amanda said. "You met my parents. I'll bet you spent the night and ate several meals with them.

Mom's like that. I haven't seen her since our New Year's Eve ball."

Mrs Stroup smiled. "She treated us like long lost friends, and was so eager for news from anywhere that she asked a million questions."

"We all feel lonely and starved for information," Amanda replied. "You'll understand after you've been here awhile and go for weeks without seeing anyone you can talk to."

"We met the Smiths too," Mrs. Stroup added, "at the Washoe Ferry. They wanted us to stake a claim near them, so we did. They'll be really nice neighbors, and Mrs. Smith promised us milk and butter anytime we need it. They were almost as cordial as your parents, if that's possible."

"Folks are right friendly out here." Mr. Stroup broke into his wife's story, "Guess they have to be helpful since we're all so isolated."

"Since you said that," Lewis interrupted, "we want you to consider Stone House and our home a refuge if you ever feel threatened enough to leave your cabin. Pardon my interruption, but I didn't want to forget to tell you."

"Oh thank you!" The new bride's response burst into the room. "Mrs. Smith and I stayed alone at their cabin while Mr. Stroup and Mr. Smith went to the mines. Mr. Smith wanted to sell butter and Mr. Stroup wanted to see the mining camp. We were alone, and sure enough, Indians came. We both thought they meant to do mischief, and we were petrified, but Mrs. Smith managed to convince them the men would be back very soon, and they left."

"Those sorts of things happen often," Lewis replied. "Unfortunately the men can't both stay at home and do the homesteading, freighting, and ranching work, so women must learn to handle a gun and talk to the roaming Indians. It's a different life out here."

"Oh! I could never do that!" eighteen-year-old Susan said.

Chapter 12: God's Birthday Present

June 29, 1873

"Katie," said Amanda, "I want to ride out on the prairie and dig some camas bulbs. We're short on provisions right now, and the camas in bloom will be easier to find. Besides, it's your birthday. Wouldn't a ride be a nice way to celebrate?"

Katie felt glad for the diversion. "Oh yes, Amanda. I'd love to go. What is camas anyway?" she asked.

They'd been cooped up in the house during the winter months, with few days warm enough to ride. The spring had been a busy and wet one with settlers stopping at Stone House almost daily.

"Camas is a plant in the lily family. It has a bulb that we can eat. The Indians knew this first, and the word spread. Many of the settlers dig camas bulbs. We'll be able to grind them and make meal which we can use in bread and pancakes. We can mix it with water, form bricks, cook it and store it for later use. It'll come in handy in the winter when traveling is harder and supplies are still so far away."

"How will we find it, Amanda? The prairie is so big."

"The flower is a light blue, and if there's a lot of it, it can appear to be a lake in the distance. Also, camas usually grows in meadows that are moist in the spring but dry out later in the summer. I think the areas near the riverbanks would be a good guess as to where we might find it."

"When do we start? I'm ready to go."

"Don't you think a lunch would be a good idea? We'll be tired before the day is over, and hungry. Midnight and Biscuit will need a bite to eat, too. Would you like to gather a small bag of grain from the barn while I make the lunches? Oh, I almost forgot. Get two burlap sacks for the camas bulbs, too."

"I will, Amanda. Would you like me to saddle and bridle Biscuit? I'll get the horses ready while I'm in the barn."

"That would be wonderful, a great help, Katie. We'll be ready in no time."

Ten minutes later, they set out toward the river and the hoped-for camas beds. "Let's head straight for the fork at the middle branch of the Malheur River," Amanda suggested. "The meadow is a bit higher in elevation there, and the increased elevation will probably boost our chances of success."

Since Amanda had stayed so busy the previous spring when they were building the house she didn't get to hunt for the prized camas bulbs. This would be a searched-for, as well as a hoped-for gathering of the plant.

They didn't reach the forks until noon. They stopped their horses and gazed in every direction. The northwest direction looked most promising, so after pausing for lunch and a short rest they pressed on in that direction. As they hoped, they found the inland sea of camas blooms just northwest of the river and in an area which flooded over when the river was high.

"The flowers are beautiful," Katie said. "Can we take some home with us for the house? They smell so nice."

"First we've got a lot of hard work to do," Amanda replied. "Let's get the gunny sacks out and dig. Harvest the larger bulbs and leave the small ones to grow till next year."

They dug with a shovel until they could pull the clump from the ground. They found numerous tiny bulbs that looked much like an onion, but few large enough to harvest. After removing the large ones, they set the clump back into the ground and covered it with dirt. They worked so attentively they didn't notice they were not alone.

"Name Numa Tah-Mano," the Indian girl with long black braids and dark brown eyes said, causing both Katie and Amanda to jump. She looked to be fifteen or sixteen years old. "Name means Paiute spring." She turned to Amanda. "See white quamash. Numa Tah-Mano gestured toward white flowers among the blue. "No eat. Not good. Death quamash."

"Oh, thank you," Amanda said gratefully. "We didn't know that. I don't see many white flowers. That's a good thing. Do you speak English?" she inquired, wondering how much the girl could understand.

"Little." The Indian girl held up her hand, forefinger above thumb, to demonstrate. "Father chief, he know much." Her fingers moved further apart.

Katie watched silently. A friend, she thought. She could be my friend.

"What your name?" The Paiute girl looked at Katie.

"Katie, my name is Katie. I live at Stone House with Amanda"—she pointed to Amanda—and Lewis.

They take good care of me." Katie hugged herself. "Nice to me." She smiled. "Where do you live?"

"Res-er-va-tion," The girl pointed toward the northwest. We move. Have to stay here now."

The girl continued digging bulbs, gradually moving further away from Amanda. Katie moved gradually toward Tah-Mano as she worked. The digging required a lot of effort, and Katie felt glad the day wasn't hot. The bulbs accumulated in the sack very slowly.

Finally, Katie heard Amanda call out, "Snack time!"

Kate stood upright and stretched. Numa Tah-Mano stood and looked at her. "Come on, eat." Katie took the hesitating girl's hand.

Numa Tah-Mano smiled and followed Katie to where Amanda waited. She looked longingly at the food Amanda removed from her saddlebag. "Me eat?"

"Of course you can eat. You probably saved our lives!"

The Indian girl eagerly accepted the sandwich Amanda offered and crammed most of it in her mouth. Amanda and Katie knew by her actions she was hungry, hungry past restraining herself.

"When did you eat last?" Amanda reached into her bag, removed another sandwich and handed it to Numa Tah-Mano. "Eat this, too, and then we'll talk."

"So sorry. Not much food, re ser vat ion. Eat much quamash." Numa Tah-Mano pointed to the beautiful blue flowers. "I find food."

Amanda and the two girls worked for several hours before Amanda interrupted their activity. "Time to go home; we'll come back another time." She carried her gunny sack to Tah-Mano's basket and poured in the camas bulbs.

Katie straightened her back; Tah-Mano continued to dig. Two weary white women mounted their horses and left the laboring Indian girl.

Katie's mind churned over the events of the afternoon as they traveled toward the Stone House. Meeting the Indian girl who could become her friend seemed like a birthday present from God. How nice, she thought. Thank you God.

Chapter 13: Friend or Foe

"Amanda, I'm so excited to find someone who can be my friend," Katie said the next morning. "I can hardly wait to see her again."

"Oh, Katie! You mustn't plan on that. She's an Indian. You're white. The two worlds don't mix. Indians do so many savage things to white people."

"Enemies don't save each other's lives," Katie replied. "Numa Tah-Mano saved us from eating the white camas bulb. That makes her a friend."

"In a different world what you're saying might be true, Honey. But there are so many instances where Indians have been deceptive. They've fooled us into thinking they're our friends, but when the chips are down they've turned against us."

"Tah-Mano wouldn't. She's close to my age. She's nice. I want to be with her more."

"You wouldn't be safe with her people. You're too young to understand; you have too little experience. We'll talk with Lewis when he gets home."

Katie wondered why Amanda seemed so opposed to her being friends with Tah-Mano. She wanted to honor Amanda's wishes, but she wanted a friend her own age more than anything. Disappointed now, it seemed to Katie that Amanda didn't care about what she wanted. She needed a friend. She felt a little angry, if the truth were known.

Katie left the kitchen and went to her bedroom without eating breakfast; a first for her since she always felt hungry.

Dear Diary,

I feel so lonely. Amanda and Lewis are nice and they're kind, but sometimes they don't understand me either. I need a friend I can laugh and walk and talk with. Tah-Mano could be one. We could play games together. I don't know one other girl like me. Where else in this dumb place can I go to find a friend?

Finding the diary of small comfort she resorted to prayer.

Dear God,

I don't feel very thankful right now. Love, Katie.

She threw the book aside and flopped on her bed. Foreboding filled her as she anticipated lunch time and the inevitable talk with Lewis. When Amanda called, Katie delayed her arrival at the table as long as she could. *I'm afraid he'll forbid me to go out alone on Midnight or become friends with Tah-Mano, I might talk back and get in trouble.* How she dreaded the conversation that must take place.

Why did Lewis and Amanda have to be so unreasonable? Mom and Dad let me go out and watch the geese alone, she thought. Nothing happened to me. *But it could have*, a voice in her head told her. *Look what happened in the end. The Indians just had to get excited and mad about something. They're all around us here, too. Whatever Lewis says, whatever rules he lays down are meant to keep me from getting hurt. I need to listen, be quiet, and obey.*

They sat down at the table together, offered thanks for the food and began to eat.

"I hear you want to go out alone on Midnight and make friends with an Indian girl." Lewis looked straight at Katie. "Is that correct?"

"Yes," Katie answered. "I do want to be friends with Tah-Mano. She saved our lives when she told us about the death Camus. We could have brought it home and poisoned ourselves. An enemy wouldn't help us like that."

"Katie, I've lived a few more years than you have, and had all kinds of experiences with Indians. I've seen them invite the army to peace conferences and then attack the soldiers when they believed them and came unarmed. I've known of cases where they killed the people who hired them and fed them."

"But Tah-Mano is nice. She's only a girl. She wouldn't do that!"

"Katie, Indian children are raised with a whole different set of values. What seems wrong to you might be honorable in their society. I know it's hard for you to understand why we want you to stay away from the girl, but if you're smart you'll listen to the voice of experience. In case you choose not to listen, we'll have to lock Midnight up and keep you home."

"You wouldn't! I need Midnight."

"You'll have him as long as you obey." Finished with his lunch, Lewis collected his hat and gloves and headed out toward the barn.

Chapter 14: First-hand Experience

"I'm going out for a ride," Katie said to Amanda later that afternoon. "I'll stay within a short distance of the house. I should be back in an hour or two."

"You will be careful, won't you? Don't even think of going as far as the camas field." Amanda hugged Katie as she cautioned her and handed her an apple for Midnight. Katie smiled her thanks and headed for the barn.

A few minutes later she headed out toward the hills northwest of Stone House. *I haven't been this way yet. Maybe I'll see something new.*

The bright sunny day invigorated her, and she breathed the fresh air deeply. Still a bit upset by Lewis' threat to lock Midnight up so she couldn't ride, she decided she must follow the rules. They know best, she thought, but it still makes me kind of mad.

Katie rode across the plain to where the trail began to climb upward. She paused to turn and look back on the way she'd come. She saw Stone House in the distance. *I've been riding about thirty minutes. I'll ride out for another half-hour and turn around.* Ahead she saw canyons between the hills, and decided to follow one of them and explore. Midnight whinnied as they started up the canyon.

"It's okay, Midnight. We'll go a little way further and turn around." A shrunken stream descended the canyon from the hilltop. A few spindly willows hugged themselves to it in their search for water. The hills showed brown traces of the once-green grass of spring. Katie pulled Midnight's reins and climbed down. I'll wash my face in the stream and cool off. As she looked around she realized she could no longer see Stone House. I'll just follow the canyon back. There's no way I could get lost if I do that.

She knelt by the stream and raised her wet hands to her face. When she uncovered her face she saw an Indian standing beside her. She'd heard nothing, but there he was. She looked around slightly and saw the second Indian. "You come," he said, and both Indians grasped her arms. One of them held Midnight's reins. In her fright and surprise Katie dropped her rag doll.

Chapter 15: Searching

"Katie didn't come back from her ride. She told me she was leaving and would be back in an hour or two, and I let her go out alone." Amanda paced the floor wringing her hands.

"What were you thinking of?" Lewis glared at Amanda, and then, seeing her misery, took her in his arms. "We'll get Les and Al to help and we'll go looking for her. Do you know which way she went?"

"I watched her ride off toward the northwest," Amanda said. "It was about two o'clock."

"I'm so glad I'm here," Al said. "Les and I thought we could use a little home cookin, so we figured we'd come in for a day or two and see if you needed us to do anything here. Seems like you do. I'll find Les. He's around the barn somewhere." Al walked out the door, decidedly not in his usual leisurely fashion.

"Can you fix us some sandwiches, Amanda?" Lewis clapped his hat onto his head. "We won't want to end the search because our stomachs are empty. We'll ride out as soon as Al and Les get back to the house."

"I'm going, too." Amanda said. "I'm the one that let her go."

"What if she comes home and no one is here?" Lewis protested.

"You've forgotten about Mrs. McNeill. She'll stay. I must go and know what's happening. I can't bear not knowing."

Les and Al came in from the barn. "Did Al tell you about his scouting experience while he served with the volunteers?" Les moved over to the counter where Amanda was rushing to make sandwiches. "Here, let me help. I'll wrap as you finish spreading." Les turned toward Lewis. "Al will be invaluable if we find we need to do some tracking."

"Okay. That'll be four sets of eyes, definitely better than one pair. Are we about ready?" Lewis' hands worked repeatedly through his hair while he paced impatiently.

Amanda and Les placed the sandwiches into a bag. She turned to Lewis. "Ready. Let's go!"

When the others left the house they found Al near the barn examining Midnight's tracks. "They went this way." He guided his horse in the northwesterly direction and the others followed, conversation scant until they reached the area where the canyons opened. Al occasionally dismounted and searched the ground for clues as to whether Katie had entered each canyon found. The party finally settled on the one with the small stream coming from it.

Al still in the lead, they set off along the stream in the valley bottom, occasionally finding Midnight's hoof prints to assure their correct direction. As darkness settled into the canyon's depth they approached the place where a legless much-loved rag doll lay hidden among broken willow branches along the creek bank. Passing by in the darkness they missed the multiple sets of tracks that led in a long zigzag path up the side of the canyon.

***

Overwhelming terror filled Katie's mind as she helplessly followed the directions of the Indians. "You ride horse. I lead." She fought her fears and tried to think of something she could do to escape this predicament she'd gotten herself into. Recriminations unsettled her emotions. *Did I disobey? Did I go too far away from home? How will I get home? Will I ever get home? What will they do to me? Where are they taking me?*

The route the Indians followed up the hillside frightened her. She looked down and immediately felt dizzy. What if Midnight slipped on loose rocks? A long fall, that's what. Suddenly Katie knew what she wanted most. She wanted to be encircled in Amanda's hug, or sitting at the breakfast table with Lewis, eating Amanda's corn muffins. She wanted her bedroom with the billowing curtains and the view of the buttes. She knew immediately what she had to be thankful for, and felt deep remorse for not appreciating what she had. Would she ever have such comforts again?

The canyon wall leveled into a wide plain. Katie, thankful to be off the steep hillside started breathing again. The Indians chatted in language she couldn't understand; nevertheless their voices comforted her in the darkness. She supposed several hours had passed when they arrived at the edge of another canyon. In its depths she saw a cluster of tepee's and saw smoke coming from each one. She wondered what living in a tepee would be like, or maybe, she thought, I won't be living at all.

The Indians seemed nice enough; in fact she noticed that one of the braves smiled at her every time their eyes met. Her imagination began to create scenes she didn't want to think about. Did he think she would be his squaw? Whatever would she do if he thought that?

Every thought upset Katie except one. She knew Lewis and Amanda would do everything in their power to rescue her. *Amanda knew I rode to the northwest*, she remembered, *but how will they ever find me?* Needing comfort she wanted her doll, but surprisingly it wasn't with her. *Where is she anyway?*

She'd hoped the Indians knew some secret trail to take them easily into the village, but now they were slipping and sliding down the hillside. If she never saw another hillside she'd be happy. At last the ride ended as they entered the village and stopped at a tepee. Katie saw that dawn had slipped in somewhere along the ride. Today would be her first day in an Indian village.

An older woman stooped and came out of the tepee. The Indian, Wyvoka—the one who smiled such a lot—and the woman talked, the man gesturing toward Katie several times before the woman beckoned to Katie. "You come."

Katie obeyed. The woman, who said her name was Bright Star, led Katie into the dimness of the tepee. Heavy odors of wood smoke and tobacco met her as she stooped to enter through the small opening. The woman motioned to a mat on the floor and invited, "You sleep?"

Katie shook her head. No way will I sleep here, she thought.

"You eat?" Katie nodded and rubbed her tummy wondering what she'd get to eat. Bright Star brought her dried fish, leaves, and bulbs of a plant she didn't recognize, but she was hungry and she ate the meal provided, thinking the bulbs and leaves tasted a lot like the vegetables she'd eaten at home. Then Bright Star brought a drink that looked like tea. "Honeysuckle tea," she said. "You drink." Katie sipped the tea and realized how tired she was. She lay down and drifted off into dreams. Bright Star, gratified, looked on. The love potions would work. She knew they would.

In Katie's dream Wyvoka smiled at her and lifted her off Midnight. Then he circled her waist with his strong arm and gazed downward into her eyes. "You, Me," he said. He led her into the willows where they sat in the tall grass and talked. She didn't know what he said, but she could tell he really liked her. They lay in the grass together and laughed. When he placed his hand on her breast, Katie awoke screaming. "No! No! No!"

Bright Star came to her. "Good sleep!" she said. Katie sat up, rubbing her eyes. Memory—disturbing thoughts—reminded her of yesterday's happenings and where she was right now. Katie could see Bright Star working with a lot of grasses and stems of some plant. They resembled the tule she remembered so well growing around Tule Lake in California Territory. Tule must grow somewhere around here, too, she thought. Bright Star smiled as she wove the materials, as if she was having great fun, Katie thought.

Katie watched as her work turned into what looked like a basket bottom. As Bright Star worked on the basket, Katie began to think it would be very beautiful. She moved closer and watched the Indian woman work busily. In late afternoon she put it down.

"We eat now." She went outside the tepee where a small fire burned, took meal from a bag, stirred water into it and fried it over the fire. "Wyvoka come," she said. When Katie looked up he stood before her holding a beautiful pair of moccasins. "I make." He held the moccasins to her. "You take."

Katie's disturbing dream haunted her, and here stood Wyvoka trying to give her a gift. Katie hesitated, fearing what her acceptance might mean to him, but then thought how foolish she was being, and reached out for the moccasins. “Thank you, Wyvoka. I will enjoy wearing them. They’ll keep my feet warm.” Nothing could have prepared her for the look on his face. Joy. His expression shouted pure joy.

All three sat on mats and ate the simple fare of meal cakes, bulbs, leaves and dried fish. Bright Star left the man and the girl together and returned to the tepee to place blue lobelia blooms beneath Katie’s pillow. “She dream again,” she said.

Katie, sitting wordlessly alone with Wyvoka, felt embarrassed but didn’t know why. After a short absence Bright Star returned with honeysuckle tea for both of them. *The honeysuckle tea and blue lobelia should certainly bring thoughts of love to the young people.* She smiled.

As she drank the tea Katie felt herself relax. Wyvoka seemed relaxed and happy. They talked, neither understanding the other until Wyvoka stood. “I go now.”

Katie’s eyes drooping, she entered the tepee and lay on the mat. *I hope Lewis comes for me tomorrow.* And then the dreams came.

Chapter 16: Frustration and Danger

Riding on in the darkness, Amanda felt a growing sense of uneasiness. Something was wrong. Had they missed something they should have seen? "Let's stop for the night, Lewis. We can't see what we're doing. We'll do a more thorough search of the area in the morning. I just have this feeling."

"No, Amanda. We've got to keep moving. The canyon goes on for miles, and she wouldn't have left the canyon. We can't go too far wrong."

"But what if we miss something in the dark?" Amanda hugged herself for comfort.

"We'll stop for some sleep before morning. In the morning if we don't see tracks, we'll know we have to come back. If we do see tracks, we'll be that much further along the way. Al's good at finding the tracks. I can already see that."

The other two men kept quiet, not wanting to enter into the disagreement, but Al had some doubts about the wisdom of riding on in the dark. He'd talk to Lewis later when he had a better opportunity.

The search party pressed on for several hours before they stopped to rest and eat. They tossed their bed-rolls in the grass among the willows of the creek and slept fitfully. At the first hint of light peeking over the hills they awakened.

Al had risen earlier and spent his time examining the trail ahead. "I'm afraid my news isn't good," he said while they breakfasted on sandwiches. "I haven't found any sign that anyone's been through here recently."

Lewis mounted his horse, and the others followed suit. "I was wrong. We'll have to go back. It's got to be Indians, and they've left the canyon somewhere. We must find the place. Let's keep our eyes on the edges of the beaten path for tracks leading away from it."

"Amanda, fretting about the time they'd lost, wondering where Katie was and what was happening to her, bit her tongue to keep from criticizing Lewis's earlier decision.

Les and Al rode ahead, carefully scrutinizing the ground on the outer surfaces of the path. Lewis and Amanda tried to search, but their minds constantly moved back to Katie. Was she safe? They feared the answer might be no.

Several hours later they arrived at a wider spot on the canyon floor; it had to be the place Amanda had wanted to stop last night. She felt the same sense of expectation and urgency she'd felt then. "Lewis, we need to stop here. I know we're missing something important." Amanda stopped her horse and dismounted. She walked toward the creek, and then back and forth along its banks.

Al and Les were re-examining the trail edges carefully when Les spotted several pair of hoof prints heading off the track and up the hill. "Boy, they sure had to want out of this canyon to go up that hill," Al commented. "Do you think our horses can make it?"

Suddenly Amanda's voice rang out, "Lewis, Come here!" Lewis rushed to her side. She pointed down the creek bank. "Look, there among those branches. It's Katie's rag doll! She would never have turned loose of it willingly!"

The four gathered to make plans. Though the climb up the canyon wall looked daunting, it probably could be done. The puzzle pieces began to come together. Katie had obviously stopped here, and apparently been surprised while she tried to get a drink. That's when she dropped her doll.

"Looks like Indians," Les commented. "We'd better follow the tracks if we want to find where they've taken Katie. This is big country. Their village might be anywhere."

"I agree," said Al. "That's probably the only way we'll ever find them."

"We'd just as well get started then," Lewis commented. "Let's go."

Amanda looked fearfully at the precipitous but necessary climb ahead of them. Even though she could see that the tracks they needed to follow led in a zig-zag up the steep wall of the canyon she knew anything could happen. The horses could slip, slide, step into a hole and break a leg, or stumble and fall. This adventure came with no guarantees. For the hundredth time she wished she'd just said no to Katie. Four people would risk their lives, all because of her error. "I'm ready," she said.

"Al, you do the scouting. Les follows you, then Amanda. I'll take the rear position," Lewis directed.

Without a word Al guided his horse to follow the clues the Indians left. The rest of the procession followed him. Silently they watched the trail ahead, Al looking for hoof-prints, the rest hoping to anticipate possible problems. Dislodged rocks rattled their way to the canyon bottom, disturbing the quiet. The plodding of their laboring horses hooves echoed in their heads, clip-clop, clip-clop, on and on.

For an hour they climbed cautiously up the risky bluff, avoiding bunches of sagebrush or greasewood blocking the path; holes the horses might step in, or loose gravel where they might slip. At last they could make out the top of the ridge. The path steepened as they climbed, increasing the dangers of the ascent. Amanda felt excruciating fatigue weighting her mind and body, and wondered if she'd make it to the top. As her horse clambered over the last rocks, she fell.

Chapter 17: Dream, Dream, Dream

The dream puzzled Katie. In it she didn't know what she wanted anymore. Wyvoka cuddled her in his arms. It felt good to be hugged, but she felt she needed to push him away. He stroked her face and hair tenderly. That made her want to move closer to him, but she knew she should run. He stroked her arm lightly from elbow to wrist and back again. A delicious relaxing feeling made her sigh and stretch as Wyvoka unbuttoned her blouse. When he bent over and kissed her breast she awakened screaming and scratching. Wyvoka wore a set of five newly acquired bloody scratches down his left cheek. The man yelled and jumped away from the frantic girl. Bright Star ran to her sleeping pallet. "You go!" she ordered Wyvoka.

"Okay, okay now," she told Katie who trembled by her pallet. "He come no more."

The village awakened with Katie's scream. Indian braves grabbed their weapons and ran toward the sound. A man's yell punctuated the tense morning, and Wyvoka ducked out of Bright Star's tepee and slunk off toward his own. Seeing him, having expected to see an enemy and fight a war, the braves broke into relieved merriment and laughter. A long time would pass before Wyvoka would live down this night.

As Katie sat outside the tepee waiting for her breakfast with Bright Star she wondered why she dreamed about this Indian man. She knew nothing about him or his ways. He looked handsome enough, but what about his beliefs and customs? Repulsed by his actions, all she wanted was home, Stone House, Amanda and Lewis. She didn't belong here. What was happening to her?

The Indians treated her well, she had to admit that. Bright Star seemed eager to give her anything she wanted, and some things she didn't want. Perhaps that Honeysuckle tea she'd drunk both nights before she lay down was some kind of drug. *I wonder if I have the choice to refuse it. It seems to be a staple in the Indian diet. But is it? I don't remember seeing Bright Star drinking any tea. I'm not having any more of it either.*

Bright Star explained that morning that she had been away and come back to find Wyvoka in the tepee. The Indian woman walked toward her now carrying the basket she'd worked on since Katie's arrival. Katie couldn't understand how it could be so nearly finished, or how could a basket made of such simple materials be so beautiful? When did the woman sleep? She smiled at Bright Star.

"You eat now. Chief come today." Bright Star handed Katie a bowl with meal bread and a kind of sauce in it, and Katie obediently ate it. She disliked the taste of the sauce, but it filled her stomach. This time the woman did not offer her the tea.

"Wash face." Bright Star handed her a soft cloth, a grey-green color, and showed her a bowl of water. Katie willingly did as she was asked, and realized how much better the cleansing made her feel.

She raked her fingers through her hair several times. That helped too.

Katie sat down on a mat Bright Star handed her, and looked around at the village. The tepees were conical in shape, appearing to be made of willow poles stuck in the ground in a circle and then bound together with increasingly short cords or strips of bark. Indians placed their doors on the east, she noticed, probably for increased warmth. She couldn't imagine how they managed to make such a simple light-weight home warm. The covering on the outside looked like the sagebrush that could be found so easily on the prairies of Eastern Oregon. As she thought about the tepees she remembered the gray green of the cloth she'd used on her face. No! It couldn't be sagebrush!

Katie guessed the size of the village to be about twenty families, if that could be judged by the number of tepees. It didn't appear they had a chief, if you could judge by the similarity of all the tepees. *I guess a chief's tepee would be bigger and fancier. I wonder what Bright Star meant when she said "Chief come."*

The village remained in the shade of the canyon wall, but Katie guessed it to be a sunny day. The morning's activities were well under way; men were out hunting rabbits and women looked for roots and bulbs. She could see that all their activity centered on gathering food or making clothing and baskets.

Several hours later Katie sat with Bright Star trying to learn basket-weaving. It certainly didn't come naturally for her—Bright Star's fingers flew, even when she tried to slow down and demonstrate the technique to Katie—and Katie felt frustrated with the whole process. She kept remembering the dream that had turned into reality; Wyvoka in her bed. Protests rose to her lips, *I don't feel like making baskets,* but realizing Bright Star wouldn't understand them, she bit her tongue and kept silence. *I hate this place. I want to go home.* Memories of Amanda's warm hugs floated through her mind; she wanted to jump up and chase them.

Chapter 18: The Chief

The clip-clop-clip-clop of horses' hooves distracted her from the dry basket materials and she gazed off in the direction of the sound. She saw nothing at first, but soon several Indians rode into the village. One of them wore a huge headdress. He must be a chief, she thought. Then she noticed the girl riding beside the chief-like Indian. She looked familiar. Katie wondered why, and then remembered the day in the Camus field. *Tah-Mano*! She remembered something else, too. *Tah-Mano said her father was a chief and spoke lots of English.* He would be able to understand her. Katie jumped from her mat and ran toward the horses. The company of Indians stopped. "Katie!" Tah-Mano said. "Why you here?"

Tah-Mano turned to her father and talked for several minutes, explaining how she knew the white girl, Katie supposed. Then the 'chief' dismounted and walked to Katie. "You don't belong here. What happened? How did you get here?"

"I went horse-back riding alone up the canyon northwest of our home. I live in Stone House. Two Indians made me come. I want to go home to Stone House."

The chief called to Bright Star. He asked many questions when Bright Star came to stand before him. Katie couldn't understand what they said, but heard Wyvoka's name several times. The chief seemed to be listening intently and getting more and more upset. At last he came to Katie to explain what he had learned.

"Wyvoka decided you were of marriageable age and decided to take you for his squaw. He brought you to Bright Star because she's the woman in the village who produces love potions for marriages. Has she given you Honeysuckle tea?"

"Two times," Katie said. "It made me dream crazy dreams. I decided I wouldn't drink it anymore."

"She's made you a wedding basket, too. I'm glad I got here in time. Things were happening pretty fast."

At his words the almost bride broke into tears. "I don't want to marry Wyvoka!"

The chief spoke again, "We have enough problems between our peoples without these brainless kinds of actions. Mr. Rinehart will be very angry when he learns of this. Wyvoka will never be important in the tribe again. He risked all our lives by his foolish dream. You will come with me, Katie. I will see that you get back home."

Tears of relief and gratitude poured from Katie's eyes. Tah-Mano dismounted her horse and put her arms around the weeping girl.

"Tah-Mano," her father said. "You stay-with Katie. We will leave soon and take the girl home."

Chapter 19: Change in Plans

"Amanda! Amanda! Are you okay?" Lewis leaped from his horse and ran to his motionless wife. "Did you hit your head?" When he received no answer, he gathered her into his arms, struggled to the top of the hillside, and carried her until he found a shadow cast by a large rock. He tenderly laid her in its shadow.

Les and Al rushed around looking for ways to help. "Don't we have a washcloth? Let's wet it and put it on her forehead," said Les and headed for the canteen.

Al gathered a blanket from the saddlebags. "She'll be in shock," he said, "We've got to keep her warm."

Lewis bent over her, stroking her forehead, planting kisses on her cheek. "Wake up, Baby, wake up!"

No response came from the unconscious woman. Lewis paced above her, sweat streaming down his face, fists clenched. "Dear God, please let Amanda wake up. Please let her be okay. Father, Father, Father, Are you listening?"

Les, seeing that Lewis's body trembled uncontrollably, got another blanket from the saddlebag. Lewis, too, was suffering from shock.

"Well, this changes things," Al said. "The way it looks, Lewis will need to take Amanda home, if he's able. If not, the search for Katie will have to wait; we'll have to take them back to Stone House. Bum luck."

Lewis, bending over Amanda, suddenly shouted, "She moved her fingers!"

The other two men, eyes riveted on the motionless woman, waited anxiously. "There. She did it again. She's coming back to us." Impatient and relieved the three hovered, eyes glued on the injured woman. An interminable thirty minutes passed before Amanda opened her eyes.

"What happened?" she asked. "Why am I lying on the ground?"

"Good question," said Al.

"You fell off Biscuit," Lewis told her.

"We're glad you're back with us." Les grinned at Amanda. "You had us all fretting. Lewis was worrying around like a bee that lost its favorite flower."

"Are you hurt, Sweetheart?" Lewis asked anxiously. "Arms? Legs? Hips? Where do you hurt?"

Amanda spent a few moments probing for hurting bones all over her body. "I'm bruised here and there, but I can move everything. I think I'm okay."

"Do you know why you fell?" Lewis wanted to know.

"I was tired. The climb up the mountain kept me tense and exhausted. I must have blanked out."

"We need to take you home. This searching and scrambling up and down hillsides, the stress of it all, is too much for any woman," Lewis said carefully.

"I hate to admit it, but I'm afraid you're right. You're making the decisions, and I worry about whether they're the right ones. I'd be better off at Stone House with Mrs. McNeill. You men could go faster without me." Amanda looked at Lewis. "Take me home, Honey. Let Les and Al look for Katie."

Lewis and Amanda watched Les and Al head out across the plain following the trail left by the Indians. "Thank you, Father," Lewis said. "I have my wife back. Now we need something else. Dear God Please help Les and Al find Katie. Help them find our daughter. Please."

They headed for lower ground in the direction of Stone House. No trail to follow, just the location of the sun to guide. Lewis estimated the trip would take about two hours, as long as they didn't find any more surprises or hillsides to maneuver.

"Where do you think Katie is?" Amanda asked as they rode toward home.

"She's in an Indian Village somewhere," Lewis replied. "Where that village is, we must find out. Anything could happen to her there."

"I keep wishing, too late, like a pre-teen does on a star, that I'd either gone with Katie or kept her at home."

"Then both of you would be missing or Katie would be angry. Quit beating on yourself about it. The timing of Katie's ride coincided with the Indians' arrival in the canyon, and she encountered them. That's just the way it was. You couldn't have stopped what happened even if you were there." The couple lapsed into silence and rode on toward home. As the sun set behind them they looked ahead and saw Stone House in the distance. "We're almost there, Honey," Lewis said. "We're home again."

Chapter 20: TheVaughnes's Discovery

Les and Al followed the horses' trail across the plain until they came to the rim of the canyon. They stared down at the numerous tepees. "This is where she is," Al conjectured, "but there are too many of them for us to tackle alone. We'll need the army."

"Let's hang around and see what we can see," Les suggested, "just for awhile."

The sun, saying it was noontime, beat down on them wetting their shirts and sending sweat coursing down their faces. They dismounted and peered into the gorge at the Indian encampment.

Movement in the camp, sparse at mid-day, didn't give much indication of any abnormal activity. A sweltering hour later, activity seemed to increase. They watched a tall stately Indian wearing a head-dress leave a tepee and mount his horse. Several more men joined him, and they rode through the village until they reached the last tepee where they stopped. A few moments later a girl, seemingly about Katie's size and wearing decidedly familiar riding attire left the tepee. She stood waiting until another Indian brought a black horse; then she mounted and rode out of the village with the group, willingly it seemed.

"It's Katie, all right and they're taking her out of the village. That's a good thing," said Les.

"We'll certainly have more luck with five Indians than twenty-five." Al pulled a huge red handkerchief from his pocket and mopped his wet face. "Shall we confront them and see if they're willing to let us take her?"

"My idea would be to follow them and see where they go. Katie doesn't seem upset, and she's apparently okay. Waiting and watching might be the best option."

"You're right, Les. That's what we'll do."

They rode along the brow of the ravine hoping the Indians' route wouldn't necessitate another hillside descent in order to follow. Eventually the canyon opened into country full of rolling hills and valleys, easily crossed on horseback. The cow hands followed in the northwest direction, keeping distance between them and the party of Indians, not wanting to alert the Indians of their presence. They trailed the group for over an hour before they entered another canyon. Another half hour and they saw tepees ahead.

"Now we know where Katie is," Les said. "Let's go back to Stone House for reinforcements, and then we'll go in and get her."

They arrived back at Stone House after dark and found Lewis and Amanda eating a sandwich in the kitchen. Amanda, overjoyed to see them back, happily made more sandwiches and Les and Al, well-pleased with their achievement, talked rapidly and seemingly non-stop. "The news is mostly good, but a little is bad. We found Katie. She's in an Indian village two or three hours out northwest," Les reported.

Al joined in, "We followed her and a group of Indians from the first village we found. Katie seemed okay and went with them willingly."

They talked on and on until Lewis brought it to a halt." The rest of you get some sleep. We'll go for her tomorrow. I'll ride over and ask the Keeney brothers to go with us."

Lewis headed into the night toward the Malheur Butte. An hour later he arrived at the Keeneys' and announced the reason for his presence. "Katie's captive in an Indian village out toward the Northwest. I could use another pair of riders to help convince the Indians to let her go."

"Sure, Friend. We can leave after the cows are milked in the morning. Come on in and sleep. We'll ride out about seven."

Chapter 21: New Developments

The riders reached Stone House about nine, and sat down, at Amanda's insistence, to a hearty breakfast of steak, eggs, and biscuits. Mrs. McNeill never disappointed anyone with her cooking. "It may be a long time before you sit down to a meal again," she said. "Please help yourself to seconds, and eat some for Katie."

"Speaking of Katie, you might want to send along some lunches," Lewis suggested.

"I'm ahead of you. Already thought of that and prepared them," reported Mrs. McNeill.

"I'm praying you'll all be safe and that tonight I can tuck Katie into her own safe bed. I so hope she's not been mistreated." Amanda gave Lewis a good-bye hug.

"Don't borrow trouble, Amanda. 'Sufficient unto the day is the evil, thereof,'" Lewis quoted. "'Let your requests be known to God.' Keep praying."

It was about eleven before the rescue party set out for the Indian village in the canyon. They'd tried to prepare for all eventualities. Weapons were part of the preparation, but in addition Lewis had Al and Les gather seed for peas, corn and beans. Maybe they'll come in handy. If all turns out well we could even help the Indians plant them. The timing is nearly right, and with a sheltered but sunny spot the seedlings might escape a late frost. The Indians are hungry, and could use the vegetables."

Mrs. McNeill prepared a first aid kit, just in case it might be needed. Bed-rolls and canteens, the lunches, and oats for the horses finished their preparations. The caravan moved out like a line of ants following a sugar trail. In this case, Katie, like the sugar, drew them steadily on the journey.

Les and Al, as they retraced their trail toward the canyon and the Indian village, discussed tactics. Should they pretend to be friends and ride in openly? Should they spy out the village during the day and sneak in after nightfall to get Katie out? Should they ride up and ask for the chief?

The Keeney brothers suggested the open approach. "Just go in and ask for the chief." In the end, the conservative approach won out. They would approach the chief and ask. That way they wouldn't stir the village toward reprisal.

As they drew near to the canyon mouth they observed a curious procession leaving it. An Indian wearing a headdress, followed by two smaller riders, themselves followed by another two Indians, rode from the opening. That both parties were following the same trail and would soon meet became obvious as they drew nearer.

Suddenly, an amazing thing happened. One of the smaller riders broke out of the group and raced toward them.

"Hold your fire, wait," Lewis cautioned as Les, Al, and the Keeneys pulled their guns. As the rider approached they began to hear her voice, "Dad, Oh Dad, I'm so glad to see you!"

Lewis leaped from his horse and threw his arms around his daughter. “Thank the Lord, He is so good,” he said. “Oh Katie, are you okay?”

“Yes, Dad,” Katie answered, “I’m better than okay, I’m on my way home.”

“Whatever happened to you?” Lewis wanted to know.

“I’m not sure of all the details. All I know is two Indians found me in the canyon and made me go with them. The chief, Tah Mano’s father, will answer all your questions. He’ll be here right away. He’s so nice. He’s bringing me home.”

The relieved rescue group looked at one another in thankfulness and wonder while they watched the chief ride the distance between them.

The chief saluted the group as he approached, and then dismounted. “I’m Chief Numaga of the Paiute Indians. I beg to speak with Lewis Rinehart.”

Lewis raised his hand in acknowledgement and approached the chief. “I’m Lewis Rinehart. I see you have my daughter with you. I’d like to know why.”

“I’ve always loved peace and tried to keep the peace for my people,” Chief Numaga replied. “These are hard times; we don’t need war between us and the whites.”

“Well then, we sure want the same things,” Lewis said. “Kidnapping a white girl is a sure road in the wrong direction.”

“I didn’t do that or sanction it. One of our young bucks found her out by herself, and the temptation was too much. He’s of marriageable age, and he thought she’d make him a suitable squaw. I made sure he’ll know better next time. When I found out about it I put an end to his plan and brought her back to you.”

“She’s only twelve years old!” a horrified Lewis said. “You’d better bring her back!”

“She hasn’t been harmed. She stayed with Bright Star, one of our women. Please understand that my return of your daughter means I’d like us to be friends.”

Lewis considered his words for a long minute. “Thank you for bringing Katie back, Chief Numaga. I’d like to show my appreciation. I hear your people are hungry and I’d like to give you a gift. We have a pregnant heifer that will soon be providing milk, and I own beef cattle. I’d like to give you a beef as well as the cow. If you keep the cow we can breed her each spring with one of my bulls, and you will have more fresh milk each year and a new calf to grow for food or milk, whatever you choose. What do you think?”

Chief Numaga seemed surprised by the gift. “I didn’t expect anything in return for bringing your daughter home,” he said. “It was the right thing to do.”

“Don’t mention it. I have men here I can send to you. They’ll help you build a pen for the cow, butcher the beef, and show you how to grow some food.” Lewis turned to Les and Al. “How does that sound, men?”

“Glad to help out,” Les said. “We’re pretty good at the farming stuff.”

“There’s something else we’d like you to think about, Chief, Lewis said. “Katie and Tah-Mano want to be friends and spend some time together. We’d like to invite Tah-Mano to come to Stone House and stay a few days so the girls can get to know one another. Being with Katie will help Tah Mano learn English, and maybe Katie can help her learn to read it. Tah-Mano can teach Katie things like basket-weaving, which herbs are edible, and ways to use camas. They can ride together, too, if they don’t go too far away from Stone House. You think about it until you’re comfortable with the idea. Let us know when you’re ready.”

"I'll think. We'll see. Thank you for the invitation, and the help. It's much more than we expected." The chief turned his horse and headed back to the village. Katie waved at Tah-Mano. "See you," she said happily.

Chapter 22: Back to Normal

Les and Al worked together in the barn gathering the tools and seeds they would need for their trip to the Indian village. They planned to leave the next day to round up a steer from the range. Then they'd ride on to the village.

"Teaching them to farm might be challenging," Al commented. "There might be a lot about growing they don't understand." Planting fields of seeds, a custom new to the Indians, would in itself bewilder them, since they were used to taking things from the earth and repaying in their unique ways.

"I'm wondering if the time between planting the seeds and any visible crop might disappoint the Indians so they might neglect to water and weed the site as needed," Les commented. "We might have to stay in the village till the seeds come up, stretching our stay to as much as two weeks in order to care for the crop."

"Yeah, and when the sprouts emerge from the ground, the Indians can take over. Hopefully, the crop grown will help to reduce the Indian's hunger." Al put tools meant for tilling the land—a shovel, a rake, and a hoe—in a gunny sack and tied it to the saddle.

Driving the steer and the pregnant heifer to the village might present its challenges, but surely with the two of them and only two animals it could be accomplished. Once they were there they could accomplish the butchering with one day's work. The Indians already knew how to store buffalo meat, so they'd know what to do with the beef without being shown.

While Les and Al worked in the barn, Lewis stayed in the house close to Katie and Amanda. Mrs. McNeill did most of the cooking and cleaning, Katie helping as she could.

Katie's story, told again and again with different details each time kept them busy for hours, and after each telling they all thanked God for bringing a happy ending to a frightening experience.

"The chief knew we needed to hurry and get me out of the village," Katie said. "He said the Hawthorne tea Bright Star kept giving me was strong medicine that would make me want to marry Wovoka. I'm so glad that didn't happen. Thinking about it gives me the creeps. I'm sure going to be more careful on my horseback rides in the future."

Remembering the warnings she'd been given before her kidnapping, she realized how unwise riding into the canyon had been, and she resolved not to do it again. "I'm so sorry I worried you," she said.

Amanda, still feeling extreme fatigue after her fall and long ride home, contented herself with listening to the others talk. "Come here," she said to Katie over and over. "Let me hug you."

They talked about the kidnapping experience, yes, but many other things crept into their conversation: What could they show Tah-Mano when and if she came to visit? How much Katie enjoyed dancing, especially with Brad? They puzzled over the whereabouts of Mrs.

McNeill's daughter who had disappeared during Indian Hooker Jim's retaliative depredations at Tule Lake; even how Katie felt about the loss she had suffered at the home place there.

When that subject came up they all cried. "I think I'll always be angry at the Indians," Katie said. "My parents didn't deserve to die like that." She still awakened during the night, the memory returning and the horror of it all freezing her body into stillness, her mouth opening in a silent scream. Remembering her mom and dad tortured her, the anguish relieved only slightly by knowing Lewis and Amanda would always be her family. "I'm so thankful to be back in my Stone House home with Amanda and Lewis," she prayed.

Once the dream awakened her, she planned—somehow forgetting her desired friend's Indian nationality—all she and Tah-Mano would do together, deliberately forcing her memories away. When the chief gives permission for her visit, I think I'd like to teach her to read, Katie thought, easy books at first, then a little harder. I know I can do it. Then we can talk about everything, some day, when she can read.

Thoughts of Tah-Mano somehow crowded out the grieving and put light in her life again. Her anticipation of the visit grew like a balloon being filled with air until she felt she'd soon pop. *What book shall we read? It should be something really easy. I can hardly wait.*

Chapter 23: Looking Forward

Fall 1873

The months passed without any message from the chief and no visit from Tah-Mano. Amanda felt better most of the time and resumed many of her duties around the house. She and Katie went riding together several times during the summer, but never into any of the canyons.

Les and Al Vaughne rode back to the Indian encampment to check on the gardens they helped plant; the Indians were excited over the beans, peas and corn they'd enjoyed eating since the men had been there. The cow continued to give enough milk for most of the children to have milk every day, and the Indians were raising the cow's offspring heifer to stretch the milk supply. All in all, the Indians looked and acted less hungry than at the last visit.

The Indians, though they couldn't converse with Les and Al, made it clear they remembered and appreciated all their help, crowding around and patting them on the shoulder. The brothers' past actions had obviously gained them friends.

After an hour or two the chief approached with a smile on his face. "My people are much better fed and happier," he said. "Thank you so much for helping us in such a generous way. Thank you for being our friends. This Paiute tribe will be yours. Tah-Mano may come to visit Katie. I will bring her in January while the weather is cold. She will be warm, thanks to you."

"It's great to have good news to take back with us," Al told Les.

"Les grunted his agreement. "Having an Indian Chief ride up to the door and leave his daughter will be a new experience. Katie will be over-joyed and impatient.

"Yeah," Al said. "She's been waiting over six months already, but now she can look forward to a given date when the visit will happen."

The two men carried the news back to Stone House and the family. They found Katie distracted and excited. "The Smiths over by the Malheur Butte have invited us to a Christmas Eve dance at their cabin." Her face glowed with excitement. "Lewis said we can go."

"Don't you want to hear our good news, or is the dance all you care about?" Al put his arm around Katie's waist and hugged her.

"What good news? Where have you been?"

"We went to check on the Indian village; the one that brought you home."

"Tah-Mano's village! "Did you see Tah-Mano?"

"No, we didn't see her, but we still have good news. Don't you want to hear it?" Al teased Katie.

"Tell me! Tell me! Hurry!"

"Well, we did see the chief. He was really pleased with the way the vegetable gardens are feeding the people."

Katie's face fell. "Is that the good news, that the people like vegetables?"

"There is one more thing. The chief wants his tribe to be our friends. That's good news isn't it?"

"I guess so. Isn't there anything else? Did he say anything about Tah-Mano?"

"Well now, I almost forgot. He did say something about bringing her over for a visit in January."

Before Al finished his last sentence Katie leapt from the chair she'd taken after hearing the first news and hugged the older man around his neck.

"You're such a tease," she said. "You almost had me crying. Meanie!"

"Now I wanta hear about that dance," Les joined in the fun. Who would dance with a pretty young thing like you?"

Katie's words rushed on. "We have to get there first, so we'll hope it won't be too cold. Lewis said we might go by horseback if it's not too cold for the ladies. If the winter is severe he said we could all load into the wagon he hauls freight in—with a lot of blankets, of course. There'll be room for all of us. It all sounds like a lot of fun, even the getting there."

Chapter 24: To the Dance

The winter of 1873 was one of the most severe on record. A few days before Christmas it began to snow, and snowed until nearly a foot of frosty white lay on the ground. Then the weather turned warm enough for the snow to start melting, and then a dip below freezing formed a thick hard crust on the surface. Christmas Eve day would probably bring continued freezing temperatures.

Early the day before the dance Lewis made the decision to take the wagon and brought bricks into the house to heat. They could help keep cold feet at bay. Amanda, Mrs. McNeill and Katie gathered blankets, brought them close to the stove to warm, and searched for all the mittens, warm caps, and gloves they could find. Then they concentrated on hot drinks and food to take along for the trip and potluck. Les and Al found extra blankets for the horses and extra oats to keep their energy supplied. The total distance was probably less than eleven miles, but conditions were harsh for both man and beast.

On Christmas Eve Day they started at dawn, not having any idea how long the trip might take. Right away they saw what they were up against. The snow was clean and bright enough to almost blind them, and the surface frozen solid except for narrow cattle trails, usually one animal wide, not even half the width they would need. One horse could walk in the trail. The other would have to break its way through the snow.

The crusted snow made the trip tedious and slow work for the horses, requiring much more effort and time to plunge their hooves through the hard surface. After each short distance Lewis decided he must stop and let the animals rest. A trip that would have taken an hour or two on a more desirable day would require the morning, at least. No one suggested they give up or turn back.

"I'll get off the wagon and break the crust just far enough away from the cattle trail to make it easier for the other horse," Les volunteered.

Their good spirits remained. They were going to a party. They would see people; get to visit, dance and let the music lift them higher than the stars. They would feel the rhythms and beats, give the night their energy. Life would be hard enough when the dance was over; they didn't want to waste the anticipation they felt today.

The men faced challenge after challenge. Clearing the way for the horses turned into exhausting work. Les turned the job over to Al after only thirty minutes; Al gave the fatiguing job to Lewis after taking his turn. One of the men drove, one rested, and one broke the track through the snow. Famished at mid-morning they stopped and ate sandwiches to restore their depleted energies.

"The snow crust wounds the horses' legs," Lewis said after the mid-morning inspection. "We need to decrease the chance of that happening. The only way I can think of is to break up the crust more thoroughly, perhaps while they're resting."

Al shared another idea, "Why don't we alternate our travel from one side of the trail to the other? That would give each horse short breaks from the hardest work; each one walking the easier cattle trail for short periods and giving them a bit less exertion."

"Let's look through what we brought. Maybe we can find a way to improvise wraps for their legs." Lewis stopped the wagon and climbed down.

Les scratched his brow. "We have gunny sacks. The horses' grain is in them. Do you think we could use them some way?" He bent to inspect said legs. "The horses traveling in the deepest snow are looking pretty beat-up."

"Wraps are a possibility, or would be if we had enough adhesive tape. We'd have to secure the wrap well and be sure it's tight, or the crusted snow would just push the wrap up on their legs. Okay. What emergency supplies do we have?" Lewis looked around the wagon bed at its passengers.

"I brought adhesive tape, "said Amanda.

"So did I," said Mrs. McNeill. "That stuff comes in handy so many times. Glad that fellow in New York figured out how to make it last year."

"Always carry it in my pocket," Al contributed. "It must have a million uses."

"I'm concerned about the grain residue in the sacks. That dust couldn't be good for open wounds," Amanda thought out loud. "Maybe it would be better to continue as we are but do what Al suggests, alternate traveling on different sides of the cattle trail."

Amanda's and Al's idea worked well, speeding their journey considerably, and they reached the Smiths by early afternoon, still in marvelous spirits.

Chapter 25: There at Last

"Welcome Friends." Mrs. Smith threw open the door to their cabin and watched with joy as the travelers filed in carrying the icy cold on their garments. "You're the first ones here. I worried about the weather, whether anyone would be brave enough to travel today. I'll bet you're hungry. Come in, come in. I made good hot stew to warm you up."

Mr. Smith busied himself asking everyone to take off their coats—no one was willing; the cold inside them dictated they keep them on—"Hey, Les, Hey Al. So glad to see you're here, too. Maybe we can start the music early. You folks would warm up fast if you were dancing. Hello, Katie, Are you ready to try out your new skills again? We're hoping to have several young bachelors here today. Lewis, Amanda, How are you?"

"No dancing yet, Macomb. These folks are hungry." Mrs. Smith ladled soup into bowls and directed them to the table.

Mr. Smith sat with them while they enjoyed the warmth of the meal. "How was your trip?"

Lewis summed it up. "Mighty difficult, but it was worth it to see you folks."

"The horses could hardly pull the wagon. I thought it was going to tip over," Katie said. "I'm so glad we could get here."

A knock on the door interrupted the conversation. When Mrs. Smith opened the door she found three of her neighbor men there. "Well hello, George, Levi, Mr. Shafer. Where are your families?"

George Brinnon answered, "They're back on the trail in a sled Jacob Stroup built. He's driving. It's hard going for the mules, trying to break through that crust. We could travel on foot faster, so we came on ahead and broke the trail alongside the one the cattle made. Hopefully our efforts will make it easier for the mules and speed up their arrival."

"Good thinking. It takes a bit of imagination to travel through weather like this." Macomb moved in behind his wife. "I guess the others will be here soon?"

"If they're not here in an hour we'll go back and check on them, Levi Wamac said. "It gets pretty cold out there."

"Well come on in and join the others. They're working on warming up right now. There's stew here for everyone."

They sat over an hour enjoying one another until George Brinnon noticed the time and said, "We'd better check on our families. It seems like they should be here by now." The three men rose and started for the door. "Be ready for some cold and hungry women and kids," he said, and the anxious husbands went out into the cold.

***

Two hours later the Stroup party had all arrived, bringing much of the population of the Washoe Ferry area: The Wamacs had a daughter, Wanda, thirteen years old. Katie felt both shy and anxious to meet her and become friends. The Brinnons brought two children. Nine people arrived with the sled designed to carry about four. That fact explained why the men walked.

When asked about the delay Mr. Stroup replied, "I had more women around than I'd ever have again, and I was tempted to head for Salt Lake." The surprised group laughed. Jacob, a quiet man, wasn't usually given to much humor.

The Smiths said several bachelors lived in the Washoe Ferry community, among them Jim Henoty and his brother who lived in their own cabins, across the road from one another, on the Idaho side of the river, so Katie and Wanda could expect to be on the floor dancing most of the evening.

Les got out his guitar at mid-afternoon. Lewis pulled Katie aside. "I need to tell you that men sometimes pull women too close when they dance, particularly during waltzes. It's a disrespectful thing and if anyone treats you that way once, don't dance with them anymore. Anyone who disrespects you doesn't deserve your friendship."

"I hope Brad will be here. He treated me nice. I'd rather dance with him than anyone else."

"Don't be afraid to accept invitations to dance. Most men will treat you right. I thought I should warn you when I heard about all the bachelors that might be here." Lewis put his arm around Katie's waist. "Have fun, Honey."

Les and Al were singing "Home, Home on the Range."

"May I have this dance?" Lewis pulled Katie into the waltz.

Late in the afternoon Mrs. Smith offered everyone another bowl of stew. She'd baked biscuits and made cookies, so everyone had their fill and felt ready for the night of dancing. More neighbors had arrived, including four or five bachelors, and several more couples. The cabin overflowed.

The Keeney brothers arrived with their fiddles and accordion just in time for the stew.

Chapter 26: The Christmas Dance:

December 24, 1873

Mrs. Smith was delighted with the number of people who'd made the effort to come. "Let's dance," she said, and twirled into Macomb's arms. The Keeneys launched into *Cattle Call* with fiddle and accordion, and husbands brought their wives close for the first dance. Les danced with Amanda, and Al asked Mrs. O'Neill.

Katie, wearing the soft blue dress she'd worn at the New Year's Eve dance last year, felt the tempo of the music and began to sway in her chair, her movements drawing attention to her fiery long hair. Where was Brad? Maybe he wouldn't be able to get there, she worried. Then she saw the man with the bald head and the big smile approaching her. "Would you like to dance, young lady?"

She smiled back at him and nodded her assent. He said his name was Jim Henoty and that he lived across the river in Idaho. He was one of the bachelors mentioned, Katie remembered. The music lifted her spirits and she enjoyed the movement of the waltz, but wished for the happiness she'd felt in Brad's arms. She noticed Wanda was dancing with a tall man Katie didn't know. She really didn't know many people. She did remember some of the people from the New Year's Eve ball at Stone House, but couldn't remember their names. She wished she could remember and felt uncomfortable because she couldn't.

That dance concluded, and another. Katie kept searching the crowd for one familiar face but couldn't find the one person that could make her happy. Brad wasn't there. How could she bear it if he didn't come? How could she make it through this night? Just when she thought she'd cry she saw Wanda approaching.

"I'm Wanda Wamac," she said. Are you as lonely as I am among all these married people?"

Katie smiled. "I'm glad you're here to keep me company. I'm Katie Erickson. I live with the Rineharts. They're my parents now. Where do you live?"

"Near the Washoe Ferry House on the Malheur, not too far from here. Do you ride?"

"Oh yes! Do you? Maybe we'll be able to get together and ride sometime, or I could ride over here as long as I stay out of the canyons. Maybe Amanda would come with me. Or maybe your mother would ride over to Stone House with you. Amanda and she could talk and we could ride."

"Cool idea. What's your horse's name?"

"His name's Midnight. Brad gave him to me after the Indians killed my parents."

Wanda remained silent for a long minute. "How do you bear it—not having your parents?"

"I cry a lot, but we're at a dance, probably the only one in a long time. Let's not spoil it by talking about my parents tonight. Let's have fun. Did you like the tall guy you danced with?"

"He was neat. His name is Charles Rice. He has a claim in Idaho, not too far away. He harvests the rye grass and sells it to the army for their horses. I'll bet he's at least twenty five. Who's Brad?"

"He took care of me after my parents were killed. He's in the army. I think about him a lot and hoped he'd be here tonight, but so far he isn't. He danced with me several times last year at the New Year's Eve Dance and I felt like I was floating on the stars." Katie looked toward the door and saw Mrs. Smith rushing toward it. Four young men in dark blue army attire walked through it at Mrs. Smith's invitation. One of them was Brad.

The service men entered the room with much foot-stomping and loud greetings. Katie's eyes, riveted on Brad, shone. She tossed her head and said to Wanda, "There he is—the fellow with the dark curly hair." When Brad saw Katie he stood without movement, surprise covering his face. And then, recovering his composure he sauntered in her direction. "Hello, young lady. It's been a long time since I've seen you."

"Yes. The New Year's Eve Dance a year ago. I'm glad you're here. Was it a hard trip?"

"We left Emmitsville early this morning. It's a long ride with this kind of weather, but we're finally here. Who's your friend?"

"This is Wanda Wamac. She lives in this area. We just met tonight."

"Well, Wanda, I'm glad to meet you. Would you honor me with this dance?"

Katie stood in disbelief and watched as Brad guided Wanda through the waltz. He didn't ask me. Why? Doesn't he know how much I miss him? Doesn't he miss me?

Lewis, seeing Katie's bewildered look, rescued her where she stood. "It's been awhile since we danced, Katie. Please honor me." He steered her onto the floor and kept her moving, but distracting her from her hurt was another matter. Her eyes followed Wanda and Brad as they waltzed gaily around the room. Misery settled in around her heart as she went through the motions of the dance.

When the next dance started Katie felt the dread of another rejection. The tall man she didn't know, the one who danced with Wanda, approached. "Would you like to dance?" he asked. Charles Rice danced skillfully, and Katie felt her inexperience, but kept up with him until the dance ended.

"I enjoyed dancing with you, Katie," he said.

"Thank you very much, Mr. Rice," Katie tried to hide her distress.

Jim Henoty came back for another dance. One after another the single men sought Katie out. Brad hadn't asked her to dance for several hours, but seemed to ask Wanda often enough! Would he ask her at all? She wouldn't let him see her misery.

Katie ran her fingers through her hair and put on her biggest smile. She searched the room and saw Brad looking at her with a questioning gaze. She tilted her head and sent him a chilling smile that never reached her eyes. He turned away, looking hurt.

At 12:00 A.M. the dancing paused for the midnight supper. Katie avoided Brad's eyes each time he looked at her. Two unhappy people endured the remaining hours of the dance. Brad was gone when Katie awoke the next morning.

Chapter 27: Anxious Thoughts

I shouldn't have wasted my time, Brad told himself as he rode through slightly improved weather conditions back to his unit in Emmitsville. *She wasn't interested in seeing me at all. I thought she would at least remember our time together after her parents died. And Midnight. She wouldn't have Midnight except for my intervention on her behalf. He would be among the army's spare mounts.*

I don't know who all those fellows that danced with her at the New Year's Ball were, but she sure had a following. I didn't blame them either. Katie has grown up in the last year. That shining long hair of hers would make any man want to run his fingers through it. Her smile lights her eyes and shines from deep inside her. That almost smile she sent me last night chilled me to the bone, though. It felt like anger. Could she have been angry at me for some reason? Because I came late? Because I talked to her friend? Because I danced with her friend? That's it! I asked Wanda to dance before I asked Katie. Everything I intended went wrong. I looked forward to seeing Katie again and enjoying her innocent banter. I talked about her to Billy all the way there. Was I out of my mind? Next thing I can expect is the men teasing me.

Katie is turning into a beautiful woman and trouble is, I'm just too old to consider dating her. But that fact shouldn't have kept me from enjoying her company.

He'd been shocked by the changes in her—even felt shy around them. The eleven year old had blossomed in the year since he'd seen her last. The straight figure had swelled in just the right places to compliment the dress she wore, such a difference in the picture last year and this. Her glowing skin showed just the right amount of tan to make her look healthy and strong.

Brad couldn't forget dancing with the eleven year old girl last winter, how lightly she'd moved on her feet, how good it felt holding her in his arms. The remembrance heightened the protective feelings he'd always held for Katie. He forced his brain to remember again the ten year difference in their ages. Better forget her it said.

Billy, riding beside Brad, broke into his thoughts. "Did you have a good time with Katie like you planned?"

Brad's doleful expression answered the question before the man asked it. "You danced with that one young lady a lot. Was that Katie?"

"No! That girl Wanda monopolized me all night. I thought I'd be nice and ask her to dance because she was new. She wouldn't let go of me even between dances or after the dance ended. I didn't get to talk to Katie or dance with her the whole evening. Brad drew a quick breath and sat rigidly on his horse, running a hand through his hair. The other hand gripped the bridle tightly. "Now I may never get another chance. I think Katie's angry at me."

"Whoa! You're sounding a lot like someone who's pretty serious. I thought you said Katie is twelve. Are you willing to wait as long as you'll have to wait while she grows up?"

"I think I'd wait forever," Brad said. "She's worth waiting for. I know it doesn't make any sense for me to feel this way about a twelve-year-old, but I do."

Brad's riding companion remained silent. He knew he was hearing truth.

Chapter 28: Tah-Mano

January, 1874

Tah-Mano was frightened. Her father, the chief, had told his daughter that she would visit Katie in January. January had arrived, and her father said she must gather a few things before he took her over to Stone House to stay for awhile. She couldn't imagine what that would be like. She'd never lived anywhere but in their village in a tepee. She knew everything would be different at Stone House, and not knowing scared her. Food, sleeping, and all the daytime activities would be strange to her.

Today she would ride to Stone House with her father and two braves; they would leave her there alone, and ride home. The frigid weather worried her, too. The ride which would take several hours would be difficult for her to bear. She would miss the small warmth the tepee offered, and the rabbit-skin blanket that kept her warm in winter. Father said the blanket wouldn't be the right clothing in the white man's world. Besides all these worries she wondered how she could talk to them with the small amount of English she knew.

She pushed her fears aside and washed herself before donning her warmest acceptable clothing. Then she stood before her father. He mounted his horse, she mounted hers, and they rode out of the village, the two braves following. It was really happening. She would be living with white people. Father said if she did it, friendship would grow stronger between the whites and Indians, and that would help them all be safer and happier.

They rode through the white frosty countryside for several hours and at last could see Stone House in the distance. "You'll be safe, Tah-Mano, Okay you stay," her father said.

Her fears screamed at her, but she would obey, the way all Indian girls did. Her father knew best. She found some comfort in the fact that she knew Katie and Amanda slightly. She remembered them from the Camas field, how they'd given her their camas roots, and too, Katie had stayed overnight with them in the tepee. They were nice people. They had cared that Tah-Mano's family was hungry.

As they reached Stone House, the door opened and Katie emerged. She ran to Tah-Mano to give her a hug, but had to wait while Tah-Mano worked up the courage to dismount.

The Indian girl stood awkwardly after dismounting, not knowing what to do, but Katie's hug came swiftly, almost taking her breath away. Katie's joy at her arrival surprised and encouraged Tah-Mano, and soon the two girls were walking together into the house, Katie's arm around Tah-Mano's waist.

"I'll show you my room," Katie said. "I have two beds. You can use one of them. Here we are. This is my room."

Tah-Mano looked in wonder at the house and its furnishings, and thought it strange that Katie had such a big room where she slept alone. Seeing Rinehart Buttes out the window made her feel more at home there than anywhere else in the house, and it soon became her favorite place.

One of the first things Katie showed her was a picture book with lots of people and animals. Katie told Tah-Mano the name of each animal and waited while Tah-Mano repeated the name several times.

"Cow," Katie said pointing to the picture of a cow on the range. "Horse," she said and placed her finger on a picture of one. "People, person," Katie said as she pointed at a human being. Then Katie reviewed the same pictures over and over. She held the book in front of Tah-Mano and said, "I'm going to teach you to read. She pulled the book in front of her and read a line or two. "I read." She put it back in front of Tah-Mano. "You read."

She showed Tah-Mano the letters of the alphabet and how words were formed with a set of letters. She pointed to each set of letters. "Words. Then she pointed to each letter. A, B, C, D, E," she said. "I teach you."

At first Tah-Mano felt confused, but gradually some of what Katie was showing her began to make a little more sense, and she could remember the animal's names. Learning seemed easier when she realized she'd heard her father speak these words. She learned her ABC's, and then to make them into simple words, cat, hat, sat, bat. Katie wasn't a teacher, but she loved to read and enjoy books, and wanted to share that with Tah-Mano.

Later Katie read to Tah-Mano from Little Women by Louisa May Alcott, one of her favorite books. Tah-Mano didn't understand very much of it, but since words she'd heard from her father sounded familiar, she did understand some. Katie could tell that Tah-Mano enjoyed hearing the words. We'll read it again after she understands more, she thought.

Katie loved the story of the author's girlhood during the Civil War just past; how the mother and four girls survived without Mr. March at home, how they shared their Christmas dinner with poor people and did their best to help them even though they had troubles of their own. Laurie and Jo's almost love story was her favorite part. Because it was such a frigid winter and much too cold for riding, the girls spent a lot of time with the reading activity.

Another place Katie liked to spend time with Tah-Mano was the kitchen when Amanda and Mrs. McNeill were cooking. Tah-Mano never seemed to tire of watching the cooking processes. The young Paiute woman had never seen cream turned into butter by endlessly shaking it in a jar. She laughed and tasted it with her finger when it was done, surprised at its salty richness. She had never seen an iron stove. The whole house warmed when the women cooked in the kitchen.

Katie showed her how to combine biscuits or slices of the bread Amanda made and meat or cheese to make sandwiches, and they made them each day for lunch using the butter they'd made. Amanda's stews made from meat and canned vegetables warmed their bodies and fascinated the young Indian girl. She would stir the hot soup with her spoon and lift one veggie at a time out to look at it. She'd eat the pieces one by one like a miser counting his coins and fearing he might lose them. Katie learned, watching Tah-Mano, how much she had to be thankful for.

One day as Katie watched Tah-Mano eating her stew she knew she wanted to tell her friend about Jesus. Katie loved reading His story in the Bible, how He always knew what people needed and gave it to them, healing blind men and men with leprosy, a dumb man who couldn't speak or hear, even raising Lazarus from the dead. She remembered listening to her mother in wonder as she read to her from Matthew, Mark, Luke, or John about all the miracles He did in the three years after He started His ministry. She pondered the statements where He claimed to be God living on earth. She'd learned that His purpose was to accomplish His Father God's desire to make a way for sinful men to come back to Him. The book of John showed that He was the Creator. He lived on earth without missing His purpose for living; doing God's will. Katie hoped she could live like He did.

The part that Katie puzzled over was that it was God's will for Jesus His Son to die. "The wages of sin is death," the scriptures said, and Jesus—alone among all men—was righteous because He never sinned, and could pay the price of bringing selfish men back to God. God loved us so much that He gave His own Son to die. Katie, amazed at the thought, had trouble even imagining it, but she did believe it. There was so much Katie wanted to tell, but she knew she'd have to do it a little at a time.

One day in late January it was a little warmer. The sight of the sunshine and absence of frost tempted Katie to go for a ride. "Would you mind if Tah-mano rode Biscuit?" she asked Amanda. "We won't be out more than half-hour. It's too cold."

"No, I don't mind, but you'd better wait until early afternoon. It will be a little warmer then."

"Do you think Biscuit will let Tah Mano ride bareback? She's not used to riding with a saddle."

"Biscuit's so good natured; you could ride her through thunder and lightning. She'll be fine with a bareback rider. Just feed her a biscuit and she'll love you forever."

The girls waited as Amanda suggested, and after lunch went out to prepare the horses and set off toward the Crossing.

A bleak scene greeted them at the river crossing, no leaves on the willows, no billowing grass. The river flowed through a narrow channel, between ice-chunked walls built up along the sides. Only rocks, and sagebrush stood like lonely sentinels in the landscape.

The sunshine warmed them as they stopped west of Rinehart Buttes.

"Katie broke the silence. "Of all the scenery I've seen here in Malheur County I love the Buttes best. Aren't they beautiful, Tah-Mano? The Indian girl looked and saw Katie's eyes fixed on the top of the peaks.

"Nice. I like."

"God made all this. He must have loved us a lot to make it so beautiful, don't you think?" Katie held both arms toward the sky. "God loves Tah-Mano. He loves Katie. He loves Amanda and Lewis and Les and Al. Everyone in the world; your father and mother—even Wovoka and really bad people—God is love." Katie patted her heart hugged herself, and pointed to Tah-Mano.

Tah-Mano smiled. She liked hearing that the Great Spirit loved her. Somehow, she'd always known that.

"Even when we do bad things God loves us, but our wrong actions make a huge canyon between God and us, and we could never reach Him by ourselves. Sometime I'll tell you how God crossed that canyon and helped us."

Tah-Mano smiled, welcoming Katie's sharing.

"We'd better start home," the younger girl said. "We don't want to turn into an icicle, or cause Amanda to worry." Katie turned Midnight toward home and Tah-Mano followed her, anticipating the hot soup Amanda would probably have ready for them back at Stone House.

On the heights of the Buttes an unnoticed lone rider observed the girls on their horses and marked the route they followed to Stone House.

Chapter 29: Katie Gives

Tah-Mano struggled to read a very simple story called "Try, Try Again," from *McGuffey's Fourth Eclectic Reader* by William Holmes McGuffey. The writer of the story, T.H. Palmer, had wanted to encourage readers and those tackling a job to keep trying. Its message encouraged Tah-Mano even though the job of learning to read sometimes baffled her.

When Tah-Mano needed a rest, Katie shared John 3:16-17 from the Bible. "For God so loved the world that He gave His only begotten Son that whosoever believes in Him should not perish, but have eternal life." Tah Mano wanted to remember the verse, so they went over it again and again until she could almost say it.

"We all do wrong things," Katie said, encouraged by Tah-Mano's interest, "but Jesus didn't. He always followed God's will for His life. That's why He could pay the wages of sin—which is death—for all of us. He allowed Himself to die and be buried for our sins.

Tah-Mano looked sad. She didn't want to hear about Jesus dying.

"They put a great big stone in front of His tomb, but Jesus didn't stay in the grave anyway. He rose from the dead and walked around among people. His followers watched Him rise up in the air and go back to Heaven. He clobbered sin and death, ran them into the ground."

Tah-Mano's eyes grew large. "He's alive?"

"Yes, all His helpers saw Him. They touched Him and walked with Him, and saw Him eat. That's what we need to believe; that He came to earth to save us and He did; that He died, was buried, and then arose from the dead to pay for our sins. Romans 1:16 says "for I am not ashamed of the gospel for it is the power of God to salvation to everyone that believes. That story about Jesus and what He did for us is the gospel, and the Bible says we're to believe and obey it."

"Obey story about Jesus? How do?"

"That's a little hard to understand, Tah-Mano, but Amanda can explain it. Come on, we'll go ask her."

The two girls found Amanda in the kitchen cutting up vegetables. "Amanda, "I've been telling Tah-Mano about Jesus, but I need you to tell her about obeying the gospel."

"I'd be delighted to explain it, Amanda said. "I Corinthians 15, verses 1-4 say the gospel *is* the death, burial and resurrection of Jesus. Romans 6: verses 1-6 describe what happens to us when we obey Him and are buried into Christ. We'll read it later, but it says we die to sin, are buried, and rise to walk a new life. The Book of Acts shows people who want to obey getting buried in water. It's called baptism. So when we believe, we do the same thing Jesus did when we're baptized; we die, we're buried, and we rise again. It's a way to show that we accept what He did for us. God makes us His child and forgives our sins. That's obeying the gospel."

The Indian girl smiled. “That’s good. I tell Ma and Father Chief. They tell village.”

Tah-Mano’s father came for her near the end of January. Katie hated to see her go. During the time together they’d become the best of friends.

Chapter 30: Fox in Chicken Yard

Chuck Chiddless couldn't believe his eyes. From his perch on his horse he could see the whole valley, and since he sat on Rinehart Buttes' West side, Katie and Tah-Mano drew his attention. Seeing two girls on horses caught his interest quickly enough, but seeing a white and an Indian sitting there talking like friends irritated him.

Whites who cozied up to Indians ought to have their heads examined. The Indians couldn't be trusted, and even if they could they ought to be left alone to do their basket weaving and hunting. As far as Chuck was concerned they just weren't worth bothering with unless you could do a little business. This situation needed his attention

Chuck lived in a run-down shack beyond the Washoe Ferry in Idaho. He'd ridden the countryside today to survey the range for cattle he might be able to filch from their owners, cows somehow separated from the herd. He figured he deserved whatever reward he could get; that beef would taste pretty good for awhile. They should take better care of their stock, he told himself.

Chuck spent a lot of his time riding into small Indian villages and selling guns he'd secured from disgruntled soldiers with an inside angle. He felt justified in his illegal activities, and disrespected and disregarded laws meant to keep the peace. Stirring up trouble fit his disposition better.

When the two girls rode away, Chuck watched their direction, seeing them move toward the well-known Stone House where the Rineharts lived. When the girls entered the building he knew all he needed to know. He turned his horse toward Washoe.

Settlers long in the area knew Chuck as a vicious, evil-thinking scoundrel, and familiarity with the insults he hurled at Indians and Whites caused them to keep their distance. Newer settlers would listen, so he would search them out.

The Washoe area seemed his best bet. Several new families made claims there during the fall of seventy three. The Stroups listened for five minutes before sending him packing, saying, "Chuck, you should be ashamed of yourself!" He found a better reception from Gunner Judson who egged him on his way to stirring the Indians and Whites to confrontation, saying, "Them Rineharts got no biznes hob-knobbing with the enemy." Gunner's consort Dick Shysterman gave Chuck enthusiastic approval, suggesting, "We should kill'em all." Though less enthusiastic, Marv Vileman and Box Cringehorn, whom he found in the Crazy Horse tavern, agreed to go along with the group and confront the residents of Stone House. "Gotta put that Indian-lovin to a stop."

Chapter 31: Katie Remembers

Stone House seemed empty with Tah-Mano gone. Katie suddenly realized that time hung heavy. She spent much time giving thanks that she'd been able to tell Tah-Mano so much of the good news about Jesus. She believed what the Bible said, that the Word of God was like seed. When you planted it in the right soil it would grow. She believed Tah-Mano's heart was the right kind of soil.

When she wasn't thinking about Tah-Mano she found her mind occupied with Brad again. She couldn't help worrying about why Brad didn't ask her to dance at the Christmas Eve Ball. Thinking about that night always upset her.

It wouldn't have been so bad if she hadn't expected to be with him almost every dance, the way it was at the New Year's Eve Ball the year before. When he asked Wanda for the first dance she felt disappointed, but, sure he'd be there for her the next one, she kept her smile and accepted the first invitation she received. The whole evening turned into one big long-lasting frustration.

She'd shut the door on thoughts of Brad during January while Tah-Mano occupied her time, not wanting to let her brooding get her friend down, but now memories crowded in, tumbling one over the other until she felt like screaming. *He turned my world upside down when he ignored me. He fussed over Wanda all evening. He talked to everyone but me. I thought he'd at least come over after the dance and talk a minute.*

Unless he doesn't care about me at all. That thought depressed Katie until she lost her appetite. Anger took possession then. *Rude, that's what he was. Impolite, discourteous and unmannerly. She didn't care. Of course she didn't.* She ran for Amanda's company then.

Amanda's words weren't too encouraging. "Katie, Brad is so much older than you; it would be very unusual for him to have serious thoughts of marrying you. He's old enough to think about getting married, you're twelve. Those years are big ones when you're just entering your teens and he's already considered an adult. On the other hand, I was fifteen when Lewis married me, and he's got a few years on me. There are exceptions; you can always hope."

"But why did he ignore me at the dance? I thought we were at least friends."

"There could be a hundred reasons. He probably had business to talk over with his army pals."

"He spent the whole evening with that girl! I hate him!"

"Hate is a strong word, Katie. Use it sparingly. When you talk to Brad, I'd suggest that you behave like the friend you are, not like a wounded lover. Act like an adult, not a child. He'll appreciate you and think more of you because of it."

Katie tried to listen and learn from Amanda, but her fears still tormented her. One day when she could stand her thoughts no longer she went to Mrs. McNeill.

The woman she'd learned to love smiled at her and welcomed her into the room.

Katie sat and immediately blurted her thoughts: "I've been miserable since Tah-Mano left; no, really, since the Christmas Eve Dance. Brad was at the dance, but I was right there and he asked Wanda to dance before he asked me. He stayed with her all evening. I think about Brad all the time, and I'd even decided I wanted to marry him. I still think so."

Mrs. McNeill put another small stitch into the quilt she held in her lap. "You're pretty young to think such thoughts, but that's the way it happens sometimes. I was very young, thirteen, I think, when I decided I wanted to marry Mr. McNeill. Of course I needed a lot of patience to wait until he could see me as a woman instead of a child." Mrs. McNeill looked up at the girl and smiled. "It will be that way for you if you're determined enough. Spend time with him when you can, and give him time. Men don't want to feel like they're under a woman's thumb, or being pushed on or controlled. Be his friend for now."

Katie recognized basically the same message she'd heard from Amanda. Be patient and wait till you grow up. It was hard to hear, but its truth convinced her. *Be Brad's friend for now. Act older than twelve.*

Making the effort to be content, she helped with the chores, or spent time with Midnight, but when she returned to her room the whole litany of doubts moved in with her.

Chapter 32: Where's Brad?

Dear Mr. and Mrs. Rinehart,

I wanted to let you know what's going on with me. I've been assigned to a job at Fort Boise, working with the Paiute Indians, and I think you might have had something to do with it. Not directly, perhaps, but I hear you and the Vaughnes went out to a village and helped plant some crops. Your actions resulted in a request from the Indian agent for the army to use some of its men for that purpose. I have been chosen to implement the plan.

The belief is that this kind of help for the tribes will promote a friendlier attitude between the two nationalities. The Indians are hungry, as you know, and the more help they get with producing their own food the better things will be for all of us. Thank you for the inspiring effort you put into helping the native peoples. We hope you will continue with the project you've conceived as we join you in it.

My new assignment will keep me in the Boise area for some time, and most of my work will be in Idaho, but I hope to see you before too long. When spring comes we'll be busy with planting and training the Indians to grow their own food, so I'd like to take a little time soon to stop by, catch up on your activities, and learn your intentions.

I send my love and hope you're doing well.

Sincerely,

Brad J Jennings

P.S. I'm sending a note for Katie, and hoping you will deliver it to her.

The decision to write Katie hadn't come easily. Thinking about her made Brad realize how much he'd upset her by letting events at the dance get out of his control; by letting Wanda lead him around all evening. 'Sorry' didn't begin to express the fullness of his feelings. 'Desperate' would come closer to the word he'd choose since he knew she probably felt angry at him. He couldn't quit thinking about the little hazel-eyed red-headed budding beauty he'd met in the line of duty but come to want in his life. He needed to write to her, explain his actions, but embarrassed as he felt over them, it wasn't an easy task to explain them, even to himself, much less Katie.

Dear Katie,

I've wanted to write this letter for a long time now, but continually postponed it till I figured out exactly what to say. I've given up on ever getting it right, so here goes.

I hope you aren't mad at me, but I understand if you are. I acted thoughtlessly—you might consider it outrageously—at the Christmas Eve Dance. Asking Wanda to dance I did innocently enough, wanting to be nice to someone new. But letting her hang on to me all evening—that was inexcusable. I'll admit I felt flattered she wanted to keep dancing with me, but underneath I really wanted to be with you.

I looked forward to this dance for months and talked endlessly about you to my friend, Billy, but when I saw you and how you'd grown into a young lady so fast I let it fluster me and prevent what I really wanted, to be with you.

I'm having a hard time writing this. I know I haven't said the right things in the right way, but it's not going to get better, no matter how long I struggle. What I hope is for you to forgive the way I hurt you and allow our friendship to continue.

You can read the rest of my news in Lewis and Amanda's letter. I wanted to apologize in one especially to you.

I'll be visiting you folks soon, and hope you and I can go out riding together for old time's sake. I'm looking forward to seeing you, Katie.

My best to you,
Brad J. Jennings

Chapter 33: Unwelcome Visitors

Katie couldn't help it. She went to the windows over and over, looking toward the Crossing. Maybe, just maybe, she'd see Brad riding to the hitching post and tying his horse. She believed Brad's letter, but she had no idea how she would act when he walked in the door. She hoped, oh how she hoped, for control, but she knew angry feelings lay buried in her heart. A part of her wanted to hurt him the way he'd hurt her; in spite of knowing why it happened, in spite of knowing he cared about her. *He could have walked away from Wanda. He saw me there when he asked Wanda to dance. Why didn't he ask me first, anyway? Am I his friend? People shouldn't treat friends that way, should they?*

On her fourth or fifth trip to the front window Katie saw horses, she thought five of them, coming toward Stone House. She hurried to her room, ran a comb through her hair and patted it in place before returning to the front of the house.

The riders arrived, but kept their seats on their horses. *Not Brad.* Disappointed, Katie turned away from the window.

They'd looked angry, like bees disturbed while making honey, she thought. They probably wanted

Lewis, but Lewis wasn't here. Les and Al weren't here either. Suddenly Katie felt the fear knotting her stomach and clenching her jaw. "Amanda! Mrs. McNeill! Get your guns and come quick. We've got unfriendly company," she called to them.

Katie grabbed the rifle behind the door. Amanda came from the kitchen with a rifle in her hands. Mrs. McNeill raised her shotgun and headed for the door.

"Don't open the door, Mrs. McNeill. Use the windows, and keep out of sight. We'll talk to them through the window. What do you gentlemen want?" Amanda called out the slightly opened window.

"My name's Chiddless. We know you kept an Indian in your house," he snarled, "and we don't like it one bit. Just wanted you to know the folks around here won't stand for it."

"You and who else?" Amanda replied coldly. "Seems to me we have a right to make friends with whomever we like."

"Where's Mr. Rinehart?" Shysterman got to the point. "Our bizness is with him."

"Mr. Rinehart is busy," Amanda said, praying under her breath. Lord help us. These guys are angry; I don't want to use this gun."

"Tell him he'd better get unbusy and come to the door," Gunner Judson threatened. "We gotta take care of this bizness today and get on with more important stuff."

"You'll have to come back another time." Amanda put her gun out the window and said, "Goodbye, Gentlemen."

"Now just a minute, lady, no one can treat us like this," Chiddless said.

Katie's hushed voice brought welcome relief to Amanda who by now was trembling with tension.

"Amanda, several guys in uniform are coming. Keep them talking."

"How's Mrs. Chiddless?" Amanda's icy voice asked. "Bet she'd miss you if you didn't make it home. Several guns are aimed at you. Now please leave." Amanda pointed her rifle at a forty-five degree angle and fired. An unlucky crow flying just over the visitors tumbled into Chiddless' lap.

Chiddless jumped and flipped the bird from his lap, startling his horse in the process. The horse deposited his rider on the ground. Brad and his companions, alerted by the gunfire, kicked their horses to a gallop and drew up behind the thoroughly chastened troublemakers.

"What can we do for you, Mrs. Rinehart?" Brad asked.

"These men are trying to tell me I can't make friends with the Indians," Amanda replied. "We had Katie's Indian friend, Tah-Mano here for about a month. We were returning a favor their tribe did for us. Chiddless said the community didn't like it. I couldn't get them to leave, so I fired."

Brad rode in front of the foursome. "You villains had better watch your step. The government and the army stand behind the Rineharts in their mission to make friends with the native tribes of the Malheur County Reservation. If you oppose us you're the enemy. I'd advise you to rethink your options, and I insist you remember not to visit the Rineharts or anyone else with your upsetting message, ever again. I hope you get my point."

The unwelcome visitors numbly nodded.

"Before you leave, if you'd be so kind, I'll ask you to leave your names." Brad pulled a pen and notebook from his pocket. "We'll be reporting this incident to the government official in charge. If there are further problems he'll come looking for you."

The thoroughly disconcerted and chastised trouble-makers, one at a time, followed Brad's instructions to leave their names, and then, hanging their heads in embarrassment slowly rode away.

Chapter 34: Truce or Consequences?

Katie watched the five men depart, and suddenly felt her knees go weak. What would have happened had the army contingent delayed their arrival for even a few moments? What if the threatening men had pulled guns and fired when Amanda did? Without the distraction of the crow falling into Chiddless' lap would they all be injured or worse? She felt suddenly thankful. Such perfect timing could hardly be mere coincidence. "I know You knew what we needed, Father. Thank you for keeping us safe."

Amanda invited Brad and his companions into the kitchen and set them down to a lunch of the ever-ready stew she'd honed to perfection and kept ready for any visitor to Stone House.

Katie—thoughts churning—grateful for the men's presence, but withdrawn and uncomfortable at Brad's nearness, helped Amanda pull lunch together and get it on the table for the hungry men. She ate silently while the diners discussed the experience just past.

"I'm so glad we were here to help you. Hard telling what might have happened if we hadn't showed up." Brad reached for a biscuit and dipped into his bowl of hot stew. "But then you ladies could have handled that bunch without us, the way it looked to me. Chiddless must have been mortified, getting dumped from his horse the way he did." Brad's face wore a look of amusement as he remembered.

Billy agreed, "His face was redder than Little Red Riding Hood's cloak. I think with everything that happened the whole bunch will be easier for the community to endure." He turned toward Brad and asked, "Is this the young lady you've been talking about?"

"Excuse me for not introducing everyone. Yes, this is Katie. Katie, this is Billy, my constant riding partner. To his left are Charles, Bob, and Johnnie. They will be helping me with my new assignment." He turned to the residents of Stone House. "Men, meet Amanda Rinehart and Mrs. McNeill. Stone House is our home away from home, and Amanda is its perfect hostess. Mrs. McNeill makes things easier for Amanda. Katie lights up their lives, don't you, Katie?"

Katie, embarrassed, smiled—not knowing how to answer such a statement—and said nothing.

Brad, hoping for some kind of response, welcomed the smile, but wished for more. "Come on, Katie. Cat got your tongue again?"

Katie, nettled by the impossible-to-answer questions, stood and left the table, leaving the young man embarrassed and wordless.

Brad excused himself and followed Katie to the kitchen. "Let's go visit Midnight," he invited. "We can talk in the barn. Or we can go for a ride."

Katie irritably headed out the door to the barn. Not knowing what to say she reached for Midnight's saddle, buckled it on the horse, and put the bridle in place.

"A ride it is," Brad said. "Good idea." He walked with Katie to the hitching post, untied Bradley, and swung into the saddle. Katie mounted and spurred Midnight into a gallop, leaving the surprised Brad behind.

The galloping riders didn't slow until they reached The Crossing and Katie tugged Midnight to a stop. When Brad stopped beside her she said in a controlled quiet voice, "You hurt me. I'm still angry inside and don't know whether I want to talk to you."

"I understand that Katie," Brad said. "You have every right to be angry, but being angry isn't near as much fun as being glad to see me. Couldn't we just pretend the dance never happened? I'm so sorry for my actions, but I'm here with you now and I'll probably never see Wanda again. Come on Katie; tell me what you've been doing—about your adventures."

Katie looked at Brad for a long moment.

"Tell me about Tah-Mano," Brad prompted.

Katie smiled at last. "She's such a neat friend. We laughed together all the time. I stayed two nights in an Indian village with her. I learned a lot about the Indians, and had to eat what they ate. *That* was an adventure!"

Brad looked worried. "What happened, Katie?"

"I rode too far into a canyon west of here and got kidnapped by a couple of Indians. They took me to their village. One of the braves wanted a squaw and I happened to be there so he helped himself." Katie looked at Brad and saw his shocked look. "Everything turned out fine, though. Tah-Mano's father is chief of several villages, and he showed up and brought me home. That's why Amanda and Lewis let me invite Tah-Mano for a visit."

Brad's worry colored his voice a vibrant red. "Katie, anything could have happened. You *must* not ride alone beyond sight of Stone House. The Indian's ways and values are different from ours. Promise me you won't do it again."

"I won't ride into any canyon alone, that's for sure."

"Katie, Come on. Don't be mad at me. I'm your friend. I expected to have a wonderful time at the dance with you. You expected a great time with me. The dance disappointed both of us. Please forgive me. I didn't mean to hurt you."

Katie struggled, her feelings telling her to punish Brad and her conscience urging forgiveness. *He hurt me. I want to hurt him.* And then she could hear Amanda saying, "*You must forgive.*"

Jesus would say I must forgive if I want to be forgiven. Blame rose again. *But he shouldn't have let Wanda keep him from me all evening! If he was a real man he wouldn't have let that happen.* A familiar voice in her mind said, *"Be kind to one another, tender-hearted, forgiving one another,"* and Katie knew she must give up her desire for revenge. She must forgive.

"I'll forgive you, Brad. Will you forgive me for sending you that hateful look that night, and for getting so angry?"

"That's my Katie. Now we can have a better day."

"Let's don't talk about the kidnapping. It upsets me to think about how stupid I was. Maybe I'll tell you someday. What else would you like to talk about?

"I want to talk about you, Katie. Always you."

Chapter 35: Sharing Hearts

Katie looked at Brad gratefully and asked, "Would you mind if I talked about my parents in Tule Lake? I miss them, and I don't want Amanda and Lewis to know."

"What do you miss Katie? I want to hear about them and your life there."

"From the time I was little my mother used to read to me. Even after I learned to read myself, I considered having her read to me a special treat. She curled her arms around me, and it was just us, there together, getting lost in *Red Riding Hood*, or when I was older, books like *Robin Hood*. The book we were reading together at the last was *A Memoir of Jane Austen*. I'll always remember those times. They made me who I am."

"What wonderful memories, Katie. My mother died when I was so young I've never remembered her. I think it was something like tuberculosis that took her, but I'm not even sure of that. Dad never could talk about Mom after she died, not even several years later."

"Oh Brad, I'm so sorry. I need to be more thankful I had my mother as long as I did."

"I used to ask Dad questions. He'd turn his back and walk away. If my oldest brother hadn't told me a few things, I'd know nothing."

"Thanks for sharing this, Brad. I needed to hear it. You must have been so lonely!"

"Dad's failure to answer my questions forced me to get used to being lonely and feeling like I'd never had a mother at all. I wish I'd had her for a little while…but I'm talking way too much."

"No you're not. I want to hear it."

"What else did your mother do?

"Lots of times I would be so excited at the end of the day that I couldn't go to sleep. Mom had a rocking chair. That's where I went to sleep many nights." Katie smiled shyly at Brad.

"I hid under the covers and read most nights, long after everyone else in the house was asleep."

"I did some of that, too, after I was older." Katie smiled at Brad. "I just couldn't put my book down."

"Sounds like both of us had our moments as pills," Brad observed, "in spite of everything. That must make us equals."

Katie laughed. "I'm getting cold, aren't you? Shouldn't we start home? Somebody will be worrying if we don't get there soon." Katie turned her horse toward home. "Thanks Brad, for listening to me a little. I really loved hearing something about you, too."

"We'll look forward to next time," Brad said. "We've a lot to talk about."

The two riders steered their horses toward Stone House, closer friends than when they left it.

Chapter 36: Big Plans

Katie and Brad returned to find Les and Al, Billy, Amanda, and Lewis sitting around the table, still talking. They were excited about Brad's new assignment, and what it would mean as far as relationships with the Indian tribes.

"Oh, there you are!" Lewis welcomed the riders to their midst and turned to Brad. "We're eager to hear more of what you're thinking—about your new assignment, I mean. How did you want to implement it?"

"First of all, I want to visit the tribes here in Malheur County. We'll begin with Chief Numaga's village. I've been thinking about more than gardening; teaching the native peoples some of the field-crop-growing techniques we used back east. Perhaps things like how to use water from the river for irrigation. We could show them how to build wagons for hauling water, or flumes to carry it from the river. Or we could suggest canals and ditches to carry it. It may be a job to convince them that learning is worth all the work it'll take, but they should appreciate our trying to help them whether they adopt the practices we teach or not."

"Great ideas, Brad. I don't think building wagons is a very practical idea since the supply of lumber is so far away, but I'll bet, knowing how resourceful the native peoples are, they'd be able to use sage brush to build flumes. Ditches and canals are practical ideas too. I would imagine most Indian villages lie pretty close to either a river or a stream. What do you think we should do first?"

"Well, selling them on the idea of growing field crops may be the first challenge. They're in the habit of moving from place to place to hunt for their food, and keeping them around to tend the crops they've planted won't be easy; it will involve a huge change for them, a change they may not be willing to make. Choosing the right crops at first will be a critical piece of the puzzle." Brad looked at Lewis, then Katie, and was pleased to see her rapt attention to the discussion.

"What do you think about potatoes?" Les made the suggestion, and the wisdom of it struck the listeners. "We should be able to get seed potatoes from Simplot, south of here who's been experimenting with them. He's found that they grow well and don't need a whole lot of attention while they're growing. We have the sunshine and the soil."

"Yeah," Al said. "The food value of potatoes will be obvious to the native people, and since they've lost their rights to the Camas prairie, potatoes should seem like the answer to many of their food problems."

"Potatoes do need some attention. Are you forgetting that the soil has to be hilled and the depth increased as the plant grows?" Billy, who had experience with the plant under discussion, spoke. "If the men are off hunting and the women looking for the plant sprouts and bulbs they usually hunt in spring, who will do the maintenance of the potato plants?"

"I want to go with you." Katie interrupted the serious conversation. "I can help, and I want to see Tah-Mano. May I go? "She turned toward Lewis and Amanda with questioning eyes.

"I don't see any reason why you can't go," Lewis said. "What do you think, Amanda?"

"How long will you be gone?" Amanda wanted to know. "Where would Katie stay?"

"Maybe I can stay with Tah-Mano," Katie said. "She'd be happy to have me there, and I'd be safe in the chief's tepee."

"I'm thinking I'll stay for a week, Lewis answered. "The other men will probably stay longer, but Katie could come home with me."

"So it's settled. I'm going." Katie's eyes danced like a ballerina in allegro. When do we leave?"

"Just a minute, young lady. We're still in the planning stage," Lewis turned to Brad again. "Are you acquainted with the Indian agent, Samuel Parrish, Brad? I hear he's very interested in programs like ours. Maybe he can help us get the supplies we need."

"I've met him, and I did like him. He has a friendly attitude toward the Indians, and goes into debt trying to get the supplies they need to successfully teach farming to the native peoples. His attitude irritates a lot of the ranchers, but I'm sure he'll do what he can to help us; maybe even go with us to work. The problem is he doesn't get much support from the government, they don't keep the promises they made to the Indians. We'll have that problem too."

Lewis pushed his chair away from the table. "We'll do what we can. Let's put the plan in motion. Al, Katie and I will go with Brad to the village. We'll talk to the chief and let him know our plans. If he agrees, we can start preparing the land. Les, you and Billy will go for the potato sprouts and bring them back here. Try to bring enough for about an acre of ground. We'll want to plant them by May first."

"What tools will we need?" Al's thoughtful question voiced everyone's concern. "Most people who came west brought a plow. Perhaps we can check around for plows we could borrow.

"Les and I can check out what Mr. Simplot is using when we go for the sprouts," Billy said.

"Let's plan our departure to the village for early April." Lewis looked around at the group. "That'll give us time to tie up loose ends—get the Indians' approval, talk to the Indian agent, borrow our tools, and get the sprouts. We'll bring in a cow from the range, too. That way we can all, Indians and Whites, enjoy it together." Lewis looked with satisfaction at his team. "Thanks to everyone for your ideas."

Brad felt thankful, too, not so much for the plans which had been made as for Lewis and Amanda's agreement that Katie could go along. A project for which he'd had but little heart suddenly assumed priority.

Chapter 37: Growing Pains

Katie couldn't wait. The days during March stretched endlessly before her. As she thought of being with Brad for a whole week it seemed like anticipating heaven itself. They could ride together on the way out to the village, work together during the days and eat together at mealtimes. They could talk about all the things they'd experienced, the things they liked and disliked. She constantly thought of Brad and all they would experience together—the way he'd joke with her, the way he'd look at her, the way it made her feel, the tender things he might say to her. All her imaginings focused on the week they would have together. *How could everything not be too wonderful to describe?*

As the hills around Stone House greeted Spring in their fleeting new green dresses, Katie's impatience for departure spurted and spilled over, leaving Amanda and Lewis wondering why she felt so much anticipation. The trip amounted to a lot of hard work as they looked ahead, and the uncertainty of the Indian's response to their offer remained. But Katie habitually pictured beauty in almost every situation, and always expected richness. She looked forward to seeing Tah-

Mano, they knew, and allowed that one fact to explain her euphoria.

"I hope you realize you'll be working hard every day," Amanda reminded her. "You might even become the cook for all those hungry men," but Katie's expectations refused to waver. Nevertheless, Amanda taught Katie how to prepare a beef and vegetable dinner, just in case.

Later that month Lewis rode out to the village where Tah-Mano's father was recognized as chief; the village where they'd previously helped plant vegetable gardens. He talked to Chief Numaga about their plans and the army's willingness to work with them. The chief looked encouraged and spoke enthusiastically and gratefully when he heard about their mission.

"The carrots, peas and beans helped us get through a difficult time," he said. "We'd be happy to learn anything else you can teach us. When will you be here?"

The late April date pleased Chief Numaga, so plans were firmed, tools located, ordered, and received, and a supply of food gathered. The pioneers rode away from Stone House on Monday, April 27.

Katie waited for the others to ride out first, and she, seemingly coincidently, rode out in the rear with Brad.

Riding, she found, didn't allow for the same easy conversation they'd enjoyed at the Crossing, but, at least for Katie, just being near Brad was reward enough. They'd have more time to talk later.

They'd been riding for an hour when Lewis turned his horse and rode back. "Brad, Can we talk for awhile? Katie, will you ride with Al?"

Disappointed at the turn of events, Katie rode forward and took Lewis's place beside the cowhand. Al turned and smiled at her. "Hey, Katie, Are you enjoying the ride or is it a little too long for you?"

"I can hardly wait to get there and see Tah-Mano. I'll be very glad to have something to do."

"There'll be plenty to do all right. Tilling the soil is hard work. Even cooking isn't so easy under the conditions we'll be living in."

"I like to help. I used to help my Dad and Mom in the garden. I love to see things grow." Katie grinned in Al's direction. "Sometimes the weeds aren't so much fun, though."

"You've got that much right," Al pulled a pipe and tobacco from his pocket, added tobacco to the pipe and lit it. "but it's always good to know you're helping someone out." The two rode on silently.

Finally the canyon where the village sat came into view, they rode gratefully toward the tepees they saw ahead.

Hunger came with the long ride and Katie looked forward to the sandwiches she remembered Amanda tucking into their supplies, enough for a day or two. After that they'd be on their own or eat what the Indians offered. As Katie remembered, that wasn't too much fun, but she'd do whatever was needed. She wasn't having any of that Hawthorne tea, though.

Just before they arrived at the village they stopped for a quick lunch of sandwiches and apples. Katie got off her horse. Surprised at how stiff she felt she waddled up the trail, trying to stretch her legs as she went. When she turned around to return to the others, she saw Brad coming toward her with lunch for two in his hands and a huge amused grin on his face.

"Oh! Hi Brad. Thanks for thinking of me. I *am* ready for lunch!"

"I'm usually thinking of you, Katie. Eat up."

As Katie began eating her sandwich, Brad talked to her about the work days coming. “I’ll be plowing most of the time in the next few days,” he said. “We’ll need you to cook up some of that beef we brought, and some vegetables to go with it. We’ll do the butchering job in the morning, and you’ll be all set.”

“Oh,” Katie said, surprised in spite of Amanda’s earlier offhand comment about cooking. “I thought I’d be gardening or something.”

“The plowing is too hard for you, Katie. We need someone to be our chief cook and bottle washer. Think you can do it? It’s the way you can help the most.”

Katie listened silently to Brad, not happy about what she heard. While the others were out on the prairie, she’d be here trying to figure out the best way to cook beef with a campfire. She was willing to do her part, but knowing she’d have to give up being with Brad during the work day challenged her composure. She held back tears, not wanting Brad to see. “I’ll try, she said, “but I’ve never cooked in camp before. You’ll be my tasters, and I’m not guaranteeing anything. What pots and pans do we have?”

“We have the big stew-pot Lewis brought. That’s all I’m aware of.” Brad looked apologetically at the discouraged girl. “You’ll figure something out. Nothing has to be fancy, and beef vegetable soup always tickles the taster. Gotta get busy now.”

Brad walked away wondering why he felt slightly guilty.

Chapter 38: Katie the Cook

At least I know how to do the stew. Katie looked at the huge stewpot Lewis had retrieved for her and the fire Les and Al had helped her build. Lunchtime had come and gone; the men were out in the field digging and plowing. *I'm glad Amanda showed me how to put in carrots, potatoes, and onions. I should have listened to her more carefully and asked a lot more questions. I was just too busy dreaming about all the time I'd have with Brad.* Katie shoved away the memory of the impossible situation she felt Brad had put her in. *I can't think about Brad now. These vegetables must be peeled and into the pot fast or the stew won't be done when the men want to eat.* Abruptly Katie realized she must get water from the stream.

She carried the bucket down a rough path to the stream-bed, got on her knees, and stretched her body to reach the water. Retrieving a partially full bucket of the clear liquid she set it on the bank and struggled to her feet. The downhill path she'd followed to her destination surprised her with its sudden steepness; it drained her energy steadily as she toiled uphill with the heavy bucket of water. She poured it into the pot hanging above the fire before she realized she would need water to wash and peel the vegetables.

Oh well, I'll have to make another trip. This time she dipped only enough water to do the job and returned more easily to the campfire. Finding a paring knife among the tools she dipped a potato into the water and began the messy job she hated, even in the best of circumstances. She soon realized her mistake. She had muddied the clean water. How could she wash the vegetables after they were peeled? She'd have to return to the stream. She dragged her tired body down the hill and up again, beginning to feel slightly irritated. Who she was irritated with she wasn't sure.

It took the frustrated cook nearly an hour to get the newly butchered beef cut into pieces small enough to eat and the carrots, onions and potatoes peeled, washed and put into the pot. She looked through the supply carton and found salt and pepper. *That should do it. At last.* She picked up a long-handled spoon and stirred the contents of the pot hurriedly, avoiding the heat from the fire by turning from one side to the other. *I wonder if I put enough veggies in there, and enough water. Tough if it isn't right. I've peeled all I'm going to peel today. This cook is escaping the kitchen.*

Perhaps I can find Tah-Mano, the reluctant chef told herself. She left the campfire burning in its pit, the potential stew heating in its pot, and wandered toward the village a short distance away.

Things look strangely familiar, she thought. *It hasn't been that long since I've been here. Things were really different then. I was a prisoner last time.*

She recognized the chief's tepee immediately. Her walk turned into a run as she approached. "Tah-Mano! Tah-Mano!" she called. A woman looked through the opening of the wigwam and turned back into it. Tah-Mano ducked through the gap and into Katie's open arms. They hugged enthusiastically.

Tah-Mano grinned shyly at Katie. "I'm glad you're here," she said.

"You remembered!" Katie squealed.

"Yes. I talk in English with my father now. I learn much." Tah-Mano reached for Katie and hugged her again. "Thank you. I like to read."

The disappointments of the long day disappeared at Tah-Mano's words. *I'm so glad I tried to teach her. It wasn't an easy job, but I made her want to learn.* All *the hard work paid off. Tah-Mano will be my friend forever.*

"I'll show you my secret place." Tah-Mano took her arm and led her through the gathering of dwellings, and then away from the village to the back of a huge rock on the west side. There they found a path leading up the canyon wall. They climbed steadily until they came to a small protected cove beside a lone juniper. A large boulder provided shade and privacy. Tah-Mano stopped and directed her gaze toward Katie.

"I love your place." Katie seated herself on a fallen log and stretched her legs and back. "Do you come here often?"

"This is where I will read someday," Tah-Mano answered, "when I have book."

"I brought a book," Katie answered immediately. *Uncle Tom's Cabin.* Tah-Mano's eyes softened and radiated a soft light. She put her hands over her heart and held them out to Katie. "I will read it and think of you. You are my true friend."

"Thank you for showing me your very own place," Katie said. "I will think of you here, reading, but now I have to get back to the camp. I left dinner cooking over the fire."

The two girls rose and retraced their steps down the hillside back to the chief's tepee. Tah-Mano gave Katie a long hug and they parted.

As Katie returned to the camp she could make out the aroma of the stew. She hoped it was as good as her nose said. The hungry men would arrive soon.

Chapter 39: Campfire Dinner

"Gee, I'm one hungry hombre." Al came striding to the campfire area, smile on his face, tapping on his pipe. "I can smell that stew Katie. Got some biscuits to go with it? I could just about eat a horse."

"Biscuits? You want biscuits?" Feeling suddenly like she'd botched it all, Katie failed to see how she could possibly make biscuits with a campfire and only a kettle. "Is there something I don't know? Tell me how I could make biscuits," she said defensively.

"Fry pans come in pretty handy at a time like this," Al said. "Let's dig through the supplies and tools and see what we have. I thought I put one in." He searched through the box, and in the very bottom, he found it: a heavy iron skillet. "Here's some flour and baking soda too. Add a little water and we've got everything we need. We'll just mix the dough, fry it up, and dinner's ready. Don't we have some bacon? We can fry a little and use the fat to keep the biscuits from sticking."

Amazed at his words and the ease with which he performed the actions he described, Katie watched the cowhand complete her dinner. "We might want to thicken the stew, too," he said. "We've all been working hard." He made a thin paste of flour and water, dumped it into the stewpot and stirred using the long wooden-handled spoon

"There. The chief and several of the Indians who worked with us will be here to join us. The stew will thicken while we fry the biscuits."

Wow! He works like a whirlwind, and knows just what to do. Katie felt even more inadequate, but she was glad for Al's help. She'd wondered whether her stew would be enough for the hungry men.

About thirty minutes later the rest of the men arrived, Brad bringing up the rear. Katie thought he looked upset, and briefly wondered why, but she was more concerned about dinner. She saw Al tasting the stew and adding salt and pepper. The biscuits were fried to a slightly charred doneness. "It's scrumptious, Katie. You did well. Chow's on!"

Lewis held out his hands. "Let's join hands and offer thanks for our food." Smiles lit the faces of the men.

Katie looked up from the prayer to see Tah-Mano and the chief as well as several other Indian men. *I sure hope they like the stew. I hope there's enough to go around.*

Al stayed beside her, helping her dish the hot meal into wooden camping bowls. The Indian guests each carried their own bowl from home and offered it up for filling, their faces reflecting their anticipation of the bountiful meal.

The group quieted as they ate their food. Katie enjoyed watching the looks of approval on the men's faces; there were no words to describe the appreciation on the faces of their guests. She thought she could have added more carrots and onions to give a fuller flavor, and resolved to look for other vegetables she could add.

Maybe Tah Mano or her mother could help her find something green to add further nutrition. Suddenly Katie realized how much she had learned by taking on the cooking responsibility, however unwillingly she had done it, and she now looked forward to the challenge of tomorrow and the days following.

Brad interrupted the relative quiet. "You men can be very proud of all you accomplished today. And Katie, I'd like to compliment you on the wonderful meal you made for us. The field is plowed and raked. Tomorrow we can start planting the potatoes."

He turned toward the Indians. "The next crucial job to finish is a flume or canal from the stream. Those potato sets will need to be watered regularly. Watering will be a backbreaking job until the flume is completed since the water must be carried in buckets. I'm depending on you, our Indian friends, to take on the watering and the flume. Your experience with creating from the sagebrush will be something we can't add to, so we'll trust your judgment. Just let us know how the work is proceeding."

The chief nodded at Brad, and then at his companions. "We'll do it," he said. He turned and interpreted the message to his crew.

"Thank you, Chief. I wish all the news was as good." Brad's face mirrored his displeasure. "Chiddless and his cronies are at it again. Remember the guy who tried to stir up trouble for the Rineharts when Tah-Mano visited them last winter? Now he's agitating some of the younger Indian braves, telling them we're spying. They're protesting our presence here, and he's trading rifles to them. Can you put a stop to this, Chief? Talk to your young men; convince them we're helping you and that Chiddless is the enemy?"

"I will," the chief said.

Brad continued his summary. "We'll make it a point to talk to Chiddless and his friends, too. Perhaps we can discourage them, though I doubt it. Good sense came up missing in those heads, if I can judge by their actions. Lewis, how do you think we can discourage what they're doing?"

"The chief could gather a bunch of men and give those guys a good scare; chase them out of the village; put on war paint and all. That should slow them down enough that we can complete our work here. Just be sure no one gets hurt." Lewis turned to the Indian leader and asked, "What do you think, Chief?"

"I'll terrify them." The chief smiled. "They won't come back."

"Won't a tactic like that backfire; make us regret it later? That bunch would leave here and talk everywhere they went." Brad looked at Lewis. "Your idea does sound mighty tempting, though."

"Here's another idea." Louis slapped his leg. "Chief could figure out a way to take them prisoner, and then humiliate them in front of those young rebel Indians. Say, take their pants away and make them do the cooking. Keep them guessing for awhile. They wouldn't be so quick to talk about something like that to everyone they see, and your people, Chief, couldn't be accused of warlike actions."

The conversation continued; more suggestions, lots of laughter, until Lewis called a halt. "The chief will figure it out," he said. "We've got a big day tomorrow. Bedtime."

Chapter 40: Week's End

The week at Chief Numaga's village passed quickly. Katie's culinary camping skills increased in a manner noticeable to all those who dined at her campfire. Tah-Mano showed her where to find wild turnip and other wild bulbs, tubers and vegetables to add to the stew, much to Katie's delight and the approval of the hungry men.

The potato sets grew happily in their new field home. The Indians busily and competently worked gathering sagebrush for the flume and laying the line it would follow from a high place near the stream to the field nearer the valley.

Chief Numaga did his part to discourage the destructive behavior of Chiddless and his crew; they left the village early in the week, leaving everyone to work in peace. What the grinning chief did to ensure the departure of the mischief-makers remained his secret.

The one big disappointment of the week as far as Katie was concerned, was that Brad was so busy, always working somewhere other than where she was. He was distracted, so much so that he didn't seem like the Brad she knew. He had little time or energy left to share with her.

The irritation Katie felt initially when Brad told her she was to do the cooking had disappeared, and if she hadn't been so busy and involved with her responsibilities she would have grieved his absence. She would have worried about his sudden apparent disinterest.

On Saturday Brad loitered around the campfire after breakfast until everyone left for their work locations. Lewis, Les, Al, and Billy went with the Indians to observe the partially finished flume and learn what they could from the Indians.

"How did Katie the cook like her job this week?" Brad asked.

"Well. Finally you got around to asking," Katie said. "At first I was scared to death and mad at you, but the more I cooked the more I enjoyed combining all the different vegetables with the beef to make the stew. Les and Al helped me learn, and cooking was fun after Tah-Mano started helping me; there was something new to try every day."

"I'm glad you're not angry with me anymore. I want you to know your cooking freed a man to help in the field. We made much better progress than we might have.

"I have no idea what you've done out there other than what I learned listening at the campfire. I'm a little disappointed about that."

"We can't leave you disappointed. Brad placed a hand gently on Katie's shoulder. Can you leave the campfire for awhile? Let's get our horses and ride over to the field. Showing you around will give me a nice break from the pressures of the week. He turned Katie to face him and looked at her tenderly. I've missed being with you, Katie. I hope you know that."

Katie felt the blush cover her face, but she sure liked what she heard. “Sure Brad. I’d love to have you show me around. The stew will simmer nicely while I’m gone. I’d like to see the irrigation project as well as the field. I’m so glad we made good progress, and Brad, I’m glad you missed me. I missed you, too.”

The two friends untied Midnight and Bradley, mounted, and rode together toward the field. Short moments later, Katie saw the field. The men had plowed and harrowed the prairie—about an acre—and dug furrows about six inches deep and six inches apart. The field lay on a rather flat area of hillside. Katie pictured in her mind what it would look like when the bright green of potato vines broke through the surface of the soil. The Indians would have their work cut out for them then, hoeing extra soil around the young plants regularly to keep the vines growing. Each additional inch of soil meant a new bunch of potatoes. No hoeing or hilling meant very few and very small potatoes.

“Do the Indians know what to do when the potatoes come up?”

“We’ve explained the crop’s needs. They’ll need to get a regular water supply to the potatoes, especially before they come up and flower. And then there’s the work of hilling the young plants regularly. They need special care when harvesting, and we need to teach them storage methods. There will be time for that later.”

“Oh Brad, the field looks wonderful. You guys did a good job. Where’s the irrigation system?”

Brad rode ahead of Katie to the upper edge of the field. As she looked ahead she could see the stream, a much higher portion of it. From the stream’s edge she saw a box like structure with bottom and sides fit together to funnel the water. The trough they formed followed down the hillside to the field. She could hardly believe the flumes were made from sagebrush. Inside the troughs the Indians had painted tar; something Katie knew would repel water and keep the troughs from leaking.

Pride filled Katie's heart; to be a part of such an accomplishment. Seeing the progress they'd made and knowing the Indians' gratitude renewed her confidence in the future of Indian-White relationships. The Indians would spend their winter with fuller stomachs and feel less need to destroy what white men created.

"I'm proud of you, Brad. Katie turned shining eyes toward the tall young man with tousled, wavy hair. "Just look at all you've done."

Chapter 41-: Rumors of War

June 1876

Though Brad continued his work with the native populations of Malheur, Union, and Harney Counties in Oregon as well as the Bannocks of Southeastern Idaho, rumors plagued both the Indian populations and the Whites. The most upsetting news concerned the Lakota & Cheyenne tribes in Montana Territory lead by Chief Sitting Bull. Latest information said that General George Armstrong Custer and his Seventh Cavalry Division had been soundly defeated in a deadly battle on the Little Bighorn River. Two-hundred-sixty-eight men died including many army officers and General Custer; fifty-five were injured in the battle recently dubbed Custer's Last Stand. This unwelcome news brought in by the stage, destroyed the settler's confidence in the U.S. Army's ability to control the Indian populations and replaced it with fear.

"Just goes to prove you never know how many Indians there are. They travel here and there for lots of reasons," Al said to Lewis one morning. "I've heard thatthe Seventh Cavalry at Little Big Horn expected no more than seven hundred or so Indians, and they ended up fighting over fifteen hundred. It resulted in a lot of dead men."

"I'm thankful for the relative peace we've enjoyed here," Lewis responded. "We won't need to send the army out for punitive reasons, thanks to all Brad's hard work."

"That may be true," Les said, "But we should be prepared; we need to know what we would do in an emergency. Each family needs a safe haven."

"People here are already scared," Al volunteered. "They think the Indians will be aroused by reports from Montana, and I think that's a huge possibility. Rumor is that Mrs. Stroup, frightened by what she's heard about the massacres around Weiser, Idaho, has taken the stage and returned to Missouri. Mr. Stroup is sleeping in the willows pretty regularly."

Indians anxiously protected their native lands in whatever ways they could, and the U.S. Army and volunteer units set out on expeditions intended to punish their thievery and other depredations—with more or less success.

The precarious peace in Malheur County shattered in June 1876 with additional bad news of several bands of the historically peaceful Nez Perce Indians' refusal to leave their ancestral lands further north in the state—lands promised to them by the Walla Walla Treaty of 1855.

Some said a wishy-washy government had failed to keep the promises it had made to Indians who consented to move to reservations. Promised food supplies never arrived, or if food did arrive, it was spoiled. Capricious land-hungry settlers persisted in staking claims on Indian lands, and as a result government further restricted Indians' access to lands necessary for their food-gathering. The word 'restless' euphemistically described the Indians' state of mind.

When the U.S. Army decided to drive the Nez Perce off their land—now desired by settlers in Northeastern Oregon—in a war described as a "fighting retreat of 1170 miles"—the native peoples were forced from their ancestral lands.

A fugitive Chief Joseph sought help first from the Crow Indians, and then, when they refused, he appealed to Sitting Bull (of the Battle of the Little Bighorn, 1876) who had found refuge in Canada. The fleeing Nez Perce struggled to within forty miles of the Canadian border only to be defeated.

Chief Joseph's surrender words are recorded in part. "Hear me, my chiefs! I am tired; my heart is sick and sad. From where the Sun now stands, I will fight no more forever."

1877

The Bannock Indians in Southeastern Idaho learned what had happened to the Nez Perce. They resentfully knew the army's history of midnight raids on sleeping villages, and that those survivors who surrendered were shipped half way across the country to Leavenworth, Kansas.

After ten years of confined living, they had their fill of starving on the reservation at Fort Hall. Upon seeing the defeat of the Nez Perce and watching the capricious land-hungry encroachments of the "pale face" onto their own important food-source lands, they made a desperate decision. They would convince the tribes of the Paiute and Umatilla to make a united stand against the whites.

They needed arms. In a reckless act of duplicity Chief Buffalo Horn of the Bannocks convinced the governor of Idaho of his friendship. The governor responded by providing the Indians with arms, disregarding a law made for protection of the white population.

The first casualty of the war died on Big Camas Prairie in May of 1878 when the Bannocks murdered a white settler. Chief Buffalo Horn continued west along the Snake River with two hundred warriors and their families, leaving shock and confusion behind. They captured the stage station at King's Hill, killing the driver, destroying property at the station, and taking the horses, leaving the men in charge surprised to be alive. At Glenn's Ferry they cut the lines connecting the ferry to shore, destroyed two freight wagons and their contents—except for the liquor which they drank—burned several farm houses in the vicinity, and drove off the horses. News of these attacks sent the settlers running for their lives.

The terror spread down-river. Those who chose to stay risked their lives; those who ran spread word of the encroaching danger.

Chapter 42: Friends Forever

June, 1878

"Can Tah-Mano come to visit me during the winter?" Katie watched while Amanda cut up vegetables for a stew.

"Oh Katie, things are so complicated with all the Indian unrest. Wouldn't it be better to wait?"

"Tah-Mano's still my friend. Her father is a friend of Lewis and Brad. Everyone in the village knows we are their friends. How many times has Lewis sent food to them?"

"I know, Katie, everything you say is true, but Indians are so unpredictable. Anything can change them from friends into enemies. They'll do what seems best for themselves every time."

"Not Tah-Mano. She loves us. The winters are so hard in the village, and we can help her by having her here. Please say yes."

Amanda forgot her vegetables. "We'll ask Lewis what he thinks, and Les and Al might have some feelings about the wisdom of bringing her here."

"Oh thank you, Amanda. I knew you'd say yes."

Katie bounced away toward her room leaving a surprised Amanda wondering how her just-turned-seventeen-year-old had found a 'yes' in her answer.

Typical teenager. Hears only what she wants to hear. I hope she won't be too disappointed with Lewis's answer. Amanda added the liquid to her stew recipe, put the lid on the pot, and set the pot on the hot iron stove.

Relieved to have the job finished, she sat at the kitchen table with her coffee. She flipped to the book of Philippians in her Bible. In Chapter Four, she read, *"In nothing be anxious, but in everything by prayer and supplication with thanksgiving, let your requests be made known to God, and the peace of God which surpasses all comprehension, shall guard your hearts and your minds in Christ Jesus."*

"Yes, Father, This is Amanda. I don't want to be anxious, so I am praying to you right now. I am thankful for the protection You've given us daily during these years we've lived in this lonely land. We have a safe home we can offer to others for protection if the Indians become angry and vengeful. I know I can trust You and Your promises if I obey Your commands. Help Lewis make the right decision about Tah-Mano. Thank You for the peace I feel. I'm coming to You through Jesus, and I know You hear."

Amanda sat quietly with her coffee until Lewis came through the door.

"Will Les and Al be here for dinner tonight?"Amanda asked.

"No Darling, I've sent them to the Washoe range to check on the cattle, and the settlement, too, to see if there's more news. They'll be back tomorrow, by noon, I'd guess. Tonight it'll be you and I, Katie and Mrs. McNeill. How is Mrs. M. feeling now? Has the flu bug departed from our residence?"

"I think she's better, but she needs another day or two to get her energy back."

"Good! What's going on with our girl? Anything new?"

"There is something I need to talk to you about. Katie wants to invite Tah-Mano again for part of the winter. I'm wondering if the current Indian unrest would make it a bad idea."

"Well, I can't see right now what harm it'd do, and it might reassure her village that we're still intending to be friendly. What bothers you about the idea? I can tell you're hesitant."

"I'm not sure what bothers me. I've just heard so many stories…."

"I remember the stories, Amanda, but Jesus tells us to treat others the way we'd want to be treated. I think that'll be good advice in this case. Tell her Tah-Mano can come in January."

"Lewis, I can't tell you how glad I am you're saying yes. Katie was counting on both of us. Now she won't be disappointed."

"There is something you should know, Amanda. The Bannock Indians are on the move again. Chief Buffalo Horn and his warriors killed a settler on Big Camas Prairie, and he's moving west along the Snake, destroying and killing as he goes. Troubled times are here. We'd best prepare."

Chapter 43: The Fight is On

May, 1878

"The army will be assembling here within the week, Amanda." Lewis moved toward his wife as she prepared biscuits for their breakfast. "They'll be trying to restore some order with the Indians. We'll need food ready to speed them on their way."

Amanda heard with her usual grace. "Mrs. McNeill, Katie, and I can handle it. We'll start today getting things ready. I think stew will be the best choice of a meal for so many. Will you be sure I have some beef? I'll tell my kitchen crew when they come down."

"Thank you for being so understanding. You're wonderful, Sweetie."

Amanda blushed and approached Lewis for a hug. As they embraced, Katie came into the kitchen.

"Do I get a hug, too?" she asked as she moved into their arms. As they stood together in a family cuddle, Katie backed away. "What's that I hear; that dull-sounding racket? Do you hear it?"

As they moved apart they became aware of a low rumble, or scraping; a sound hard to describe. The intensity of it increased steadily.

"I've heard that sound before; it was up in Harney County." Lewis moved toward the window. "It's the Indians. When they move—on the war path or not—they take all their belongings. The women and children lead the procession, and surprisingly, they're the ones that do the most damage. Here's where we find out whether all our time spent helping them pays off. If we have a barn and horses after they pass, we'll know this bunch knows about our help and knows we're friends."

"Are you saying we're in danger, Lewis?" Amanda's brow furrowed with concern. "Should Les and Al guard the barn and the horses? Or should we all get our guns?"

"The house made of stone as it is, everyone in it will be safe. Anyone outside will be in danger. We'd be badly outnumbered, anyway. I'll get the guys to come in out of the barn, just in case." Lewis headed immediately for the barn and corrals. Les and Al heeded his advice and came into the house.

"What about Midnight and Biscuit?" Katie's face looked as pale as the moon on a foggy night.

"We'll have to trust the horses and the livestock to the Lord," Lewis said. "Everyone pray. Pray especially for our neighbors to the south and west. I predict that the Indians will head that direction when they get here. If our neighbor's houses are near the river, it'll be a miracle if they escape with their lives, much less their property. My guess is the Indians will head down Bully Creek.

The group watched the column of Indians as they clattered closer to Stone House. The women in front wore moccasins, carried babies and guided their children ahead of them. On they came, closer to Stone House.

Katie, seeing the women direct the children past the house and the barn felt her knees like warm butter, barely supporting her. As she watched with her family she saw older people following the mothers and children; they seemed to be the caretakers for two to three hundred horses. Some of the horses pulled platforms made of willow poles and loaded with tepees and other possessions. Behind the platforms and trailing last in the long procession came the Indian braves, dressed in their war paint. Katie knew now what the scraping, rumbling sound was. This was a sight she would never forget. Thank you, Father, for keeping us safe. Please help our neighbors, too."

Lewis clapped Les on the back and shook hands with Al. "Treat others as you'd like to be treated, a bit of wisdom from above, proves to be the best way to live, once again. Let's hope the Indians' good will lasts a long distance down Bully Creek." He moved to Amanda's side and enclosed her in his arms. "You okay, Babe?"

Chapter 44: Do Unto Others

Two days later the first contingents of the army arrived and set up their tents around Stone House. Brad was there with Company B, 1st Cavalry.

He didn't want to be there. He couldn't believe that some of the same Indians he'd helped plant fields to feed their families were now among the ones on the war path. And yet they were, especially men from the Bannock tribes of Idaho. He couldn't imagine himself firing upon those people. He felt sure about one village; Tah-Mano's father would be a friend forever. It was painful to realize that in spite of his friendship with the whites, Numaga and his people might suffer the consequences of the actions of those more volatile and prone to fight; some of the younger braves were usually the troublemakers.

Was his program to come to an end because of the actions of a few foolish youngsters and the ambition of Chief Buffalo Horn of the Bannocks? He'd heard that the chief wanted to prove his expertise and superiority to Chief Joseph. *At what cost?* he wondered.

What would Katie think of him if he had to make war on the family of her best friend? Katie. Katie was his main concern. In war time anything could happen, the least of which could be that they would be permanently separated. His face blanched and his stomach lurched just thinking about it.

Katie looked out on the sea of tents around Stone House. The reality of the war rushed into her mind. *I hope Brad doesn't have to go fight the Indians. He's doing so much good on his present assignment. I'll worry every day if he has to go.*

Tah-Mano. Tah-Mano is an Indian. We are friends with those Paiutes. Brad wouldn't be safe at all in a combat situation where he knew Paiutes were involved. He'd be hesitant to fire his gun. And that could cause him to die. "Oh please don't let him go to war, Father," she whispered. She clasped her arms around her body and shivered.

Captain Reuben F. Bernard was in charge of a total force of 250 men of the Cavalry Units, and Brig. General Oliver Otis Howard was there, as well, with his 480 men. Captain Evan Miles with his 500 man force of Infantry, Cavalry, and 4th Artillery came as well. Indians on the warpath were big trouble that demanded enough men to do the job right. The commanders stepped inside Stone House to discuss strategies.

"Before we start with the details, I'd like to say something," Lewis stated. "I'm hoping the young man who's in charge of the Indian pacification program with the Paiute and Bannock will be left to continue his valuable work of helping the Indians with their food supply. Many of the Paiutes are not involved in the violence and destruction of this war. With all the discouraging things that are going on we need that program to continue. The Malheur Indian Reservation is close. We'll have Indians around for a long time. We need to work out our differences."

"Well now," Captain Bernard responded, "that's an idea I hadn't considered, but I can see that it's a good one."

"I'm glad you think so. Let me tell you why I'm making this request. Just two days ago the Bannocks moved their entire war party past Stone House. They didn't touch one thing; I think the fact that we've been helping them is the explanation for that. Don't think the Indians are blind to what we're doing. I've heard that scouts hang out at the top of Malheur Butte and observe our every action, and their communication systems are amazing."

"Go on, Lewis. Let us hear what you know."

"Thank you, Captain. Usually, when the Indians move, the women and children lead their procession. Their chief activity is to destroy property and livestock. I've seen whole herds of sheep destroyed and stacked in one big pile. I've seen every building on so many farms burned and scattered. They didn't touch ours even though they went right by here. You can see their path outside. I think they know we're their friends because of the way we've helped them. I'm hoping they'll remember our kindness a long way down the Trail, and that many homesteads in this area will be spared their depredations."

"I hope so, too. I'd appreciate an introduction to the young man who worked with you. I presume he's the soldier you're speaking about."

"Yes. His name is Brad J. Jennings. He's in the 1st Cavalry unit, Company B. I'd be glad to introduce you. He's a fine young man; a Corporal, I think."

"Captain Bernard, Have you considered the danger Corporal Jennings would face if he continued the program?" General Miles stood and stepped forward. "He would be going in and out of the villages; how would he separate friend from foe? Another problem he would face is the constant movement of the tribes during wartime. I'm just not sure it's practical to try to continue such a program in the present situation."

Brigadier General Otis Howard stood and spoke, "We'll consider how we might modify the program. Perhaps we could have Indians known to be friendly lead other friendlies to the forts and carry food supplies back to the villages. That would mean more of the food would be grown near the forts by our men, but it's a way those peaceful Indians could still eat.

Lewis glanced out the window and saw Brad leading Bradley to the hitching post; he ducked out of the room and brought him through the door. "Good time for an introduction," he said to Brad, drawing him into the room. "Captain Bernard, I'd like you to meet Brad Jennings. We were just discussing his work feeding the Indian population. Brad, this is Captain Bernard. Sitting next to him is Brigadier General Howard. Standing is General Miles.

"Aren't we wasting a lot of time dreaming about an impractical idea?" General Miles protested. "Every hour we spend here talking lets the war party get further ahead of us."

"I'm in charge here, General," Brig. General Howard said. "I believe we'll let Corporal Jennings continue his program, with the understanding he'll modify it in the ways he sees fit to protect his men. As for our overall tactics, I've decided we'll follow the hostiles, but at a distance great enough that we won't alarm them. Unless we're attacked, we won't attack. When we get to the Columbia River where all our troops will combine, we'll hope to surround and subdue them. If I'm reading this situation correctly, their intent is to drag the Umatilla tribes into this fracas, but I don't think they'll succeed in that. Hopefully we can bring this uprising to a swift end. Any questions?"

The women saw the meeting had concluded and moved to the kitchen to retrieve the food. Stew, biscuits, carrot sticks and apple wedges appeared on the table.

"Sit down Captain Bernard, General Howard, General Miles," Lewis invited. "Brad, you may sit beside Katie during dinner. The men outside will file into the kitchen later and fill their bowls from the large stewpot on the stove. Be seated, Ladies. Everyone join hands and we'll pray." Lewis waited while Amanda, Katie, and Mrs. McNeill sat.

"Our Father, You know what a mess we're in; how the Indians are choosing war. Give us wisdom in our decisions as we respond to them. Bless Corporal Jennings as he tries to maintain peace with the villages, and Captain Bernard, the Generals, and their men as they march out tomorrow. Protect us all. Please bless our bodies with this food. We pray in Jesus name. Amen"

Chapter 45: Dinner with the Generals

Shocked and surprised to find himself suddenly in the near presence of Katie Erickson, Brad remembered a long-ago meeting at a Christmas dance. Don't blow it again, he told himself. As he stole glances at the girl beside him he counted the years that had passed. Seventeen. Katie must be seventeen now. It wasn't a child that sat beside him. Katie was a woman now. Finding himself suddenly speechless he struggled for the right words.

"So Miss Katie, how have you been? You look wonderful tonight."

Katie blushed. "Thank you, Brad. I've been fine, but lonely too. Where have you been keeping yourself?"

"I've been mostly in Idaho working with the Bannock Indians. They've been extremely unhappy for years. They appreciate our efforts to help them, but those actions are not enough to erase the neglect they've endured and the hunger and hardship resulting.

"I thought you might write me. It seems like you would have if you cared about me at all." Katie looked at her plate avoiding Brad's gaze.

"I wanted to write, Katie. Every time I thought I might be able to sit down and do it, another crisis arose. I didn't want to tell you everything and make you worry. I'm here now. Let's enjoy being together while we can."

"I cried a lot. How is that better than being worried?" Katie looked around the table, feeling suddenly exposed.

Brad lowered his voice. "I'm sorry, Katie. I never want to make you cry." Brad reached for Katie's hand on her lap and gave it a tight squeeze. "Please forgive me for hurting you. I didn't mean to."

"I know that Brad. Thank you for wanting to protect me, but I really want to know what's going on in your life. All of it. Please share with me." The bright smile Katie sent his way told him he was forgiven. "Do you think you could write to me? Please?"

"The way things look right now I'll be going back to Emmitsville. The Indians are still restless, we're at war. There won't be much good news I can share." Brad, still reluctant to bombard Katie with all he went through in his job, shook his head and ran fingers through his hair.

"Did you hear what I just said, Brad? I want to hear even the bad news. At least I'd know you're still alive and still care ….."

"Excuse me, Corporal Jennings." The voice of General Miles intruded into the far too accessible world of Brad and Katie. Could you spare a moment to tell me more about what you're doing over there in Bannock territory? I'd be most interested to hear."

"Sure General, but there's not much to tell. I've been helping the Indians learn how to grow gardens and crops. The hardest part of all is keeping those fiery young hotheads calmed down. Every day I have to explain our desire to help them and the reason for the program. I guess they don't have much trust in the army after all the clashes we've had in the past. That kind of thing is hard to live down. It's exactly why we need this program. We need to build a new history with them; a history they can trust. Brad searched the General's face for understanding, but found none.

"Your head's in the clouds young man. Those Indians will never quit wanting to fight. We'd just as well fight and get it over with." General Miles looked away from the disappointment on Brad's face and crammed a biscuit into his mouth.

General O.O. Howard spoke up. "I have to disagree with you General Miles, and may I remind you that I'm in charge here. Keep your discouragements to yourself and listen. Maybe you'll learn a few things. Go on, Corporal Jennings. Tell us what the Indians are saying."

"Yes Sir. They talk about the promises of food our government has made and its failure to deliver on those promises. They've suffered through a lot of years with a lot of restrictions on their movement and little food. They're tired of it. I tell them over and over that the purpose of this program is to help them take care of themselves so they don't have to depend on promises. They forget as soon as I say it; we do it all again the next day. They can't forget how we've driven them off their ancestral lands. We're really fortunate there are older heads that understand and welcome what we're trying to do."

Katie watched Brad's face as he talked, and saw the tension building there. She wanted to rub his shoulders; somehow convey her understanding. She wished this meal was over; the hard questions, the necessity for Brad to repeat the difficult things he remembered, and his having to feel the criticism of General Miles's closed mind. *I wish all these people weren't around. I want some time alone with him.* She didn't know yet whether he would consent to write her. She must know. She couldn't bear it if he refused, no matter what the reason.

The meal ended at last. Katie knew she should help pick up the dishes; nevertheless she stayed at Brad's side.

"When will you be leaving, Brad?"

"I'm afraid we'll be leaving in the morning long before you're awake."

Katie's face showed her displeasure and pain. "But I've hardly talked to you."

"Listen to me, Katie." Brad lowered his voice to an almost whisper. "You will be in my mind and heart every moment I'm away. If I seem distant remember I have to consider the fact that I'm ten years older than you. I feel guilty caring about you as I do. We have to wait a little longer; perhaps someday soon this war will end and I can get out of the army. For now I must obey orders, go where I'm sent, and do what I'm told. Do you understand me?"

"That sounds like a good-bye. Couldn't we walk out to the barn and see Midnight? We could be alone there and talk a little more."

I guess we could go for a walk, probably not to the barn though. Let's just walk out toward the Crossing."

"Katie's face fell. "We won't be alone. The army's out there."

"That's the idea Katie. We need people around." Brad spoke now in a hushed voice. "You've no idea how much I'd like to pull you into my arms and kiss you breathless, but that action would be inappropriate right now. Tell you what Sweetie. I promise to write to you as you asked. I'll tell you what's happening. Will letters make you happy?"

"I'll be happier than I'd be without them. Do you really want to kiss me Brad?"

Do I want to kiss you? Katie, I love you. There, I said it. The times I have spent with you are memories I treasure." Brad drew Katie into his arms. "Since I've known you I've felt alive. My heart is at home with you; where you are is where I want to be." He planted a tender kiss on Katie's forehead and released her. "We've been ordered to bed down early tonight. I should go."

"I pray God will keep you safe Brad. I'll pray every day."

"I'll count on those prayers Katie. They're what will get me through this."

Chapter 46: Reunion

May 1878

Lewis Rinehart watched the last contingents of the army ride away from Stone House at 4:30 A.M. Knowing he'd seen the last peaceful day for some time, he considered what actions he needed to take. *Chief Numaga's village will need food. They won't go to war against us; I know they won't. The raiders are moving southwest from here. We might have time to make a quick trip out to the village with beef, corn seed, and potato starts before things get too stirred up. I'll bring Les and Al in from the range and we'll plan the trip. Maybe Katie would like to go out and spend a night with Tah-Mano. I'll talk it over with Amanda.*

He found her in the kitchen clearing the last of the dishes from the counters and piling them beside the sink.

"Time for coffee, Honey?"

"Sit down Lewis." Amanda took two cups from the shelf and poured coffee.

As she sat down Lewis observed the dark circles under her eyes and realized how exhausted she must be. "You did well, Amanda. I'm always so proud of the way you take care of so many people."

"People going to war, Lewis. They're all in danger." She picked up her cup and drank, set it down, and circled her arms on the table making a pillow for her head.

"You need to rest, Amanda. Could I share an idea with you before you lie down?"

"This may not be the best time. Could it wait?"

"Not really, Honey. I have to act now."

"What are you planning to do? Don't tell me you're considering going to Chief Numaga's village again. Not now."

"I thought about all those hungry people this morning. It'll be especially hard for them to hunt food during this war without being mistaken for the hostiles. It's time to plant corn and potatoes, and they don't have the seed or potato sets. I could take beef, too. Amanda, it would make a huge difference to them. Think about Tah-Mano."

"When do you plan to leave, Lewis? You're not planning to take Katie, are you?"

"Probably I'll leave day after tomorrow. How can I leave Katie behind when she longs to see Tah-Mano, talks about her every day? The hostiles have left this area for the time being. We'll be safe. Try not to worry."

"Easy to say, hard to do, Lewis, but I'll try."

Two days later the procession left Stone House; Lewis led the way, Katie followed, and Les and Al rode together in the rear. Driving two beef cattle before them, carrying seed and potato starts in gunny sacks, they rode northwest from Stone House. Through the day they watched carefully for roaming hostiles, but saw none. They arrived at the village and Chief Numaga welcomed them.

"So glad you come. Babies crying, wives unhappy. We need food. Thank you, we eat now." The chief bowed to Lewis. "Two thanks."

"Where's Tah-Mano?" Katie asked.

"She walks that way." Chief Numaga pointed, and Katie remembered Tah-Mano's hideaway on the hillside.

"I'm going to find her," Katie said, and she walked past the wigwams and toward the hill. Les, uncomfortable seeing the girl walk away alone, followed at a distance.

When Katie found Tah-Mano she was engrossed in the copy of *Little Women* Katie had given her. When she saw Katie, she jumped up, dumping the book on the ground. "I'm so glad to see you, Katie."

Katie flung her arms around Tah-Mano and squeezed. "Me too. We can't stay long, maybe overnight, but I have so much to tell you. How do you like the book?"

Tah-Mano picked the book off the ground and hugged it to her chest. "I read more than one time. I like so much."

"I read it over and over, too," Katie said, "as if I imagined Laurie and Jo would get married the next time, and I hoped they would. The story shows such a wonderful family. They lived in wartime, too."

"I don't like war," Tah-Mano said. "We are afraid, hungry, and cold."

"Brad and the army are going to continue the food program with the peaceful villages. I'm so glad."

"Thank you God," Tah-Mano said.

"Brad said he loved me but we have to wait until he's out of the army when this war's over. He kissed me on my forehead. He's so sweet." Katie rushed through her news like a non-stop stage from Boise to Umatilla. "Brad will be working out of

Emmitsville with the Bannock and Paiute peaceful Indians. He's promised to write me."

"I'm happy for you," Tah-Mano told her. I have a love too. His name is Brave Spirit. We marry soon."

"Oh Tah-Mano, That's so exciting. Have you started the preparations?"

"Yes," Tah-Mano answered. "My wedding basket is being made now. It is shaped like the earth and the sky. It means Brave Spirit and I will live in the world, have good experiences and bad, and know the thunder of storms. Good wishes for our life together are woven into the basket, the mountains and valleys of life are there. To Paiutes the wedding basket is a sacred thing. We will hold it when we are married."

"How beautiful that is." Katie sighed. "When will you marry? Is the date set?"

The Indian girl blushed. "First he visit my home, I visit his home. If parents like we'll set a date; probably in fall. Look Katie, it's getting dark. We go now."

Surprised at the encroaching darkness, Katie leaped from her seat. "Oh! I didn't notice."

As the two girls started down the hill in the dusky darkness, they failed to notice two grotesquely painted forms slipping into the path behind them. Rough hands reached to cover their mouths and grab their arms. Helpless against the men's strength, they yielded.

Les watched as the Indians grabbed the girls, and responded immediately. "See this gun? I'll blow you away if you don't turn loose of the young ladies." The Indian men failed to understand the words, but the man pointing the gun at them convinced them to turn loose. Katie and Tah-Mano, shaken but unharmed, ran to Les's side.

“Now get lost,” he said to the Indians, “before I decide to use this gun.” He pushed the gun suddenly in their direction. They turned and ran.

Chapter 47: Long Distance

June 10, 1878

Dear Katie,

I miss you, but it's wonderful to know you're safe at Stone House. I'm hoping you miss me as much as I miss you. My days seem pointless and empty, in spite of all the things I have to do.

Have you heard anything about Sarah Winnamucca? She's the daughter of Chief Winnemucca, and she's been translating for the agents at the Malheur Reservation. I think we'll be hearing a lot more about her.

She has a great respect for the army but has lost her respect for the current agent at the Malheur Reservation, whose name is Rhinhart; he's made too many promises and then broken them. He's shown a general lack of caring or respect for the Indians.

Sarah's father, Chief Winnemucca comes from a long line of peace-loving Indians. I wouldn't be too surprised to see Sarah taking her translating and other skills and helping the army.

It seems the hostiles aren't through stirring up trouble. The news coming in by telegraph says they have nearly 450 warriors. A late event down in

Southwestern Idaho near South Mountain had a volunteer contingent of 26 men led by J.B. Harper catching up with a group of 50 hostiles after they had attacked a mining camp and killed two men. Despite the hostiles' great defensive position, Mr. Harper attacked. Chief Buffalo Horn was mortally injured. He ordered his warriors to leave him in the brush to die. As a result of his death, the hostiles need a new chief. I would hope they are greatly discouraged by their loss and that they will go back to the reservation.

Please don't worry about me. Just pray that this awful war will end soon. Sometimes I get discouraged that it's so difficult to keep peace, but working toward it is my job, so I soldier on.

Affectionately,
Brad J. Jennings

Stone House
June 12, 1878
Dear Diary,

This has been such a long and interesting day. We've had so many people here. One visitor fascinated me. She arrived here in a wagon with a man and his little girl. She said she didn't know the Bannocks were at war until some men they met told them to go immediately to Stone House to be safe; a war was starting. Awhile after she'd arrived Captain Bernard and his troops showed up.

A lot of people are seeking refuge here, and some suspected the woman of taking ammunition to the Indians. They went to Captain Bernard and accused her. She told the Captain, "Search my wagon, and if you find anything more than 'a knife, a fork, and a pair of scissors, I will give you my head for a football.'" No guns were found in her wagon, and she volunteered to work with the army. All the Indian scouts are afraid to do such dangerous work, the Captain said.

The woman's name was Sarah Winnemucca, and I liked her a lot. So much was happening that I didn't get much time to talk to her, but I want to get to know her better. Maybe she'll be back. I hope so.

I'm lonely for Brad. I hope he writes to me.

Katie

June 19, 1878

Dear Diary,

I still haven't heard from Brad. He promised he'd write, and I don't know whether to worry or be angry. I'm praying for him every day. I know his work is extremely difficult.

Sarah Winnemucca came here to Stone House again, and with her was a group of army men, Stuart's column, they said. The hot weather and dusty roads exhausted all of them, and we had a quiet bunch of visitors.

The army column was ordered to be ready for action. Sarah shared my room with me. She told me that the man in the wagon with her last week had asked her to marry him, but she didn't love him, so she said no.

I told Sarah about Brad and how important he is to me. She was amazed by what he is doing and how he is trying to help the Indians. She's grieving their situation all the time.

This past week, since she was here last time, Sarah has been working so hard. She's making horseback trips all over Oregon. Her most recent one took two days and nights. Captain Bernard sent her to find the Bannock camp and rescue her people who were there against their will. She finally caught up with them at Steins Mountain. The General had sent her with a promise that if the people came to the army they would be fed and protected from the hostiles. Chief Winnemucca and his tribe, and some others sneaked out of camp with Sarah to join the army. Egan was among them, but he was recaptured and forced to stay with the hostiles. Chief Winnemucca's band asked for the army's protection on the journey they would have to make.

The minute Sarah lay on the bed she fell asleep. We had to wake her to eat something. After a few bites of stew and biscuit she fell asleep again.

She is my hero.

Katie

June 20, 1878

Dear Brad,

Finally! Today I got your first letter. You said you miss me a lot. I think of you all the time, imagining what you're doing, and I go to sleep every night after praying for you and for us. I pray that we'll be able to be together soon.

We've been so busy with all the company. People are coming here to be safe. The army seems to use Stone House as their meeting place. General Bernard and his command have been here twice.

You asked if I'd heard about Sarah Winnemucca. Would you believe me if I told you I'd met her? Not once, but twice. The interesting thing is that both times General Bernard showed up too. I'm not sure, but I think he asked her to be his aide in some way. So you were probably right. She will be helping the army.

There's not too much else happening. When I have time, I read. I've discovered a new author, Isabelle Macdonald Alden, and I am ordering her series, The Ester Reid Series. The series is based upon her own life.

I should be reading for a long time; there are four books I think.

I don't ride much these days. It's too scary out there wondering when I'll run into a hostile.

God bless you Brad,
Katie

June 20, 1878
Dear Katie,

Hi Sweetie, I've no idea how long these letters take to reach you. I hope I'm not just repeating things you've already heard.

No good news today. The Indians are traveling through Southern Oregon. It seems from the path of devastation they're leaving that they're on their way to Burns. The Bannocks have forced most of the Paiutes off the Malheur reservation, and are holding them prisoner somewhere in the area of the Owyhee. I hear Chief Winnemucca's band is among the prisoners. Captain Bernard is working on a plan to rescue the friendlies and take care of them till this war ends, but it's difficult because all the Indian scouts are afraid to travel through Oregon at this point. This really cripples the Captain's ability to learn and communicate.

The Bannocks have destroyed several ranches, a few of the owners escaped with the aid of Chief Winnemucca's intervention. This chief has refused to join up with the new chief of the hostiles, a man named Egan. There's a question as to Egan's willingness to join the hostiles, much less wanting to be their chief. A man called Oytes seems to be the main leader of hostilities. I think Egan's doing what he has to do to survive.

The size of the hostile band is growing daily. All the disgruntled and angry are joining up with them. Most Paiutes who joined the Bannocks were frustrated with Agent Rhinehart's handling of the reservation resources.

It isn't safe to be in the Oregon countryside anymore. Many sheep and cattlemen have lost their lives. Warn Les and Al to be cautious.

Miners are also being attacked. Most of the reported problems seem to be out toward Harney County, so anywhere in the Southwestern direction is particularly dangerous.

Here's a story I heard, and am passing on to make you smile. The Indian chief named above, whose original name I can't remember, was always running around with only one moccasin. An amused white man called him "wanne mucca" meaning 'one moccasin.' The chief heard and liked the name and has called himself Wannamucca ever after.

There's an empty place in my heart because you're not with me.

Be safe, Sweetie,
Brad J. Jennings

July 4, 1878
Dear Katie,

Your letter of June 20 arrived today. It really made my day. Your news about meeting Sarah Winnemucca makes me a bit envious. Talk about being in the right place at the right time! Wish I could have been there.

It turns out I was right about the hostiles heading for Burns. Captain Bernard caught them encamped on the Silver River about thirty miles west of Burns—he had in his company a volunteer contingent under a man called Rube Robbins. Together they were a formidable group, and managed to deceive the hostiles into thinking themselves outnumbered. When the army went shooting and yelling through the village the

Indians fled in every direction. I guess Robbins and Chief Egan had their own personal duel where Chief Egan was severely wounded. I'm sad for him, but word is he was rescued by his followers.

This battle didn't end in victory for the army though; Captain Bernard, out-numbered as he was, couldn't break up the Indians' re-formations on the bluffs around the camp, so he withdrew. The Indians left in the night. A total of eight men died and several were wounded.

My hope is that with Chief Egan disabled the hostiles will give up their plans and go home. We'll have to wait and see.

My heart hurts over all the lives lost.

Dreaming of you,

Brad J. Jennings

July 10, 1878

Dear Brad,

I've been doing something different. Amanda has ordered a new Singer treadle sewing machine. It came yesterday, and she and I are both trying to learn to get along with it. It isn't the machine's fault; it's just new. Amanda ordered fabric for both of us, so we'll both have new dresses if we can ever learn all the ins and outs of using the machine.

I do know this already. Using this machine will save us so much sewing time. Once we know what we're doing, I think sewing will be a lot more fun. Who knows? Maybe someday I'll even make something for you.

Last winter Amanda started teaching me how to knit. I feel like I'm all thumbs while I'm trying to learn, but I can see how it will be a useful skill to have. Every day I learn more about cooking. It seems like it's all we ever do at times, but I think I enjoy the creative part of it; making something new is always fun.

I'm so glad the friendly Indians have escaped and travelled safely to be with the army, and I'm glad they'll have enough to eat. That will keep them much happier. I hope you're safe there at Emmitsville among the Bannocks who didn't want to fight. I'm still praying for you daily.

Hugs,
Katie

July 10, 1878
Dear Katie,

Those hostiles do get around. Now they're on the John Day River. It's obvious they're on their way to the Umatilla Reservation in the Pendleton area. Chief Egan has delegated his position as chief to Oytes, and Oytes is apparently changing tactics. He set up an ambush for Captain Bernard's troops, and on July 2 two of the Captain's scouts were killed in the resulting melee. Several men were injured, but Captain Bernard's men were able to send the hostiles running.

Captain Bernard's a pretty wise man. He said from the beginning the hostiles would try to recruit more allies from the Umatilla area.

Brig. General Otis Howard came to Captain Bernard's rescue in the above mentioned battle. He had 450 more men at his disposal, and together they cornered the Indians on Pilot Rock twenty miles south of Pendleton. It happened on July 8. Amazingly, again there were very few casualties. Captain Bernard has certainly proved his wisdom and courage beyond questioning. Whether anyone is winning this war is still questionable.

I miss you more every day my dear Katie. I dream of you every night. I want to hold you in my arms.

I love you,
Brad

July 15, 1878
My Precious Katie,

Finally there is some good news. Pendleton escaped invasion by the hostiles, by God's working, I'm sure. It was close. The interesting thing is that General Miles saved the day by deciding on his own to return to Pendleton where he helped repulse the hostiles.

The hostiles were not able to fully convince the Umatilla tribes to ally with them in spite of indications there might have been previous promises made in that regard. Though 1000 Indians, compared with his fewer than 500, went out to face General Miles, only the Bannocks and Paiutes under Oytes attacked.

How General Miles managed to keep his cool in the face of 1000 Indians is a question I'd love to have answered. He seemed like a more volatile man at Stone House the day we met there. Anyway, the General was easily able to defend against the attacks that came. For six hours they stayed in battle position until the hostiles retreated and headed east into the mountains.

The Umatillas went back to their reservation. The hostiles have to be discouraged. No alliance with the Umatillas makes victory improbable for them. They can only take out their anger on the countryside. We are not out of danger, dear Katie, but there is hope.

Be safe in God's love,
Brad

July25, 1878

Katie, My Treasure,

I received your letter of July 10, and loved knowing that you're learning so much about sewing. Figuring out a new machine and its works is always difficult, but usually is worth the work it takes. And yes, knitting is useful, particularly if you know someone who's out in the cold a lot. Hint, Hint…A warm scarf can make a huge difference.

Chief Egan is dead and Chief Oytes's hostiles are retreating to the south. They were greatly disappointed when the Umatillas failed to join them in their cause. Chief Eagan was murdered by Umatillas anxious to curry favor with the army. They entered Egan's camp under pretext of friendship. The hostiles are humiliated, and angry as well as discouraged. I fear for the citizens through whose territory they pass while on their way back to their country.

Please be careful and stay within easy reach of Stone House, always. As I said previously, no place in Oregon or Idaho can be assumed safe right now. I wish it weren't the truth, but I know it is. The hostiles are breaking into smaller bands and scattering for their return. They are murdering every white they can find or catch. They might be anywhere.

As I've said before, my work is very difficult right now. Pray for me as I do for you.

The Lord Bless You and Keep You,

Brad

July 30, 1878

Dear Katie,

It's happening as I feared. Reports are coming from all over the states of Oregon and Idaho of people caught alone by the hostiles and murdered. Especially ranchers and sheep-men seem to be vulnerable. The closest problem to you I've heard of happened on Bully

Creek at the Dan Brady place. As Mr. Brady was returning home he looked down from a ridge and saw the Indians in and near his horse corral, apparently taking their pick from his horses. Two Indians happened to look up and see him, interrupted their business with the horses, and took off after him. You know how a horse behaves when it's nearing home. It's nearly impossible to turn him around. Dan had to almost rip his horse apart spurring him to get him running, but he did escape the hostiles. The Indians went back and destroyed his place.

I'm afraid all the intercessions Sarah Winnemucca is making on behalf of her people will be in vain. She has too many acts of violence to overcome. I fear the consequences—not just for the hostiles, but our friendlies as well—of this venting of their disappointment and anger. I've heard of hostile incidents in so many places; everything from killing everything and everyone in sight, to taking all the butter from a dairy farm, stacking it into a huge pyramid, and letting their children slide down the slopes. They steal horses and kill them, torture farm animals, and massacre whole families. I guess they're expressing their sense of outrage for all they've suffered.

The army has spread out and is trying to control the situation, but so far hasn't succeeded.

These are tough times, Katie. I'm glad God is in control and that we can trust Him.

My love,
Brad

August 5, 1878
Dear Katie,

This has been a better week because I got your letter of July 1. Just knowing that you're okay blesses and calms me. Keep those letters coming.

I'm not surprised to hear that you're having a lot of guests at Stone House. Some of them are pretty important—Sarah Winnemucca, for instance. I'm glad you got to meet her. It's turning out that she's been fearless and invaluable to the army. That's why you had Captain Bernard and his troops there at the time she passed through. The travels she and her sister Mattie undertake at the Captain's request are extremely dangerous. She's a real trooper.

I'm not surprised that you're having a number of visitors from neighboring farms, too. People don't feel safe in their homes anymore. So many people would rather sleep out in the willows or in the mines than trust they'll be safe on their farms. Locking the doors and staying in your farmhouse has proven to be a bad choice; sure way to have your house burned down and you with it. I am looking forward to the day when this war ends and we can live more peaceful lives.

Goodbye, Precious Katie, Be safe.

Brad

August 10, 1878

My Precious,

I'm afraid I don't have good news. General Howard has been ordered to forcibly remove all remaining Indians from the Malheur Reservation. All, not just the hostiles, I'm sorry to say. As I write, the removal of approximately 550 Paiutes and Bannocks is in process. They will be taken to Camp Harney near Burns for the time being. Where they're going to put them and how they're going to feed them is what I'd like to know. So far it doesn't appear that the present Indian agents ever consider that. (I should except Samuel Parrish, the very first agent at Malheur Reservation. He truly seemed to have the Indian's interests at heart.) I sincerely hope I'm mistaken and they will wait to make the transfer until food supplies can be assured.

I know this news will be unwelcome and will upset you, but you said you wanted to know all the news, good and bad.

You will be worried about Tah-Mano and her family, I know. We can only trust them to God. Try to understand that this news has a good result, too. The hostile Indians will no longer be in your area. You can relax your vigilance a little and live more normal lives.

Try not to worry, Precious Katie. Worry doesn't help. Pray every day and try to find peace.

Till next time,

Brad

October 2, 1878

Dear Katie,

It looks like the Malheur Indians are doing okay over in Harney County, seemingly having enough to eat and warm clothing. That alone is a huge improvement and restores their feelings of well-being. Hopefully they can stay there. I believe Chief Winnamucca may have taken his tribe back to Nevada and their ancestral territory, however his daughter Sarah is still in Oregon helping the army generals communicate with her people. The orders the army receives contain many enticements and promises to the Indians, and Sarah is the one to tell them to her people. For her sake and theirs I hope someone in Washington doesn't mess things up now that they're beginning to settle down a little.

The Bannocks here in Idaho are still restless, but no longer talking of war. I don't know how long the ease will last given the circumstances at Fort Hall.

I fear some of the hostiles have escaped to the Salmon River Sheepeater's country, and I'm hoping they won't stir up more trouble for later. For the present their absence makes my job easier.

I enjoyed your last letter. It's nice to know you can take Midnight out and feel the air in your face again. I think you'll be safe now, but I'd still feel better if I knew Amanda rode with you.

Yes, Katie, my love, I still miss you, and I look forward every day to the time I can end this stint in the army and get on with my life. Till then I hope you'll wait for me.

Hugs for you from me,
Brad

December 18, 1878
My Dearest Katie,

I'm so sorry to have to write this letter. I have some incredibly sad news to share with you. Please, before you read on, get Amanda to read it with you.

Sometimes I hate orders that come down from the president to the army. This is one of those times. President Grant has ordered that *all* the Paiutes living on the reservation or in Harney County are to be forcibly moved to the Yakima Reservation immediately. This is to be done in spite of the lack of warm clothing, adequate food for the journey, or the winter cold and snow.

Apparently the promises that Malheur Reservation could become a permanent home for the Indians are no longer being deemed important. As I write, the native peoples are preparing for the trip. Women and children will ride the wagons. Men, some of them in leg irons, will walk. The route will no doubt be through the John Day wilderness; the mountains are steep and rugged, not to mention the snow. How will the small children and older people survive a winter trip in the northern mountains? I fear for all of them.

I must go.
Bye, Dear Katie, Be safe. I love you.
Brad

Chapter 48: Decision

Katie will be so upset. She will know Tah-Mano and her family will suffer indescribable pain and hardship. There must be something I can do. People will die in those mountains in the freezing weather. I want to help, but how? Brad's thoughts tumbled one over the other, forward and back again. He couldn't stop worrying about the Indian's plight and the tortuous journey they had ahead of them. Knowing that Tah-Mano's family would suffer among those exiled to the Yakima Reservation, in spite of their choice to befriend the whites, and that they would be punished along with the hostiles in spite of their innocence didn't sit well with him. *I have to do something. I can't sit here and watch it happen.*

An awareness crept into his troubled thoughts. *I've been sitting here doing almost nothing for days. The Indians are gone from the villages. I'm just waiting for new orders that might take me to the moon for all I know.*

What if I could get a wagon from one of the farmers and fill it with food and a bed or two? I could get some first aid supplies, some warm blankets. I could become a comfort station for those who are failing in strength. Maybe I could save lives. Trying to help would be so much better than sitting here worrying. I'm not good for much here anyway.

"What am I thinking?" Brad's voice surprised him. He retreated into his thoughts. They were too outrageous to speak out loud. *I'd have to go AWOL in order to do anything. I could ask permission, but if my request is denied I'd have no way to do anything because I'd have told the army where I am and what I'm doing. I am going to do something, and I'm going to do it right now.*

Brad collected his warmest clothing, leaving all his army apparel. He gathered blankets and his weapons. He packed his travel gear, food, and water. When he rode out of Emmitsville he wore a ten gallon hat, faded and worn blue jeans, a brown and white-checked long sleeved flannel shirt and a leather fur-lined jacket. Dark heavily framed glasses hid his eyes. When the town lay far behind, Brad urged his horse to a gallop and headed for the Southwest, Harney Agency, and a new life.

Chapter 49: Joshua Cross

Burns, Oregon

Joshua fixed a demanding gaze on the clerk of the supply store.

"My name's Joshua Cross. I'm new around here. I need a good covered wagon and supplies to fill it, and I need it now. Any idea where I could get one?"

"Buyin' or rentin'?

"Buying if it's a good one. I'll pay top dollar if you can deliver it now. What do you have?"

"Just got one in first of the week. Belonged to a farmer a ways east of here. Let's go out back and have a look."

The two men walked out the door and around the building. Ahead of them sat a covered beauty of a wagon. Joshua whistled and proceeded to check the tongue and wheels for signs of wear. "Looks like it's never been hooked up to horse or ox. How much?"

"Will ya be needin' horses? That'll cost extra.

"With horses will be fine. Name your price, and I'll have a look at the horses."

Transaction completed, Joshua proceeded to fill the wagon with the supplies he'd need. Another hour found him driving his wagon west toward the Harney Reservation about ten miles out from Burns.

He began to see the tepees first. Miles before he saw the main buildings, in every direction he turned, he saw the dwellings crowded together As he drew nearer the headquarters he saw groups of Indians standing close together and talking quietly. That they were grief-stricken was obvious. . Men paced to and fro. Women cried and twisted their hands or fiddled with their hair. Occasionally he heard a loud exclamation of protest.

They know, Joshua realized, *they know what's going to happen.* He rode into the headquarters and tied his horse. As he walked toward the building, he met two women leaving. Both of them were crying. *I wonder if that could be Sarah Winnemucca.*

"Pardon me, Maam. My name is Joshua Cross. Are either of you Sarah Winnemucca?"

The shortest of the women answered him. "I am Sarah. This is my sister-in-law Mattie. What can I do for you?"

"I am here to help your people through the winter. I have a wagon full of supplies. I intend to join the march through the mountains to Yakima."

"You want to help? The best way to help is to stop this horrible thing that has been ordered by your president. Does he have a heart? How can he do this, and in winter?"

"Miss Winnemucca, I don't like these orders either, and I want to assist your people in any way I can."

"Our children and our fathers will die in the cold. How can we bear it?"

"I wish I could remove the order. I hope you will come to me when you or your people have needs I can help with. I have a good wagon, horses, blankets, and food; also a few medical supplies." Joshua tipped his hat to the women and continued toward the building where he arranged with Major Cochrane for his own wagon to cross the mountain with the caravan.

"We'll be leaving two days from now," Major Cochrane told him. Be ready, no matter the weather. Pay is $15.00 per day. Good luck."

We'll certainly need luck and a lot of it. Joshua left the building biting back his resentment.

***

Tumult reigned in the Indian encampment during the two days. Mothers worried about their children and how they would keep them warm without adequate blankets and clothing during this unwelcome winter trip through such difficult terrain. They fretted about their food supply. Wives railed at their husbands for allowing themselves to be drawn into the hostilities and thus causing their families to be punished. Those who had not participated in the war hoped their choice to remain at peace would exempt them from exile. Surely their good behavior and their relocation to stay with the army would mean they wouldn't have to go to Yakima.

Some attempted escape by slipping out of camp, hoping against hope the dreaded journey could be avoided. They hoped in vain, escaping only to be chased down and returned to camp.

Joshua watched the desperate expressions of grief, and even though he was among the native peoples to help, couldn't stop the guilt that invaded his mind. How many times had he been involved in situations where the army had punished the women and children along with the warriors? He hoped it wouldn't be the case again. He intended to try to make it up to these people. What little he could do wouldn't amount to much, but perhaps he could decrease the pain and suffering he knew lay ahead.

Joshua knew that Tah-Mano's family was among the grieving Paiutes. He wanted to help them for Katie, and that desire was the motivation for his desertion. *Dear Katie. She will be wondering why I'm not writing. She will think all the wrong reasons are the explanation. She will cry.*

He must find Tah-Mano's family before they left. *It's the least I can do. They re somewhere in the camp. But I can't let them know who I am. I'll watch over them the best I can from afar. For Katie.*

For several hours he searched through the huge camp in vain, and finally saw them from a distance in Leggins' group, several miles away from where he had started. Taking care not to attract their attention he left and returned to the Harney encampment.

How Joshua wished he could explain everything to Katie, but if he did, he knew he would be found and imprisoned. Secrecy, even from Katie was the rule for his life, like it or not.

Chapter 50: The Journey Begins

Joshua watched as the Indians carried the limited supplies they had to the wagons. He saw several mothers with babies in their cradleboards, and several pregnant women. *Sad. They'll have a hard time on the trail.* He saw the Indian fathers, some old and frail and being helped to walk. He worried for them. *They need to ride, but wagons have been provided only for women and children.* He saw that wagons needed obviously did not equal wagons provided. The best he could manage would be to save his wagon for the obviously needy, and, after they were on the trail, hope Sarah Winnemucca or her sister-in-law Mattie would come for help when it was needed.

Major Cochrane approached the wagon where Joshua sat. "I've decided to put Sarah Winnemucca and her sister-in-law Mattie in your wagon. They can bring others of the women and children to you if they choose."

"Thanks Major. That will be fine. I'd like to see the mothers with little ones where they'll be a little warmer."

Major Cochrane went on about his business, a word of encouragement here, an admonition there, as the unhappy group of people prepared for the difficult journey.

A bit later Joshua watched as Sarah Winnemucca left Major Cochrane's quarters and walked through the Indian encampment, apparently delivering some message. Now and then a man would leave the group and follow Sarah. Finally, a group of twelve to fifteen men followed the woman back toward Major Cochrane's quarters. Suddenly a group of armed soldiers appeared, surrounded the loudly protesting group, and directed them into a building. Men were placed around the building to guard it. An officer informed them loudly, "Try to walk out of there and you'll be shot."

Joshua made an assumption: *Prisoners of war, apparently. Probably the only ones that really deserve the exile.*

Sarah Winnemucca walked away from the Major's office crying. Her path led her past Joshua's wagon.

"Can I be of any help Ma'am?"

"How can you help? I'm asked to do things that make my people distrust me. They won't believe anything I say to them ever again."

"You did what you had to do, Ma'am. They'll forgive you in time."

***

The men under guard shuffled out of the building where they'd been imprisoned. Each of them wore leg-irons.

"Form the train, Major Cochrane called out. Line up behind this wagon here; we're moving out." A confusion of moving wagons pulled behind Joshua and formed a ragged line. Joshua saw cavalry members positioning themselves; a row of guards on either side of the caravan.

"Wagons Ho!" Captain Winters shouted, and fired his gun into the air. The train lurched forward as every horse strained to pull. A communal cry of grief pierced the air as the captives bid goodbye to their homeland.

***

Chapter 51: Hell in Winter

First entry in Joshua's diary
December 20, 1878, Day One of the journey

The weather turned extremely cold as we began our journey north toward the John Day country. The humidity increased as we pressed on through the wilderness, intensifying the misery.

It felt like snow. The women, children, and the oldest noticed it most.

Sarah Winnemucca brought two pregnant women to the wagon for extra care. When Sarah isn't caring for the women she prefers to walk. I'm glad for the blankets I provisioned; they make it a little easier for the women and a few of the others.

Day two:

On the second evening we reached Canyon City and camped there.

Mr. and Mrs. Charles Parrish, favorites of the Indians because they cared responsibly for their charges during their first years on the reservation, came into camp and visited the tribe. It pained me to see their interactions; much talking and crying for hours. The Indians seemed to be begging the Parrishes to stop what is being done; as if there were anything they could do.

The snowflakes began to fall this bitter, cold, night. Captain Winters received a telegram from Washington after our meager meal, the message being that he was to bring Leggins' band to Yakima along with the rest. Tah-Mano's family will be among them. So, in spite of the freezing weather and the snow, we are forced to stop and wait for Leggin's peaceful band to be delivered. They will protest all the way, I am sure, and with good reason.

Already I miss Katie. How will I stand it?

Joshua Cross

December 24, 1878

Day Four

We waited for two long miserable days in Canyon City for the rest of the Paiutes. Cutting wind and biting snow took its toll. An older man died during the night. I later learned that the man whose wagon he occupied demonstrated his carelessness by dumping the man's body in the snow.

It appears even Sarah is now; after all she has done for them, distrusted by her people; she's spoken too much bad news. Leggins refuses to talk with her, and her own brother is angry. The spirit of the band is broken. Unbelievably, the Major persists. He sent a message through her to Leggins. He is to help guard his people and prevent their escape.

I fear the outcome of this trip. Will this heart-broken people learn to work together? They must, if any of us are to survive.

It's Christmas Eve. How I want to write to Katie.

Joshua Cross

December 26, 1878

Day Six

A beautiful young woman became a mother on Christmas night; by morning she was childless. She watched her baby buried in a snow bank on a wild mountain and died of grief before the next day passed. It all happened at my wagon. The ground was too frozen for any other burial, but I'm still angry and horrified at what happened. Sarah came, attended her, and did everything she could. Following Paiute tradition, members of the grieving family have cut off their hair. I feel like cutting my hair too.

Joshua Cross

December 28, 1878
Day Eight

Travel in these wagons is incredibly difficult; would be hazardous in normal weather, but in these freezing snow-covered mountains is nearly impossible. The people are suffering. Three more small children have frozen to death in spite of all we can do; another new mother has lost her baby. Everyone is grieving. So many people have shaved off their hair, and that only makes them colder.

We've nearly reached the Columbia. Perhaps things will be a bit easier after we cross into Washington. I pray they will be easier. There aren't enough blankets in the world to shut out this cold, and I've given my last one away. I'm so glad Tah-Mano's family got several of them.

I'm thankful that Katie can't see how the people are suffering.

Joshua Cross

Chapter 52: Yakima

January 10, 1879
Day 20

We are in Yakima now. That is not to say our situation is in any way improved. We crossed the Columbia at the John Day Ferry, and tried to keep moving. We arrived to find that preparations for the exiles' arrival in Yakima were minimal, so we were forced to camp outdoors again. The chief of the Yakima Indians came with a Father Wilbur out thirty miles to meet us. We've been outside here ten days now, and another of the Paiutes died.

I understand Father Wilbur is to be in charge of the group, and that we will be moved up to Fort Simcoe soon. I pray that preparations have been made and housing prepared there. The winter continues to be brutal with lots of snow and freezing weather. Most of the hired, privately owned wagons have abandoned us, so we won't be moving on until more are provided.

How time drags on. Will this struggle of a journey never end?

Joshua Cross

January 20, 1879

Day 30

The evening of January 10 Father Wilbur returned with wagons and his Indians to transport the exiles up to Fort Simcoe. When we arrived there, no housing had been constructed, so a shed-type barracks was hastily thrown together. No insulation of any kind was added. Reminds me of a barn I'd put my cattle in.

The snow has continued. At one time it was waist-deep. The supplies I brought with me have long ago been used, or somehow disappeared. The clothing and blankets issued by the army to the Indians while at Camp Harney are gone.

Sarah Winnemucca tells me the tribe complains that blankets are stolen while they sleep. It seems Father Wilbur's "civilized" Indians are good at pilfering, trading and gambling; they manage to finagle every valuable item from our Paiutes, and the exiles are freezing to death. We've buried several this week. Issues of clothing seemed bountiful when received at the Yakima Reservation Agency, but the clothing rations given to the Indians are miserly. Who is benefiting? Certainly not the Paiutes.

Another contributing factor to the Indians miserable condition is that meals, when they are provided for the exiles, are skimpy.

To make bad matters worse, even the tribe's horses are disappearing; apparently being stolen by the very people who are supposed to be providing for the Paiutes. I grow more and more disgusted with the actions of the reservation agents. Katie would be livid with anger, I know.

By all indications our Father Wilbur is another 'Rhinehart.' He confiscates government provisions intended for the Indians, and manages to use them for his own profit. He actually tells the Indians when they complain that he doesn't want to be troubled about their problems, and all while he is praying. I'm sickened by what I see, and it didn't take the Paiutes long to recognize the familiar pattern.

Oh Katie, how I long to see your face.

Joshua Cross

April 30, 1879

The atrocities mentioned previously continue. I continue to voice my objections to Father Wilbur. He's obviously getting rich at the Paiutes' expense.

Sarah Winnemucca, at last, is coming to me to talk. I learn many details of Wilbur's abuses through her. She's frustrated and heartbroken because she is made to be the mouthpiece for his promises—so often un-kept—that she is no longer believed or trusted among her people.

Wilbur set the homeless band to work about the middle of this month. They were to clear sixty acres of brush and prepare it for plantings of wheat. One could hope the wheat grown would be used to benefit the Paiutes, but they no longer believe they will see anything of the benefits.

Men, women, and children participated in the assignment. They completed the work in ten days. I didn't blame them for being disturbed when, after the clearing was done, Wilbur hired his crew of spoiled Indians to do the plowing. The Paiutes had received nothing for their hard work.

There is plenty of land. I aim to ask for acreage and encourage the Indians to grow their own food crops. They would be better fed, would become stronger and be better encouraged.

Someday I intend to report the wrongs so evident here, but in my present situation my hands are tied.

I can't write to Katie either. My dear Katie. I hope she will forgive me for what I've put her through. I pray that someday she will understand that I deserted my post because of my love for her and her love for Tah-Mano. She probably believes I'm dead or I've quit caring about her. She'd be ever so wrong in each case. I'm thinking about her all the time; wishing I could see her; wishing I could hug her and kiss her. The pain I feel tells me I'm a long ways from dead.

I wish I felt like I'd accomplished more of the goals I had when I decided to make this trip with the Paiutes. I'm not sure the things I've done have been worth what it will likely cost me. Enough of this morbidity. In my saner moments I know that one life saved is definitely worth it.

Joshua Cross

June 30, 1879

The crops the Paiutes planted are up and growing. We used the seeds I'd brought with me, potatoes, carrots, peas, squash, corn; things that will keep the people from wasting away. They're very protective of their efforts on the property. They keep weeds out and water faithfully. That's no small job since they must carry much of the water from the Yakima River. There *are* two large springs at Fort Simcoe, located a bit closer than the fishing place at the river. With horses the job could be much easier, but with things as they are—no horses to be found—the work is grueling. I help as I can with my horses.

I've talked over and over with Wilbur, reminded him that the seeds the Paiutes planted were mine, emphasized that the crops the Indians grow are for their nourishment and not his enrichment. He talks a good talk and makes all the right promises. I'm afraid he will not hesitate to break them.

I've been away without leave for six months. I must go back to Fort Boise and get whatever's coming to me. I pray I will be able to see Katie before they lock me up.

***

Chapter 53: Consequences

July 8, 1879

"I don't care if I never see him again," Katie said passionately to Amanda. "He doesn't care much about me or he would never leave me so long without so much as a letter."

"Be careful what you say, Katie. There must be good reasons for what Brad's doing." Amanda lowered her knitting and looked at the red-eyed girl still sitting at the dinner table. "Always be ready to listen for those reasons, and always be merciful. Perhaps you might have done the same thing if your situation was similar."

"I'd *never* have left him waiting for six months without a word, but he quit answering my letters. Just like that. I don't even know if he got them. I hope he doesn't flatter himself that I'll wait around forever."

"Katie, Listen to yourself. You're letting your emotions rule you. Instead of being critical of what Brad's not doing try remembering the person he is, how he's helped so many people, what a hard worker he is, how you were so proud of his accomplishments. Then when he does return you'll be glad to see him and not have to feel guilty because of all the bad thoughts you've entertained."

"That's easy for you to say, Amanda. What if Lewis left without a word and didn't write you?" Katie jumped from her chair and stalked away from the table. "You just don't understand."

Amanda watched Katie leave the room. How well she could remember the days when she'd loved Lewis and had to watch him ride away, sometimes for months at a time. Yes, she did understand, and wished she could help Katie more. She'd go to Katie's room in an hour and see if there was anything she could do.

***

When Amanda went to Katie she found her lying on her bed staring glassy-eyed at the ceiling. The girl did not respond to her greeting. Amanda went to Katie's bed, urged her to make room, lay down beside her, and reached over to caress Katie's forehead.

"I know it's hard, Katie. Sometimes we have to grab our feelings by the shoulders, like the unruly children they are, and make them behave, send them to stand in the corner. They'll protest but they'll go."

"It hurts so much, Amanda. When I think about how long it's been since I saw or heard from Brad I can't help feeling like he's rejecting me."

"Try thinking about what a special man he is, the blessing of knowing him. Trust him to do what's right. I think you'll find more peace if you can do that."

"But what if he doesn't come back? What if he's found someone else?" Katie choked out the words, almost a stutter. She laid her hand over her heart, as if to keep it from breaking.

"When you ask that question and dwell on the uncertainty you're borrowing trouble that may never happen. If it does happen you can deal with it then. Don't waste your life worrying."

"But it all makes me so mad. It makes me want to hurt him like he's hurting me. It would serve him right, wouldn't it Amanda?"

"It might seem so at the time, but retaliating never makes things better. It damages relationships, sometimes permanently. Think about what I've shared with you, and then try to get some sleep. You'll feel better in the morning."

Amanda hugged Katie, rose from the bed, turned off the light, and tiptoed from the room. Katie lay in the dark battling; her feelings against the truths Amanda had spoken to her so many times in the past. An hour passed before she could struggle no longer. She slept.

Chapter 54: Good Intentions

Morning light filtered into Katie's bedroom and she gradually became aware that another day had arrived. Memories flooded into her consciousness: Brad and his long absence, her hurt feelings, the desire to retaliate, and Amanda's reminders about how to take the high road. I have to think, she told herself. I'll eat breakfast and go out for a ride. Midnight and I can be alone for awhile. She threw back her covers and put her feet on the floor.

When she entered the kitchen thirty minutes later Amanda greeted her. "Good morning, Honey. I hope you're feeling better."

"I think I'll take Midnight out for a ride as soon as I finish breakfast. Will that be okay with you? I have a lot of thinking to do."

"Yes Katie. That sounds like a good idea. Which direction are you planning to go?

"I thought I'd head up toward Willow Creek. I'll run into fewer travelers up there. I want to be alone with Midnight for an hour or two and be back for lunch."

"Take a snack along just in case you're delayed. Okay?"

"Well, I guess I can do that if it'll make you feel better."

Katie hurried through breakfast, gathered some water and a snack. She mounted Midnight and rode north from Stone House intending to intersect with Willowcreek. The direction was new to her; she hadn't ridden along Willowcreek before. The day was hot and dry and smelled of sage brush. *I'm glad I brought plenty of water. This might be a long ride without it. It must be at least eighty degrees, and in the sun eighty degrees is a bit much.* She rode for thirty minutes before she began to see in the distance the willows that told her she was getting near the creek and some shade. She intended to rest there and eat her apple. Then she'd ride up the creek.

Soon she heard the murmurs of water sliding over rocks in the streambed and turned toward the sound. When she reached the creek she found an inviting shady spot, dismounted Midnight, lowered the reins to the ground to remind Midnight not to stray, and plopped down in the shade. *Now for a drink.*

Katie snacked on her apple and thought about Brad and the choices she would need to make if he ever came back. Amanda's gentle words of advice came back to her. She did want to see Brad again, but the reunion would be awkward. She struggled with the idea of just accepting his actions and his absence without letting him know how upset she was. No, that wouldn't be exactly honest. Maybe it would be better to tell him how she'd suffered not knowing why he wasn't writing, but do it in a way that wouldn't put him on the defense. She needed to listen quietly and hear his reasons for not writing as he'd promised, not attack him with hostility. Amanda was right. She must be careful to take care of a relationship she cared about so deeply. Gratefully Katie remembered all the times Amanda had told her the truth; every time she'd been tempted to let her anger control her.

The thought popped into her head. What if he's not alive? Maybe that explains everything, and I'll never have a chance to love him the way I want to. Suddenly Katie's thoughts embraced her parent's memory and she realized the uncertainty of life and perhaps, how temporary the relationship between she and Brad could be.

Katie finished her apple and drank deeply of her water. Refreshed, she decided to walk for awhile amongst the willows. She chose her direction, picked up Midnight's reins, and headed up-stream. The shade provided welcome change from the hot sunny ride she'd completed to get here, and she continued to walk for some time. The babble of the creek drew her closer, and she decided to get a drink from the fresh water. Remembering another time when she'd been surprised while doing the same thing, she looked carefully around her.

Chapter 55: Joshua

The thin, tired, bedraggled man rode on. With a journey of over three hundred fifty miles behind him he felt as if his limp body might slide off his mount. Mustached, wearing a beard down to his chest, hair hanging limply to his shoulders, he felt mighty smelly and filthy too. How long since he'd had a real bath? He couldn't remember. How long since he'd eaten a real meal? That memory too was long gone. All he remembered were the rocky ravines, the nearly impassable forests, and the ceaseless riding. He'd survived on hard tack and beef jerky since his provisions had run out, how long ago he didn't know.

One thought sustained him. He would see Katie soon. He'd been riding down Willow Creek for two days and knew the journey was almost over.

Soon he would have to make a decision. Should he go straight to Fort Boise and reduce the risk of being arrested by the army, or should he take the risk of going south to Stone House?

No. As much as he wanted to see Katie and know everything was okay between them, he feared the consequences if he did not go directly to Fort Boise and voluntarily place himself back under army authority. The constant presence of people at Stone House meant someone would probably recognize him if he said even one word.

If the army found him before he turned himself in, the penalties would be much greater; no hope of an honorable discharge, maybe even a lengthy imprisonment.

One thing he knew. He must rest. He found some shade deep in the willows along the creek, slid off his horse, and tumbled onto the grassy ground where he fell soundly asleep.

Chapter 56: Katie's Discovery

Could that be a horse up there in the shadows? I think I must be seeing things. Am I? Katie approached Willow Creek cautiously, moving toward the horse she imagined she saw. As she drew nearer the spot she realized it wasn't her imagination. There *was* a horse standing quietly in the shadows. No. It wasn't only a horse. A man lay on the ground, still holding the horse's reins. He looked thin and unhealthy to her, but she wasn't a doctor. Perhaps she should awaken him and make sure he was okay. But should she really? She was alone here. Anything could happen. She pushed away her fears and decided to check him out. As she stooped to place her hand on his shoulder she spotted a name embroidered on the pocket of his shirt. *Josh. His name is Josh.*

"Wake up Josh. Are you okay? Josh, if you're hungry I have a little food. I'd be glad to share with you."

The man lay motionless so long Katie began to fear he was dead.

"Oh! Wake up Sir. Wake up right now if you're okay. Please!" She began to shake the man, and he finally opened his eyes.

"Here, Sir. I have a sandwich and I think you need to eat it. How long has it been since you've eaten?"

The man continued to stare at Katie. She saw the look in his eyes change to something like gladness. Katie couldn't understand what she saw, but hurried to get out the food she had.

"Thank you, Katie," he said.

Shocked, Katie gazed at the man. Something about him stirred her senses; something familiar. "How do you know my name? Where are you going?" She pulled the last apple from her backpack and handed it to him.

"Well, that depends."

"Your voice sounds just like someone's I know."

"Whose voice does it sound like Katie?"

"Oh, you sound like a guy I used to know, but I haven't seen him for a very long time, and you don't look a thing like him. Are you feeling better now that you've eaten a little?"

"I'm feeling infinitely better now that I've seen you. You know Katie, sometimes things happen that we'd never planned; things that change all our actions. Even the way we look. That's what happened to me."

"You haven't even told me your name, or how you know mine. All I know is that you're Josh and that I found you here in a dead sleep. Tell me your name, and maybe we can sit and talk for awhile."

"Now that sounds like a good idea. Turns out my name isn't Josh at all; it's Brad. Brad Jennings. Now can we talk?"

Katie stared, almost unbelieving, but convinced in spite of herself by his voice. "But where have you been Brad? Why aren't you wearing your uniform?

Why didn't you write me? Why are you so thin? And why on earth does your shirt have Josh on it?"

"The answers to those questions are why we need to talk. We need to do it now, because when night comes I need to go back to Fort Boise.

"Maybe I'm too upset with you to talk to you at all. Do you know how much it hurt me when you just quit writing and totally disappeared?"

"Oh Katie, I'm so sorry I hurt you, but I couldn't figure out any way to help it. I hope you'll understand the whys much better, and feel much more like talking when I've explained everything to you."

"Amanda always tells me I should never refuse to listen. If you want to talk, I'll listen."

"Thank you. That's all I ask. Please, sit down in the shade for an hour. Then you'll decide what you want to do. As I said, it will be imperative for me to go to Fort Boise at once."

"What's happening in Boise that's so important?"

"That's part of what I want to tell you. Please sit here beside me."

Katie sat down. Brad took her hand and began his story.

"Back at the beginning of winter, after the war ended, things started looking really bad for the Paiutes. As you already know, I've been concerned about them for a long time. All of a sudden, as I think I wrote you, all the Paiutes were removed from the Malheur Reservation and sent to Fort Harney. That was bad enough, but what happened next was worse."

"What can all of this have to do with you staying away from me so long? I thought you loved me."

"Just wait Katie; I'll explain it all. An order came from Washington to transport the Indians up to the Yakima Reservation. It was mid December when that happened, and as you know it was a hard winter with lots of snow and extreme cold. The army did not have adequate provisions on hand for such a trip, but either the order said to move them immediately or someone was in a mighty big hurry. Wagons were hired for women and children and men had to walk. I knew that under these circumstances the travel through so much mountainous country in the wintertime would cost many lives if someone didn't do something. So I decided it would be me."

"I was pretty sure I'd never get permission to make the trip with them, so I didn't ask. I ditched my uniform, dressed like a cowboy and hid behind dark glasses. In other words, Katie, I deserted my post; I went AWOL.

"Oh Brad, you didn't!"

"Yes, I did. I thought the lives I might save were worth the chance of imprisonment or worse."

"When I was far enough away from my post I went looking for a covered wagon and some work horses. I found them. When I was prepared with as many blankets as I could get, some first aid supplies, medicines and food, I went out to Fort Harney where all the Indians were encamped, the hostiles as well as the friendlies, being guarded by the army. The Indians had received the bad news. What a fearful and sad lot they were."

"Brad, are you telling me you just packed up and left without even saying goodbye to me, and that you felt good about it? That's thoughtless and mean. I don't know if I can forgive you for all you've put me through."

"Please listen, Katie. Let me finish."

"I think I've heard enough. I'm going home."

Chapter 57: Brad's Hopes

Katie jumped up, headed toward Midnight, and froze. *I promised to listen, what am I doing?* She turned back to Brad. "I'm sorry. I need to hear the rest of what you have to say. I do feel hurt that you chose to leave without telling me, but I can almost understand why you did it. Please go on with your story."

She sat down again beside Brad. He studied her face and then reached hesitantly for her hand.

"I found Tah-Mano's family camped out with Leggin's group of friendly Indians."

"Tah-Mano! What was she doing there? They're our friends!"

"Yes, Katie. Tah-Mano and her family were there and they were included in the Indians being evicted from their homes."

Katie sat, immobilized by the thought of Tah-Mano, now gone from her home.

"In my situation I couldn't let them know who I was. I made sure they had all the blankets and food they needed; then I went back to the main camp."

"The trip through the snowy and icy mountains took us about ten days. As I feared, people died; especially the old and the very young."

"Is Tah-Mano all right? And her family?"

"Yes, Katie. Tah-Mano is all right. She and her family were among those Paiutes helping me plant a garden just before I left. I've been in Yakima with the dispossessed Paiutes since, trying to make life a little easier for them. They're still hungry—the agent seems dishonest and evidently cares only about enriching himself—but I helped the Indians get a good garden going. I hated to leave not knowing whether they'll reap the benefits, but if I don't get back to my post and explain myself I'll be in a big lot of trouble for a long time."

"Is Tah-Mano's family still okay?"

"We'll hope they'll all be better when the garden starts producing. For right now they're living pretty miserable lives. I'm disappointed that I couldn't make more difference for all of them."

"Brad. Stop that. You did what you could to help, and saved lives in the process. It means the world to me that you cared enough about my friend and her family to make such a sacrifice. I'm sorry I was so impatient. I was being selfish. You did what you had to do. What about the other situation; the AWOL one?"

"I'm hoping if I turn myself in before someone captures me that I will be treated with leniency. I'm hoping General Howard will be at Fort Boise, or at least in charge of my case. I've heard him referred to as the Christian General, and know he would at least be sympathetic to me and what I was trying to do. That could make a huge difference. If I'm captured before I get to Fort Boise, the best I can hope for is Court Martial and prison."

"Oh Brad! Is it really that bad? Isn't there something Lewis could do to help you? Maybe Les and Al Vaughne could ride with you to make sure you get to Fort Boise?"

"I'm nervous about going to The Crossing. So many people go through there that I'd be sure to run into someone I shouldn't run into."

"You could come in during the night. We could arrange a time and I could meet you at the barn. We'd only let Lewis, Amanda, Les and Al know you were there. Then you could talk it all over with everyone and decide what course you should take."

"I just don't know, Katie…"

"Please Brad. I'd feel so much better if you had someone helping you get safely to Fort Boise."

Chapter 58: Fort Boise

July 1879

General O.O. Howard rubbed his eyes and scratched his head thoughtfully. Since the beginning of the Sheepeater campaign in May he'd had little rest.

The Sheepeaters, usually a peaceful tribe, had welcomed the Bannocks who'd escaped the troops during the Bannock war just ended, and had been accused of numerous depredations since, the first in August 1878. Responsibility for thievery of horses, murders of miners, ranchers, and anyone else unlucky enough to be caught alone had been laid at their feet. These roving Indians traditionally moved from place to place in summer following the wild game that fed them, and camped in varied places in winter, making location of their camps and discipline for their crimes very difficult.

General Howard's position as commander of the Columbia Division of Indian Affairs meant he was responsible for a large territory; most of Oregon, Washington, and Idaho. That meant he had to track down the Indian encampments, destroy them, and deliver survivors to Fort Hall Reservation.

He had deployed numerous troops from the Oregon Territory and Northern Idaho. All had to move through previously untraveled, barely navigable terrain and all kinds of tumultuous weather. He'd ordered them to McCall at Payette Lakes, Idaho.

The General had a lot on his mind trying to deal with this campaign.

Furthermore it had recently come to his attention that Corporal Brad Jennings was missing from duty and had been for nearly six months. This information and his learning of it so late troubled and distracted him. He'd developed a relationship with the young man who struggled daily to build friendships with the Paiute tribes before and during the Bannock war. He couldn't help thinking there had to be a powerful reason compelling such action as desertion. Still, the corporal had deserted, and as much as the general might want to sympathize, he must deal firmly with Brad's case. He'd review court martial procedures at his first opportunity. In the mean time he'd better prepare a poster with the missing corporal's picture.

He sighed at the distraction and re-directed his attentions to the campaign at hand. The news was bad from Lieutenant Catley.His troops had arrived at Big Creek and the South Fork of the Salmon River and finally began to see signs of recent Indian presence. Underestimating the importance of what he saw, Lieutenant Catley led his troops up the canyon and rode into an ambush where the Indians fired on the troops from all sides, wounding two men and forcing his retreat to more favorable ground. Catley had not been able to regain the offensive, and was forced to return to Fort Howard at Grangeville to re-supply the unit. Catley's defeat forced General O.O. Howard to re-deploy the remaining troops into the Salmon River area where the Indians had been located. Nothing about the situation pleased him. . Catley should have expected what had happened; the terrain and the knowledge of the Indian's presence should have put him on his guard. *Chalk it up to inexperience, I guess.*

One of those deployments, Colonel Bernard's Company G of the 1st Cavalry, toiled through six-foot snowdrifts and rushing waters as they moved up the Salmon River. They were forced to abandon many of their supplies. The other units experienced similar calamities. *This uprising is bringing nothing but headaches.* There were times he wished he had never become a commander. He'd sure rather be home with his family.

Chapter 59: Trouble Brewing

Chuck Chiddless sat atop his horse, in his usual spying position on Rinehart Butte's upper western side. The sun descended over the hills beyond Stone House. Chuck entertained vengeful feelings regarding Stone House and its occupants; just seeing it stirred them all up. How well he remembered his visit there and its humiliating ending. *Right unfriendly of them gals, getting out those guns. If those soldiers hadn't showed up, they'd a knowed who was boss. I'll show 'em yet.*

As he turned his horse to head toward Washoe a movement in the valley caught his eye. A lone rider, apparently headed for Stone House, stood out against the sunset. He appeared to wear a cowboy hat and a beard, and sat his horse as if he was bone weary.

Now I wonder who that is, riding alone like that. Think I'll sit awhile and see if he stops in. He watched the ambling horse for thirty minutes; saw the rider guide it to the barn behind Stone House. *Looks like he's expected. Now that's intrestin'.*

***

Katie met Joshua Cross at the barn and helped him unsaddle and unbridle his horse before she ushered him through the back door into the kitchen. Amanda set a warm meal on the table and invited him to sit. Katie stood quietly beside the door.

"No Ma'am, I've done enough sitting for now."

"Then I'll put your stew in a cup and you can drink it. Want some coffee to go with it? Here are some hot biscuits." Amanda opened the oven and removed her golden brown offering, gracing the kitchen with the welcoming aroma of hot bread. Setting the butter beside the biscuits on the table she invited again, "Are you sure you don't want to sit, Brad?"

"Think I changed my mind, Ma'am. Name's Joshua. Joshua Cross if you please." Josh sat, removed his hat, and bowed his head. "Thank you, Lord for this food and these friends. It's nice that I can see them again. Guide me through the difficult days to come. In Jesus' name I pray, Amen.

Lewis came into the kitchen. "Howdy Brad. Great to see you again. In case you're wondering, everyone who lives here understands your situation, and we all want to help. What we're thinking is that Les and Al Vaughne should accompany you on your way to report at Fort Boise. That would give you a bit more security in case anything goes wrong."

"I've been thinking about that idea since Katie mentioned the possibility. Can you spare Les and Al for a week or so?"

"Yes, I can. They can do some business in Boise City for me after they deliver you safely to Fort Boise."

"Thank you. I'd be grateful, Sir." The tired traveler relaxed and helped himself to a biscuit or two. "Delicious Ma'am."

Lewis's voice claimed Brad's attention once more. "Now get some food into your body and we'll show you a place to sleep. You look like you could use about a year of rest.

"You'll write to me Brad, won't you, like you promised?" a timid voice from the doorway pleaded. I want to know how things are going for you…the discipline and all. You'll tell me won't you?

"I'll try Katie. I don't know what restrictions I might have to deal with, but always know I want to hear from you even more than you want to hear from me. Thank you for asking me to come here; it was a good idea."

A trio of men on horseback left Stone House before sunrise three days later. They had delayed their departure in order to give Corporal Jennings, alias Josh Cross, time to eat and rest from the months he'd spent on the Yakima Reservation.

Brad appeared wan and weary, and looked much too thin. During his stay on the reservation he'd eaten the same inadequate diet the Indians had been given. Amanda had offered much more than a habitually starved stomach could tolerate, and he'd eaten very little. Though the rest and food had helped, his energies still sagged, rendering him quiet and uncommunicative.

The Vaughne brothers, normally quite talkative, sensed his reluctance to communicate; the two of them conversed, rarely asking his participation.

"I expect we'd better look on anyone who attempts to join us with suspicion," Al said, straining to see through the remaining darkness. "Is there anyone you can think of that might be considered Brad's enemy, Les?"

"Only person I can think of is that fellow that came to Stone House. Remember Katie telling the story in a half-laughing, half frightened state?" Les slapped his leg and grinned. "The girls were at the house alone when he and his cronies showed up and wanted the Rineharts to quit associating with Tah-Mano and her family. Seems to me the ending of that event would have humiliated him. I don't expect he has very friendly feelings for the Rineharts, or for Brad who showed up in time to send him on his way."

"Yeah, that event ended perfectly;" Al responded, "Amanda shooting that crow and it landing in his lap. What was his name anyway?"

"As I remember his name was Chiddless or something like that. Good name for a guy whose horse dumped him, and in the presence of the ladies. Nope, can't blame him for feeling humiliated. I'd say he's probably an enemy. He's never met us, so that's in our favor."

"Well, could be," Al responded, "but we've never met him either. Everyone's an enemy. They have to be if we keep Brad safe. We'll be on the lookout for any kind of interference, and we'll recognize it if we see it. Chiddless is just the type we need to watch out for. In fact he's probably the most likely person to interfere. Hopefully he knows nothing about this present situation. How long do you suppose it'll take us to get to Fort Boise, Les?"

Chapter 60: The Prodigal Returns

Three tired men on horseback approached Fort Hall. They'd ridden hard in order to reach their destination the same day, not pausing to eat or rest. The sun had set behind them as they traveled. A full moon, high in the sky now, lighted their way toward the army post. As they approached they could see the locked gates; they'd figured they would be forced to camp outside for the night, risky as it was.

Al Vaughne turned to his brother. "Maybe we don't have to camp outside. What if we fired a shot or two to get someone's attention? What do you think Bro?"

"Well," Les said, "If you'd like to start a war that might be a good idea. Why don't we try knocking? Someone will be responsible and on guard."

"I vote for the knocking," Brad, suddenly all ears, spoke his judgment.

"Knocking on the gates it is," Al agreed with the two other men.

"I want to do the knocking and the speaking," the unexpectedly talkative Brad stated. "I'm the one who needs to do the explaining, and I want to talk to

General Howard and only General Howard. I sure hope he's here."

Anxiety shadowing his face, Brad stepped forward and knocked on the gates, He dreaded what followed. However this business turned out, there would be nothing fun about the next few weeks. He knocked again after a few moments and no response. Finally a guy in uniform, looking half asleep opened the gate.

"What's up?" he said. "Everyone's asleep. Couldn't this wait until morning?"

"I need to speak with General Howard. It's extremely urgent," Brad said. "It can't wait until morning."

"What if I said General Howard's not here?" the sleepy guard asked belligerently. "The General won't be in a wonderful mood if you disturb his sleep."

"I'll take my chances on that."

"State your name and your business here."

"Sorry," Brad said. "I can't talk to anyone except the General."

"You don't give me your name, you don't get in," the guard stated.

"I can tell you I'm coming from Stone House with an important message."

"Maybe the General will consider that enough information. We'll check it out. Wait here." The guard turned and walked through the door into a hallway.

"So far so good." Al removed his hat, slapped it on his leg, and looked sympathetically at Brad. "We'll take it one step at a time."

***

General Howard woke easily. He'd been restless since early evening when this stranger called Chuck Chiddless had arrived at the fort telling a story that had upset him. Chiddless said that several days ago he'd seen a very thin, tired horseman sneaking late in the evening into the barn at Stone House. It made him wonder, he'd said, if he'd seen the same guy in the poster on the tavern wall in Boise City; the guy that was AWOL by the name of Brad Jennings. "He's a nasty hateful guy if it was Jennings. Deserves to be in the brig. It'd suit me fine if you sent him away for years."

The message had been upsetting because if there was a chance it was Corporal Jennings he'd have to send men to confirm his identity and arrest him. Once he'd been arrested there would be no choice of leniency.

When the guard came to his door and said men had arrived with an important message from Stone House, it waked him fully. "Tell them I'll be right out," he said, leaving the guard flabbergasted at his words. "And while you're at it, take Chiddless to the brig. Tell him that we're concerned for his safety since he's come with such an important message, and are putting him in protective custody. I'm not saying who's being protected."

***

"Good morning, Gentlemen. We'll go into a more private room and you can share your message." The General led Les, Al, and Brad through a doorway into the hall, and into his office. "Won't you sit down?" He closed the door and took his seat behind a huge desk littered with topographical maps. He looked expectantly at Brad, noting how thin he was and remembering Chiddless' words.

"Now, Gentlemen, What can I do for you?"

"General Howard, I thank you so much for seeing us promptly and apologize for disturbing your sleep. My name is Brad Jennings. I am the man on your AWOL poster. You will notice my modified appearance. I'd like to tell you my story and the reasons for my disappearance, and place myself back under your authority."

"Well Brad, I've spent restless nights wondering where you were and why. May I compliment you on your make-over? I would never have recognized you. Now, tell me what you've been up to."

"Gladly, General. As you remember, before and during the Bannock up-rising, I worked among the Paiutes and Bannocks helping them to ensure a food supply that would make them less dependent on the rations from the Federal Indian Agents. I knew many of the native people and became concerned about them. Last November when the order came to remove them from their native territory in the Malheur, I knew the timing would put them all at risk. The winter had already demonstrated its severity, and knowing the terrain through which they would travel, well Sir, I just had to do something to make it a little easier for them. I bought a wagon and filled it with food and blankets, plus things they would need in an emergency. I knew I should ask permission, and I didn't doubt your willingness to give me the orders. It was Washington I doubted, and there wasn't time to do a lot of dickering. I didn't want to leave without orders, but I couldn't see any other way. Whatever the consequences of my actions, the lives I might save would make my choice worthwhile."

"Whatever your intentions, Corporal, you did leave without orders. You understand that I can't just ignore that fact, don't you?"

"Yes General. You have your responsibilities. Do what you must, but may I ask a favor in behalf of my friends who rode here with me? You might remember them. They assisted me in my work during the uprising. They need food and beds to recuperate from our long ride. May I present Les and Al Vaughne?"

"Yes, I remember Les and Al from my visits to Stone House, I believe. Nice to see you again, Gentlemen. You can certainly stay for whatever time you need."

"Thank you General," both men responded.

Al added, "We rode along with Brad because of concerns for his safety, and certain troublemakers who might want to interrupt his intentions to reach the post. We have other business in the Boise area, so after a day of rest we'll be on our way."

"I'll make arrangements for you and your horses. Now, back to Brad's situation. Corporal Jennings, I need some time to consider your actions. Under the circumstances I have no alternative but to detain you, at least while I contemplate whether there are ways we could put you back in good standing. You can rest and eat and think. Then we'll talk again. Good night Gentlemen. Wait here. I'll send men to show you to your quarters."

Chapter 61: Brad Reconnects

Dear Katie,

I have seen General Howard. We arrived at Fort Boise after midnight, but he arose from his sleep and talked to us. I feel encouraged that the General will be fair with me and give me a chance to redeem myself. He remembers the work I did during the war and seems to believe it was important. He did say he couldn't ignore my AWOL status, and has locked me up for now, but he promised we could talk again after he'd considered the facts.

I need to sleep now but I wanted to let you know that we've arrived safely and I am in good hands. When my brain is working better I'll be able to figure out a way to come back to you. Believe that. I love you Katie. I'll see you in my dreams.

Always thinking of you,
Brad

Brad laid his tablet on the floor and relaxed into the first mattress he'd enjoyed for over six months. *Give me wisdom, Dear Lord,* he prayed, and tumbled headlong into dreamland.

He saw Katie peeking out of the haystack so many years ago. He saw her sadly riding Midnight; he remembered the long trip from Tule Lake to Stone House. Then he saw Katie and himself dancing together at the ball, her flowing hair gleaming and her eyes shining with joy. He saw them together near the Crossing, sharing their life stories. He saw them hugging among the troops on the trail near Stone House.

Another picture appeared and he wanted to hold it in his mind and heart forever: Katie and he stood before Lewis in front of the dining room fireplace at Stone House. Katie wore white lace; he wore his dress uniform. "I now pronounce you man and wife," Lewis said. And Brad kissed his bride.

***

At 7:30 the next morning Brad jolted out of his sleep with the banging on the cell door. "I've brought your breakfast, Corporal Jennings. I'm sure you're ready for it."

"It can't be morning already. Feels like I've slept only an hour or two. What time is it?"

"Time to be up and then some," the guard answered. "Its 7:30. Birds have been up a long time."

"What's for breakfast?" Brad sat on the edge of the cot and stretched. "I feel like I could eat a cow, and a big one at that."

The guard eyed the thin man before him. "Looks like you maybe *should* eat most of one." He opened the cell door, passed the tray to Brad, closed the door and disappeared.

Brad looked at the food before him and lifted a silent prayer to God. *Thank you for caring for my needs, Father. Guide me through this day.* He ate hungrily, swiftly, feeling the desperate need of his body, hardly knowing what he ate. When he finished the food he placed the tray in front of the cell door and lay back on his cot. Sleep claimed him before his head hit the hard pillow.

When he awakened, the guard stood before him with a second tray. “Chow time.”

Brad accepted the tray with gratitude, sat on his bunk and studied the meal before him. A concoction of who knew what; probably a mixture of several left-over preparations, appeared to be the main dish. On the side of the plate lay some pale looking vegetables and two pieces of toast. It would fill his stomach, he decided, and ate it gratefully. *Not too bad.* He finished the cup of weak coffee provided and set his tray in front of the door.

“Now I need to think,” he told himself. “How can I make my situation better?” As he thought back over the past months and the benefits he had provided the Indians, he wondered. *How can I let the General know what I accomplished in a way that I won’t appear to be bragging? What evidence can I provide for his consideration and that of others? I wish I had some written evidence.*

“You do,” The answer sat there in his mind.

“Yes, those diaries I kept just to keep me sane. They are the evidence I need.” Brad looked around the cell for his saddlebags. They seemed to be missing. *Where are they? I’ve got to have them.*

Realizing that it was evening and that the guard would not likely return until breakfast so he could ask his questions, Brad took a deep breath. *Calm down. Tomorrow will do. I’ll write Katie again, and tomorrow I’ll check out my saddlebags. If I can’t have them I can request that they be sent to General Howard for his examination.*

Dearest Katie,

I slept most of the day, except for when I was eating. Guess I've been pretty tired and didn't know it. All I have to report is that I saw you in my dreams like I promised in my last note to you. I know now how precious you are to me. I know, too, that I want our relationship to grow into something very strong and lasting so we can be together.

It was so hard to be away and have no contact with you during the past seven months. Hiding my identity was the most difficult thing I've ever had to do. Most of the difficulty was connected with separation from all my friends; especially you, Dear Katie. I lived the loneliest days of my life going over those mountains to Yakima; no one with whom I could share, and always wanting to share with you. I won't go into those long months in Yakima.

In retrospect I realize that I did one thing while I was gone that may help to find my way out of the AWOL charge. I kept a diary of what happened day by day. I recorded what I saw; the consistent neglect of the Indian's needs; everything from shelter to food allowances. Perhaps my record will convince my superiors that I wasn't just running away from duty and that my service was useful. This is my current hope.

Right now I don't know where the diaries are. They were in my saddlebags which seem to be missing. Anyway, they are not with me in my cell. When the guard brings my breakfast in the morning, I'll ask him to bring them to me. If I can't have them, I can at least request that they be given to General Howard for his inspection.

That's all for now. I'll try to get these notes sent out to you as soon as possible.

In all my dreams I hold you in my arms. I love you, Katie.

Brad

Chapter 62: New Friend?

I'm bored. No friends, nothing I think of to do sounds interesting. Brad has managed to get himself in a pickle, in spite of his good intentions. I haven't heard from him. I wonder why. I thought he would write me, but he hasn't. I wonder if he cares about me at all. Katie grumbled in her thoughts; the more she complained, the worse she felt.

Lewis and Amanda just don't understand. They say all the time that Brad has his hands full right now, and that's why I haven't heard from him. I understand that, but it was his own choice that put him where he is. It just makes me mad.

No, I'm not mad. I did tell him I'd listen, and I did approve of what he did when I was thinking about it. It's just that now I'm so very lonely, and I can't see him, and I'm sick of having no friends. I need a change.

Katie listlessly left her room and went to the kitchen. Amanda greeted her cheerfully. "Good morning Katie. How's my girl this morning?"

"You don't really want to know." Katie flopped into a chair.

"Of course I want to know. You're my daughter; a mighty grown up one, but you still need a mother. Tell me what's going on in your head."

"Since Tah Mano's gone I don't have any friends except for Brad, and Brad's in a jam and can't ever come, and I just cook and clean, and ride, and then do it all over again."

"It sounds like you're in just the right mood for a ride right now. Why don't I fix you sandwiches and you can take Midnight out for awhile. Maybe you could meet new people at The Crossing, or go swimming at the Nat. The water's wonderful there."

"Maybe I will go for a ride. A person can read only so long. I haven't been out for some time. It would be fun to meet someone new. Trouble is, everyone's on their way to someplace else."

Katie left Stone House a few moments later with sandwiches and apples in her saddle bags. She headed for The Crossing. *Sure hope someone interesting is there; someone that will stay around for awhile and be my friend.*

When she could see The Crossing, she saw something unusual among the emigrants busily laundering and otherwise scurrying around. It was a different kind of wagon; one with pots and pans hanging on hooks all over the outside. Mops, brooms, brushes, and kinds of equipment she didn't recognize made her curious. She rode directly to where the wagon was parked and pulled on Midnight's reins. A small, slight, jovial man came around the wagon.

"Howdy, young lady. You're just the beauty I've been waiting for. Would you like to take a peek inside my wagon?"

"No thank you. I don't know who you are. What are you doing here?"

"Why I'm your friendly traveling peddler. I have everything from the Montgomery Ward catalog to fabric for your next new dress. I have plant starts from England and the East. If there's anything new I've got it. Name's Wendell Wiley. What's yours?

"My name's Katie Erickson. Where are you from?"

"I came from St. Louis, Missouri. Where are you from?"

"My first home was at Tule Lake, California, till the Modoc Indians destroyed our farm and killed my parents. Now I live here."

"Beauty like yours is wasted out here in the sagebrush. Let me show you something I have in my wagon. Wait here and I'll get it."

Wendell disappeared behind the wagon flaps, and reappeared carrying a small black box. "Now you sit right there on your horse and I'll show you something wonderful."

Katie watched him as he pointed the black box in her direction and looked in it. "I've taken a picture of you," he said. "Have you ever seen a picture of yourself?"

"Once I saw myself in a looking glass, but that was a long time ago. My mother had one in California. When can I see the picture?"

"Wait here. I'll be back in about five minutes." Wendell ducked into his wagon.

Katie thought curiously about what the picture would look like.

"I don't think you know how beautiful you are," Wendell said as he emerged from the wagon with the picture. "Here, have a look."

She looked at the picture and saw her mother as she had looked for so many years. *She was so beautiful. I never thought I'd be so much like her.*

"You could have a different life. A beautiful girl like you shouldn't be out in this wilderness. You could be a model, wearing fashionable clothes, having your picture on magazine covers, knowing important people."

"How could all that happen? I can't even imagine it."

"You'd have to come with me. I know a lot of people who could help you."

"Come with you? Why would I do that? I don't know you, and I couldn't leave Amanda and Lewis, or Mrs. McNeill. They're all the family I have."

Wendell's face showed his amazement. "You'd throw away an opportunity like this? Everyone would recognize you. You'd be popular, the life of the party, the one everyone would be eager to meet."

"No thank you, Mr. Wendell." Katie turned Midnight to ride away.

"No. Wait. Don't you want your picture?"

"I'd love to have the picture, but I'm not coming with you."

Wendell reached to scratch his head, as if to make an important decision. "Tell you what. If you'll let me come with you and meet your folks, I'll leave the picture for you. It's pretty special, isn't it?"

"It reminds me of my mother. That's why I'd like to have it. You can follow me. Amanda might like to see what you have to sell." The girl rode toward Stone House, and the peddler followed her.

***

"Thank you Mr. Wiley," Amanda said. The salesman had pulled out his wares and showed them, and Amanda had bought another large kettle. She knew she had needed it numerous times for the large amounts of food she cooked when so many people gathered at Stone House. *I'll be prepared next time.*

"Wouldn't you like one of these cameras? Here, let me take a picture of you."

"Why would I need a picture?" Amanda said. "No thank you."

Wendell pulled out the picture of Katie. "Now isn't this something you'd treasure? Katie and your husband would treasure a picture of you in the same way."

"Yes, I see what you mean. You may take my picture."

Wendell obliged, and in several minutes had disappeared into his wagon and re-appeared with the picture. Amanda looked at it, seeming pleased.

"It's beautiful, Amanda," Katie said. It looks just like you."

"Do you have one of those picture-taking gadgets for sale?" Lewis had entered the room and overheard the conversation.

"As a matter of fact, I do," Wendell replied. "What would it be worth to you?"

"Depends on what your price is." Lewis came to where Amanda sat, patted her hair, and sat near her.

"For twenty-five bucks I'll sell it to you and teach you how to use it and develop the pictures."

"Make it twenty and you've got a deal."

"Done!" Wendell went to his wagon, secured another camera, and invited Lewis into his wagon to learn the developing process.

"You'll spend the night with us, Wendell," Lewis stated.

Katie went to bed early. She felt exhausted, and fell fitfully to sleep. Visions of young women wearing beautiful outfits drifted through her dreams. She saw her own picture on the front of Women's Home Companion time after time. She watched as she posed in front of Wendell's camera, and felt proud of the pictures he took and the way they looked on the magazine covers. *You would be so beautiful and so popular and so well-known,* a voice said in her mind. *You'd have all the money you need to buy anything you want. You wouldn't have to cook or clean anymore.*

The restlessness continued all night, and Katie awoke in a pout of thanklessness. She couldn't help remembering the enticing scenes of her dream; visions of all the young men she could choose from filled her head.

I could go with Wendell. He would take me. I could become beautiful and famous. Amanda and Lewis aren't my real parents anyway. I don't have to stay here in this wilderness.

These tempting thoughts challenged Katie's integrity. They were uncomfortable somehow, she realized. What was it her Bible said about beauty? That it came from within; that it wasn't to be displayed like a trophy or bragged about.

She looked with pain at her ungrateful spirit. *Lewis and Amanda have been my family for seven years or more. They embraced me when I had nowhere to go. Where would I be without them? What can I be thinking of?*

What about Brad? He gave up so much for me; his position in the army is in jeopardy because of his love for me and concern for my friend's safety. He's in trouble right now. How can I desert a man who loves me so much?

And Wendell; I don't know him or how he would treat me. I must be crazy to consider going with him because of a lot of flimsy promises.

Shame consumed her. She fell to her knees and asked forgiveness.

Chapter 63: Developments

Brad awoke to a stream of bright sunshine coming through the small window. Thoughts of Katie tumbled through his mind warming and energizing him. He had to figure out how to return to her.

Then he remembered the brief-case and the diaries he had written. He arose and waited impatiently for the guard to deliver his breakfast. The man came finally, but seemed disgruntled, if you could judge anything by the look on his face.

"Thanks for the breakfast. Just what I needed. There is one more thing I'd like to ask of you. Do you know what happened to the saddlebag I had when I arrived?"

"How should I know? I'm not the one who checked you in."

"Could you tell me who that was?"

"I'm not allowed to discuss the other personnel with prisoners."

"Then would you be able to find out what happened to the bag and send a message to General Howard for me?"

"Depends. What kind of message?"

"The bag contains very important information the General needs to see. It's crucial information that will impact his thinking and affect his decisions. I'd like to have the bag if I can, but if I can't, I'd like you to tell him about it."

"Might and might not. Depends on whether I have time."

"I'd be mighty appreciative if you could make time. Please do me a favor."

"Gotta go." The guard stepped through the door and disappeared.

I see that nothing is going to be easy from inside this cell. Discouraged now, Brad sat on his bunk and lifted his heart to God.

***

"You've got company, Corporal. The guard turned to two men waiting in the hall. "You have about thirty minutes, Gentlemen." Brad looked toward the bars of the cell and saw the faces of Les and Al Vaughne. His spirits brightened immediately.

"I'm so glad to see the two of you. I've been disheartened because I need my saddlebags. The guard just let me know he probably would not help me find them. Do you guys know what might have happened to them?"

"Yeah, we know," Les volunteered. We took them with us on our errand. Didn't think you'd want to lose track of them. Why do you need them?"

"It has occurred to me that the diaries I wrote while traveling to Yakima might help the General understand what I did and why. Hopefully he will consider them important to his investigation."

"Great idea Brad. We'll see if we can get an appointment to deliver them to him if that's what you'd like us to do." Les reached through the bars to pat Brad's shoulder.

"You two are an answer to prayer. I can't do much from inside this cell. Please try for the appointment and take my saddlebag to the General. Now, what about you? Where have you been for the last couple of days?"

"Lewis sent us to Boise City to buy seed for the spring plantings. Al hurried to fill Brad in on their mission. "We bought corn, potato, sugar beets, and carrots. It takes a lot of food to run the wayside inn. The seed will wait in Amanda's root cellar till planting time."

"Sounds like good planning on Lewis's part."

"We also bought alfalfa seed to plant for a cover crop until spring," Les volunteered. It helps preserve moisture and puts nitrogen and a bunch of other minerals back into the soil."

"Thinking about the crops makes me want to be out of here and planting that alfalfa. And I'm feeling sick about being separated from Katie for so long."

"Don't you worry about that young lady," Al said. "She's got a mighty good head on her shoulders." He looked apologetically at Brad. "We'll need to be going now if we want to get home by nightfall."

"We'll try to get your bag to the General before we leave. Take care now." Les turned and headed toward the door. Al followed him.

***

General Howard welcomed the Vaughne brothers into his office. "I understand you have important papers to give me. Might I ask what they are?

"Brad Jennings wrote diaries while he was away from service. I know you'll be interested in what he wrote." Les handed the saddlebag to the General. "What you learn may impact the decision you must make about his future. Brad asked us to turn his saddlebag containing the diaries over to you for your inspection."

"Thank you, Gentlemen. I'd be interested in anything which helps explain his actions. I must say I was totally perplexed by his decision. Is there anything else I can do for you? Do you need anything for your journey?"

Chapter 64: Brad's Challenge

Mid August, 1879

The guard's words, coming before he awakened, startled Brad. "The General says he wants to see you, Corporal." He opened the cell door and handed in Brad's breakfast, a copy of the ones Brad had seen for three days now. "I'll return in an hour to escort you to his office. Be ready."

"Thank you Sir; I've been ready since I got here, and I'll certainly be waiting for you."

"Good luck, Fella."

"Do you have an idea whether the General has received my bag?"

"Nope. Say your prayers. The General don't have much use for cowards."

After breakfasting and cleaning up as best he could under present conditions, Brad waited both anxiously and eagerly for the meeting on which his future rested. *Remember, what you did seemed the only right thing to do. Don't apologize for doing something that was right. Pay attention to every word the General says.*

The guard's arrival interrupted his self-instruction. He rose, met the man at the cell door, and followed him out of the cell-block into a hallway. General Howard's office appeared on the right at the hallway's end.

The General sat behind his cluttered desk. He stood and welcomed Brad. "Sit in front of me, Corporal Jennings, where I can see your face." He turned and dismissed the guard. "That will be all for now."

The General waited until the guard closed the door, and turned to Brad. "Well, Corporal, you've presented quite a puzzle to me, and I've had no idea how to deal with it until I received your bag from your friends. Now I've decided a course of action. Don't respond, just listen."

"Choosing to go Away without Leave is a serious choice and a grievous charge to have leveled against you. As you know very well this choice could have landed you in jail for a very long time. I don't want to excuse what you did. I'm sure you understood the possible consequences."

"On the other hand, it is obvious to me after reading your diary that you had honorable motives and wanted to protect the Paiute people from the dangers of their winter eviction."

"I'm sure, also, that when you left without permission you knew you were questioning the judgment of your superiors who chose the timing of the journey. I question that judgment too. Because I do, I'm going to give you some choices."

"Thank you Sir."

"Is there anything you'd like to add, Corporal?"

"Yes, General. I'd like you to know I understand the difficulties of making decisions for Oregon when the leaders are in Washington D.C. Oregon is so far away, and so much can go wrong."

"I'm glad to hear that you understand the difficulty," General Howard continued. "Now, to change the subject a bit, I'm not sure whether you're aware of this or not, but the Sheepeater Indians apparently committed numerous thefts of horses and murders of miners over in Central Idaho along the Middle and South Branches of the Salmon River. Can't say I blame them much. About 7000 miners are panning for gold right in the middle of the areas where they usually camp during the winter."

"Rocky Mountain Sheep, Mule Deer, and Pronghorn Antelope inhabit the region. The Indians are fearful of losing such a plentiful and necessary food source; it's their motivation for wanting to keep the miners out."

"Since I'm the commander of this region I'm responsible for turning this situation from a confrontational one to a peaceful one. It's been a frustrating job all the way."

"The Salmon River terrain is full of problems. Nearly vertical mountains rise from either side of the river. It's called the River of No Return with good reason. Everywhere are rocks of every description, underfoot, overhead, obstructing travel. Some areas are virtually impassable. One area near the mouth of Salmon River is actually named Impassable Canyon."

"Colonel Bernard left Boise and has struggled up that river full of rocks and rapids for several weeks now, looking for the Indians. He's had to cross and re-cross the river and its tributaries in order to find places to pass. He's struggled to go forward over layers of rock, sometimes climbing on all fours. His pack train got separated, leaving him without supplies, sometimes for days at a time. Things are looking up a bit now. They've found signs of the Indian's presence on the

South Fork. Colonel Bernard is requesting supplies and reinforcements."

"I'd like to send you to join the reinforcements, with a special task in mind. You've impressed me with your service prior to your time AWOL. I'm asking you to do what you can to bring an agreement with the Indians, hopefully short of harming them. Before you decide whether you want to do this, let me tell you: this will probably be the most physically-demanding assignment you've ever had. If you succeed in achieving your objective I will waive your court-martial and give you an honorable discharge. What do you think, Corporal?"

Chapter 65: Katie of Malheur

Gladness filled Katie's heart as she watched the peddler drive away. *I'm glad he's gone. Everything he did stirred my restlessness. I'm glad I feel content again. I have a good life here. Yes, I have to work, but work brings its reward. Lewis and Amanda love me and provide for me. I could be wandering around in this world without anyone to love me if it hadn't been for them.*

Besides Lewis and Amanda I have Brad's love if I'm smart enough to appreciate him and keep it. He's in trouble with the army because of me; because he cared about me and my friend. How can I criticize and gripe because he's not here with me right now?

She turned and went back into the kitchen where Amanda was washing canning jars.

"Do you want me to go pick the beans and get them snapped, Amanda?"

Amanda twisted her body and looked at Katie. "How did you know I was longing for help?"

"I didn't know. Just knew I'd want help if I were canning green beans. Remember the old saying, 'Many hands make light work?'"

"Of course I remember. Didn't everyone's mother say that?"

Katie changed the subject. She still tried not to think of her mother. The memory of her parents' death still agitated her pain, whipped it to a white heat.

"How many are we going to can; all of them?"

"Let's pick them all; the ones that are mature enough. There shouldn't be more than we can do today with the two of us working."

Katie went out the back door to the large garden. It was a hot day, and she wished for shade, but gardens aren't planted in the shade. She returned to the kitchen and grabbed her hat from the hook by the door. It would provide a bit of relief for her eyes. Stopping by the root cellar she retrieved a pail, returned to the multiple long rows of beans, and stooped to reach the bean plants.

Pulling the leaves aside she found the beans; long luxuriously shaped pods. *Beautiful, Lord. We're thankful to have them.* One by one she deposited the green treasure in the bucket. The beans piled quickly but by the time the bucket was half-full, she stood and stretched her tired back. *It would be really hard for Amanda to do this all alone. I'm glad I realized she would need help.* She stooped again and continued picking the crisp green beans. Bucket filled and piled even higher, she climbed the steps back into the kitchen.

Amanda had finished sterilizing the jars. They stood steaming and shining on the drain board of the sink. A large pot of almost-hot water stood on the stove waiting for the bean-filled jars to be added. Picking the beans wasn't the only hot part of the job. Before the beans were sufficiently cooked the kitchen would be filled with steam. Once in the past, apparently because lids were not screwed tightly enough, greenish steam had colored the walls and left a huge cleaning job waiting to be done. *I hope we don't make that mistake again.*

At least we can sit down to snap the beans. Katie carried the bucket to the table, gathered large bowls, one to snap them into and one to separate the broken stems. Katie sat down. Amanda joined her.

Just as the two women finished the snapping job they heard the stage pulling up in front of Stone House. Katie jumped to her feet. I'll see if there's any mail. She ran down the front steps. The driver of the horse-drawn stage jumped to the ground, several letters in his hand. "Looks like you have some official business from Fort Boise there. You might want to open it first."

Katie looked at the letter. It was addressed to her. *Could it be from Brad? I hope so. It's been so long since I've heard.* She inserted her index finger under the envelope flap and ripped it open. "Yes! It's from Brad. You bet I'll open it first," she said to the driver. She ran into the kitchen.

Amanda, seeing her face knew what Katie held. "Would you like to read it in your room?"

"No. I'll read it right here. I'll read it to you. Then we can talk about it. I'd like that. You're the best friend I have Amanda."

"Thank you Darling. I'm so glad you feel that way."

Katie began to read the precious words Brad had written to her.

"They got there safely, Amanda. He's seen General Howard and he feels encouraged. Oh! He's in jail, Amanda. I was hoping that wouldn't happen. He says he'll get to talk to General Howard again after the General's had time to think. Brad says he's trying to figure out a way to come back to me. Knowing that makes me happy. How sweet. He says he'll see me in his dreams. Oh!! He says he loves me."

"Now don't you feel better Katie? Glad that you decided to trust him and wait for him?"

"There's another letter, Amanda. 'Dearest Katie,' it says. He slept all day. Let me read this part to you. 'All I have to report is that I saw you in my dreams like I promised in my last note to you. I know now how precious you are to me. I know, too, that I want our relationship to grow into something very strong and lasting so we can be together.' Katie paused in her reading and looked at Amanda.

"Is he saying he wants to marry me? Does he really?"

"It does sound like he's thinking in that direction. How would you feel about such a circumstance?"

"I think it's what I want, Amanda. But it scares me, too."

"I'm glad you see what a huge decision marriage is. It's a commitment to be faithful for your whole life. A lot of things can happen in a marriage; things that will test your resolve, put doubts into your mind, wear your patience thin, and make your spouse seem less attractive. You have to be ready to keep your promise through all of that and more."

"What kinds of things, Amanda? Have those things happened to you?"

When I left Summerville, I had a lot of romantic notions that Lewis and I would always be together; that all of our life would be romantic; that he would always pick up his dirty socks and help me with the dishes. He would always help me onto the wagon or stage and open doors for me. He would always be there to comfort me when I grieved. Early after our marriage he had to be away with the legislature, and ten years ago we dealt with constant Indian uprisings. There were times I wanted to escape it all and go back home."

"Do you mean where your mother lives now?"

"No Katie. I wanted to go back where we came from in the East. Life seems easier there."

"But you didn't go?"

"No, I didn't go. I made a promise to God and to my husband when I married Lewis, and I intend to keep it."

Amanda finished stuffing beans into the jars, adding salt and water, and then putting them into a large boiler. Katie sat and contemplated all she had heard.

Chapter 66: Into the Unknown

Brad rode north from Boise. He had accepted General Howard's challenge to make an agreement with the Sheepeaters. He'd jumped at the chance to prove himself. He did have some doubts about his body and whether it was up to the task before him, but he'd seen tough terrain before. There was always a way. He headed for the Payette River and the hot springs, the place where he would join the forces of Colonel Bernard.

The troops, finding fresh evidence of the Indians' nearness were closing in, according to General Howard. Brad knew that timing was critical; if he reached the Indians after the army had destroyed a village—the usual way to discourage the Indians' depredations—he would experience all kinds of problems in his efforts to negotiate.

After checking in with the command he intended to go on his own search. Perhaps he could get to the Indians first, convince them that only those guilty of crimes would be punished, that life on a reservation could be to their advantage. Just how it would help them was hard to figure out, knowing what he knew about the Reservation Agency System, but perhaps

Rhinehart on the Malheur and Wilbur on the Yakima were the exceptions, not the rule. He certainly hoped so.

It's wonderful to be out in the fresh air again. Living in a jail cell may give lots of opportunity for sleep, but once you've slept; boring. At least I had time to write Katie. Well, I didn't tell her about the job the General's giving me. I wish I'd had time to write once more.

I've got to succeed on this mission. That's all there is to it. I hope the passage isn't too difficult or doesn't last too long. I want to get back to my Katie.

***

Evening of the next day found Brad approaching the Payette Lakes hot springs. The terrain steepened, hardened; and the hills, covered with timber and brush, presented a very different picture than the one he'd left in the Boise Basin. The troops, camped around the lake, colored the greenery with dark blue and gold. The sounds and smells of the evening meal filled the air. Bone-weary from his long ride, the exhausted man longed to slide off his horse onto one of those logs; he was hungry enough to enjoy even trail rations, whatever they might be. Suddenly he found himself remembering the stew Katie had made at the Paiute camp in Malheur County. He saw her flushed happy face as she bent to stir, stood, and turned to receive his approval. His heart lifted as he remembered, and his stomach rumbled.

"Where can I find Colonel Bernard?" he asked a young man sitting by the fire pit. The youth crammed another bite into his mouth and pointed out toward the lake. "See the tent with the flag? You'll find him there."

Brad rode in the direction indicated. As he approached the tent the Colonel stepped outside; his eyes fixed on the water. "Beautiful here, isn't it?

"Yes Sir. Corporal Brad Jennings reporting for duty Sir."

"Do you have orders?"

"Yes Sir, if you please. General Howard sent me to negotiate with the Sheepeater Indians. If it pleases you I'll work alone. That way I can probably get closer to them, not frighten them away."

"Haven't I met you somewhere before, about a year ago? If I remember it was at Stone House in Malheur County. Am I correct?"

"You are Sir. Amazing memory."

"I'd suggest you take at least one man with you. The areas you'll be traversing are extremely rugged. Accidents can happen."

"I understand Sir. Did you have someone in mind?"

"Lieutenant Farrell has several Umatilla scouts; all have proven extremely trustworthy. They know the canyons and the river instinctively and experientially, and understand English. I'd like to suggest one of them."

"Thank you Sir. If you can spare someone that soon I'd like to leave in the morning, if that's convenient for you."

"It turns out, Corporal, that the troops you see here will be moving out tomorrow. We'll be marching up the South Fork of the Salmon to the Big Creek area. We'll connect with Lieutenant Edward Farrow and the Umatilla scouts there. Lieutenant Catley was defeated there, and the Indians make their presence known in various ways. We've just located an evacuated village and burned it. We recovered many of our lost supplies too. The inhabitants of the village have scattered over the whole area. We'll all be so grateful when the Indians are peaceful on their reservations and we don't have to destroy their property."

"Sounds like the sensible thing might be for me to accompany you at least to the junction of South Fork with the main river; from there I'll strike out on my own."

Chapter 67: Salmon River Reality

The difficulty of troop movement up the South Fork amazed Brad. At times they followed a narrow, rough, and rocky wagon road up the South Fork, and gave thanks for it. When the track disappeared and granite jutted into the river bed leaving no alternative, the only choice was the stream bed and rapids. When-narrow valleys or ultra gravelly banks left no other choice, the horses suffered. To save them, the men walked, leading their horses and stumbling over round-rolling rocks and barriers.

The Rains farm sat just above the mouth of the South Fork near the Main Salmon River.

"This is the Rains property." Colonel Bernard pointed to a narrow farm located on a gentle hillside. "You may have heard that the Indians attacked James Rains and two of his workers while he was finishing his last bale of hay one evening last August.

. James died at the house in his presence after being wounded mortally," according to his friend and brother-in-law Albert Webber.

"The Indians built fires circling the house. When Webber knew he could no longer help James, he watched for the fires in the back to burn low and sneaked out. The irrigation ditch saved his life, for it was bordered with willows and led into a creek flowing from the mountains. After a desperate scramble up the creek bed to the summit he reported the attack to those at the Warrens mining camp. I had the sad duty of recovering James's body from the burned house."

Brad, heavy-hearted at what he heard, rode silently.

"You can learn from the survivors," the Colonel noted. "They climbed on hands and knees up the creek-bed."

"There are four farms along the Main River. When the Indians are out of sorts, these have been the people who've suffered. During the last year, three of the four heads of families on this forty-mile stretch of river have died. We've a huge and very important job in trying to relocate the native peoples peacefully.

As I remember these incidents, I'm reminded of another warning I should give you. Never get off your horse in an Indian attack. It can make the difference between life and death. At least that's what 'Three-Fingers Smith' would tell you. He's the only survivor of the ambush at Payette Falls that killed Munday, Healy, and Grosclose as they tried to recover stolen horses. The other men dismounted; Smith didn't."

Brad listened soberly. He hated hearing of the atrocities the Indians were capable of, but he could almost understand their motivations. Their lives depended on having the right to hunt and fish in the locations they knew. He'd learned too that the Sheepeaters considered the mountains they called home as sacred places. Every tree, every rock, every animal was inhabited by spirits. *The presence of those miners is an insult to their beliefs; our presence will be too.*

"Be particularly watchful of places where the trail is extremely narrow with granite hugging the uphill side and no cover below. Those giant rocks are perfect ambush opportunities for an enemy. That's how it happened with Munday and his party. When do you plan to separate from our party? We'll be joining up with Lieutenant Farrow's company today."

Brad considered the Colonel's question quietly. "If we can join him and find a scout to go with me, I'll be ready."

"The Indian signs have been mostly in the area of the Big Creek and its canyons. The Umatilla scout will guide you on the trails that lead there. We've been chasing the Indians, so they'll be on their guard. How do you intend to get close enough to them to negotiate?"

"I've been praying about that. God will give me an opportunity. I have to be ready for it when it comes."

"Indians can be tricky devils," the Colonel said, "be friendly until your back is turned."

"I know, Colonel. I'll have to trust God to take care of me. I believe I'm trying to do the right thing. Accomplishment is hard to achieve without risk."

"Now that's a true statement. Just be extremely careful. I'm getting to like you."

"The feeling's mutual, Colonel. Thanks for your concern."

An hour later they climbed a ridge and saw Lieutenant Farrow's troops spread out below. The second hour they walked among them. The Colonel addressed the young Private at the border of the camp. "Where's Lieutenant Farrow?"

"I'll take you there if you like."

"Thank you Private. I'd appreciate that."

***

Brad and the Umatilla scout rode out of camp the next morning. Lieutenant Farrow had recommended the Umatilla named Duranjaya. He spoke understandable English and the officers trusted his judgments. Brad hoped to arrive at the Big Creek Canyon area in two days, and Duranjaya said he knew trails that would cut hours off the trip.

"We climb hill. I know way. You follow." Duranjaya guided his bare-backed horse with his heels and hands. "You want to find Indians. I know their place at Big Creek."

As Brad followed his guide up the steep hill he couldn't help remembering another time; the time Katie was lost. Les and Al had found her by following an Indian path up an extremely challenging hill in Malheur County. *Dear Katie. Thank you for helping find her, Father.*

They struggled up the hill, challenging one obstacle after another, improvising ways to proceed, sometimes abandoning their mounts. Brad saw Duranjaya's confidence and it heartened him. He despised the weariness of his body and prayed it would be equal to the task before him. *Give me wisdom and strength, Father. Help me get home to Katie.*

Valleys, hills; sharp granite, round rolling baseball sized; the stones were everywhere. Brad worried about his horse; would his hooves stand up to all the punishment they were enduring? *What would I do if I had to walk? I'm sure my legs would feel like a bowl of jelly if I tried to stand on them right now.*

Chapter 68: Deserted?

The path curved sharply to the left. Duranjaya jerked to a stop, avoiding a large fissure in the rock surface they traveled. He looked off to the right and pointed. "See path. Man go there."

The two men followed the bloody path. Behind a large Mountain Mahogany tree they found a badly wounded Indian. Blood pooled around his head; his twisted right leg showed bone jutting raggedly through his skin at the ankle.

Energized by the man's obvious need the two men sprang from their horses. Brad ripped his shirt from his back and tore it into strips. Wrapping the torn material around the man's head he pushed against the deep wound on his skull hoping to stop the flow of life-giving fluid. *He's unconscious. He would have died had we not come along.*

Duranjaya staunched the blood flow from the man's leg. He asked Brad to hold the man's leg just below the knee, and give a slow steady pull to move the bone back where it belonged. Then he found a straight stick with which to splint it, wrapping it with left-over strips of Brad's shirt.

"Let's wait awhile and see if he wakes up," Brad said to his guide. "We can use some rest, and it would be hard on him to be slung over a horse's back right now."

Duranjaya nodded, dropped his horse's reins to the ground, and sat on a log near where the injured man lay. Brad joined him, unconsciously heaving a huge sigh.

"You sleep, I watch," The Indian leaned against a pine tree behind the log. "Thirty minutes, maybe more."

Brad nodded his agreement, braced his elbows on his knees, and rested his head in his hands. He slept almost immediately.

When he awoke, uneasiness pervaded his spirit; saturated it. He could hear the wounded man breathing heavily as if he were trying to get up. He glanced toward where he had been lying and saw his eyes were open. He was studying Brad's face.

Brad's thoughts swirled elsewhere. *Where's Duranjaya? He said he'd wait and watch.* Brad couldn't see him anywhere.

"Feeling better?" he asked the injured man. The Indian obviously didn't understand English. Brad opened his backpack and removed two pieces of beef jerky. Offering one to the man he asked, "What's your name?"

"Name Chanadaka."

Brad knew Chanadaka couldn't understand, but he felt tense. He talked to him anyway. The man watched him and listened. "We found you here. I wish I knew what happened to you. It looks as if you may have stepped in that hole on the trail and thrown yourself. Where's my guide? I have no idea where I'm going without him. Surely he's just gone into the woods for berries, or to shoot some game. I could use a bit of meat right now. I'm almost starved." Brad rubbed his stomach and grinned at the Indian on the ground. Chanadaka rubbed his stomach too.

Brad volunteered, "Maybe I could go a little into the woods and look for huckleberries. A handful of those would taste good right now." The man on the ground wore a hopeful look on his face, so Brad ventured a short distance into the trees, cautioning himself not to turn and get confused. Then he realized that he must get back to Chanadaka; he must be there when Duranjaya returned. If he ever came back. He looked for a sunny spot, a clearing, hoping against hope he'd find the berries they needed. He looked around him and realized the berry bushes would likely be found on a south or west-facing hillside. There certainly wasn't one of those in these woods, not as close as he needed it to be. He couldn't risk getting lost.

The disappointed man retraced his steps to the side of the wounded man and said apologetically," Sorry pal. No berries in here. He shook his head. We'll need to look for them when we're traveling. We may come across them then on one of those hillsides we've got to climb." *Why am I doing all this talking? He doesn't understand a word I say. But maybe it's keeping his mind off the pain.*

Brad sat down again on the log and immediately started dozing. He roamed the worlds of sleep and wakefulness without decision, his exhaustion choosing for him. When he woke the last time it was evening. Chanadaka had pulled himself to a sitting position. Duranjaya was nowhere to be found.

Brad's tumultuous thoughts slowed him, but finally, under control now, he asked, "Feeling better Chanadaka?"

The man looked questioningly at him.

"Well you must be feeling better. You're off your back. I'm glad you can move like you did. It gives me hope we can get you out of here. Maybe tomorrow we can get you on a horse and go."

Chanadaka studied Brad's face and nodded.

Does he understand a few words, like horse and go?

"Where go?" Chanandaka surprised Brad with the question. He did understand a little, Brad realized.

"I don't know where to go. I guess we'll continue on this trail and see if we get to the Big Creek Canyon. I wanted to connect with the Sheepeater Indians and talk to them. I hope we'll find them."

"I Sheepeater. I take you."

Amazed at the way things were developing, Brad stood speechless. When he finally recovered from his surprise he asked, "Take me where?"

"My home," Chanadaka replied.

"Well, this isn't what I'd expected, but it gets me where I need to be. We'll wait a day or two to see whether Duranjaya comes back. That'll give us both a little time to gain strength. Then we'll see if we can get both of us on my horse. If we can do it we'll head for your home."

Chapter 69: Destination?

"Come on, Chanadaka, Let's get out of here. That sorry excuse for a guide must have decided to retire without telling us." Two days had crawled by as the two men sat and stared at one another and rested and slept and scrounged for something to eat. Jerky and that 'self rising' were a poor substitute for a meal but Brad felt stronger, and Chanadaka's head wound seemed to be healing. Brad knew they couldn't stay here longer. The Indian's ankle wound needed medical attention. *I just want to get home to Katie. How long have I been gone anyway?* Brad had jotted a few notes to Katie when he had a chance, but the difficulties they'd faced had left him without energy to write anything that made sense.

Brad supported Chanadaka, the injured man hopping on one foot, and sat him down close to where the horse was tied. He secured the backpack behind the saddle and then removed it. *We've got to ride double. I'll have to hold on to the pack.*

"Ready? He looked Chanadaka in the eye. I'll support you. You push as hard as you can with your good leg and I'll lift you as much as I can. Maybe it'll be enough." *I hope he understands what he needs to do.* "Ready, jump!"

Brad caught hold of the man in mid-air and guided him onto the horse's back. He led the horse close to the log they'd sat on and climbed onto it. Seeing that he needed more height to mount the horse he looked around for a larger log or a large rock he could stand on. He needed to be able to lift his leg over the horse's back, not swing it up as usual. He couldn't take a chance of dislodging Chanadaka.

Leading the horse Brad followed the trail they were on when they arrived at the location of Chanadaka's injury. Looking for the rock he needed, struggling over the rocky surfaces and around brush and trees that obstructed their passage they moved down the trail. Brad supposed he'd walked for an hour when he found the help he needed; a huge rock with crevices he could use to climb to the top. From there he could easily mount.

In the saddle at last, Brad reached to his backpack setting on the rock and placed it in front of the saddle horn on the animal's back. He'd have to support it with one hand. "Giddy-up." He heeled the horse gently in the side, and they were on their way.

"I know trail," he heard Chanadaka say. The Indian pointed back the way they had come. "Little way."

Brad turned the horse around and followed the trail back the way they had come. "You're the driver," he said.

About thirty minutes passed before Chanadaka lifted his right hand and pointed to the right. "Go that way."

Brad looked right and saw nothing to indicate a traveled route.

"Wait minute. Now." His Indian guide pointed again. The trail wasn't obvious, leading through timber and sage, and up and down hillsides. But Brad followed the man's signs and controlled his uneasiness with the thought of getting to the Sheepeater camp where he could begin trying to convince the Sheepeaters to give up the struggle to stay off the reservations. He realized what a huge job that would be and prayed for wisdom. *"Help me say what they need to hear, and keep me safe, Lord."*

In far less time than he had imagined Chanadaka pointed up a south-facing mountain. Then Brad could see parts of the Sheepeater's camp. After another slippery ride up the hillside they rode into the camp.

A group formed around them; Brad knew they were concerned about Chanadaka and asking for information. Chanadaka, suddenly very talkative, answered their questions.

After a short time, when he noticed the Indians looking at him with friendly, inquisitive eyes, he threw his leg over the saddle horn and slid to the ground. He turned, helped Chanadaka dismount, and offered his arm for support. At that point a man stepped forward, slapped Chanadaka on the shoulder and offered his arm. Chanakada took it. Brad, knowing how exhausted Chanadaka must be, slipped his arm under his remaining shoulder, leading the horse with his other hand.

Their destination turned out to be the medicine lodge inhabited by the shaman. The medicine man led them on a short journey to Big Creek. He walked into the creek and bathed, emerged and used a red pigment to paint figures on his chest and face. He built a small fire with cedar branches and held his hands in the smoke. He rubbed the smoke onto his body. And then the man put his hands on Chanadaka, chanted with closed eyes, fell into a trance and lifted his hands to entreat the Great Spirit for the injured man's healing. After he emerged from his dream state, the shaman made a poultice of herbs and soil and bound it on the ankle wound. Brad supposed its purpose was to draw out any infection that might be present, but so far no one had volunteered any information. *I hope they have someone around here that speaks English.*

Chanadaka did seem to feel better. His face brightened and as his friends gathered round him he spoke enthusiastically to them. Brad supposed he was sharing all his experiences, and felt confident about what he might be saying. He reminded himself that he had been kind and helpful. He hoped the Indians knew that.

Chapter 70: Surprise

"You come." The man appeared before him and seized his right arm. Brad knew he should not resist, and walked willingly where his escort led him. *I'm sure I'm going to meet someone important. Maybe the chief. Thank you Lord for helping me say the right things, truthful things and compassionate ones, wise ones.*

Brad noticed the Indian dwellings as they passed. They were different than the dwellings he'd seen previously on the plains; not teepees exactly, but rough forest houses made of smallish tree trunks pulled together at the top and fastened and then covered with skins. Each dwelling was set on a round stone foundation dug into the hillside. *I'm amazed to find that the village is so high on the mountain. I wonder why.* The size of the encampment surprised him; probably no more than twenty dwellings in all.

His escort led him to a dwelling quite indistinguishable from the others, stopped at the entrance, and called in, "Miave" (Chief).

An older man stepped out. "My name is Tanmanmo." He turned to Brad's escort and dismissed him, then looked at Brad again. "What are you doing in the land of the Sky People? Your people destroy our villages and disturb our Spirits."

"I'm looking for *you*, Chief. I bring an important message."

"What is the message, young man?"

"You may call me Brad. My army rank is Corporal; Corporal Brad Jennings. The message is that your people and my people both want the same thing. We want peace. It is hard for our peoples to live together because some of your people and some of our people do mean things like killing innocents. The people who kill are the ones who should be punished, not your whole village or my whole town. Will you turn over your people who murdered the miners and the farmers on the Salmon River? Why should all your people have to run constantly and see their villages destroyed for things they didn't do? Why should they keep suffering? No one who has not murdered will be punished. Only the guilty will pay for their crime."

The chief stared at Brad for several minutes. Brad waited for what seemed like an eternity.

"How do I know what you say is true? What about the army that has been chasing us everywhere we go?"

"General O.O. Howard is head of the Department of Indian Affairs for the Columbia region. He is the one who sent me to try to make peace between white men and Indians. He commands the army."

"You are free to go. Thank you, Corporal Brad Jennings for helping Chanadaka when you found him in the forest. He would have bled to death, he says, if you hadn't helped."

Brad saluted the chief and turned to go. Three Indians followed him. When they came to an especially-well-built lodge two of them stepped forward. Grasping him by the biceps they guided him into the building. After showing him a place where he could lie down, and giving him berries and bread cakes to eat, they backed out of the lodge. Brad heard the clunk of a barrier being slid into place at the door.

Chapter 71: Creativity

Time crept by on turtle feet for Katie. She had tried to keep busy, but after Brad's letters quit coming her motivation and energy disappeared too. She had planned to keep busy in his absence, thinking it would somehow bring him back sooner.

Why doesn't he write? What can be keeping him from writing to me?

The last she had heard from him was the letter that made Katie wonder and hope for their future together. She'd been invigorated then, and decided she'd make him a shirt. *How hard can it be? I've been making my own dresses. I'm so glad Lewis bought us the sewing machine. How else could we possibly keep ourselves looking decent?*

Amanda and she had canned nearly everything in the garden except what they had stored in the root cellar for the winter. They had worked hard to clean the garden area and mulch it to keep the weeds down.

Pumpkins and squash were still growing, waiting for October when with a little help from Katie and Amanda they would turn into zucchini or pumpkin breads and pies, not to mention scary-faced jack-o-lanterns.

Now with the garden chores finished Katie brought out the grey-blue-black-plaid fabric she had ordered from the Montgomery Ward Company in Chicago. *It will make a beautiful shirt and look so good on Brad. How I miss him!*

Katie carried the fabric to the large dining table and spread it out with selvages (finished edges) together. She had found a Butterick men's shirt pattern in the Delineator Magazine Amanda received monthly, and ordered it for her project. Now she opened the envelope and studied the pattern guide, the directions she needed to follow.

When she thought she understood the instructions she began to lay the pattern pieces on the folded fabric, measuring and adjusting to make sure each end of the arrow printed on the pattern piece measured the same distance from the selvage and pinning it to the fabric. Looking back at the pattern guide she read it again. A phrase jumped off the page and stuck in her mind. "Keep selvages even, being careful to match plaid lines." *Why didn't I see that before? I knew I was using a plaid fabric.*

Unaccustomed as it was to bending over a table for such long periods, Katie's aching back told her it was time to do something else for awhile. She heeded the ache and reported to Amanda in the kitchen that she was going to the barn to feed and visit Midnight; maybe she'd find the brush and give him a treat. Maybe she'd go for a short ride, too. "I'll be back in thirty minutes or so," she told Amanda.

The tired seamstress escaped through the back door to the fresh but hot air outside, where she twisted and stretched her body for several minutes before heading for the barn. Deciding to take the ride before brushing Midnight, she saddled and bridled him, swung into the saddle and spurred her horse into a gallop. The hot air felt cooler as she moved through it.

About thirty minutes later she returned, refreshed by the air, the exercise and the view of Rinehart Buttes; they were very special to her now, kind of a family treasure. She rewarded Midnight with an apple and a brush-down before she opened the door into Stone House and entered. "I'm back, Amanda," she called and then went into the dining room where her work was spread.

Looking down at the job before her she realized she might need help. I'll ask Mrs. McNeill. She's a wonderful seamstress; she'll give me some good advice on how to do the best job of matching this plaid. She knocked on her good friend's door, waited for permission to enter, and asked, "Do you feel like helping me, Mene?"

"What are you doing Katie? Is it something I know how to do?"

"I'm trying to cut out the shirt I'm making for Brad. I bought this beautiful plaid he's going to love, but now I'm realizing I know nothing about matching plaids. I'm afraid that without some help I might ruin the fabric."

"Of course I'll help you dear. I've done a lot of sewing in my time, so I'll enjoy helping you. Did you know that when I started sewing we had no patterns? I learned to look at a dress in a catalog and cut the shapes I'd need to put the dress together. We used paper or a cheap fabric to test it before we cut out the fabric. Once I made a form-fitting wedding dress for a young woman from a picture in a magazine. It turned out beautifully, if I may say so."

"Oh, Mene, I could never do that."

"Well, you might if you had no choice. The only alternative to improvising was to tear apart an old dress you liked and use the pieces to pattern the new one. It took a lot of time. We women didn't get much sleep in those days. Now, let's look at your shirt."

Katie led Mrs. McNeill to the dining room table. Mene demonstrated to Katie that the plaid on the bottom layer of fabric did not match the top layer. She pushed a straight pin through on a selected plaid line and asked Katie to look and see if the pin came out on that same line on the bottom layer of fabric. Katie readily saw that Mene knew what she was doing. Together they worked, checking and adjusting the fabric until the lines matched. Each pattern piece also had to be laid so when the notches were matched the plaids would match. Finally, everything lay smooth and ready to cut.

The grateful girl pulled her helper into an enthusiastic hug. "Oh Mene, whatever would I do without you? I think I can do it now. I can really finish Brad's shirt. "

Chapter 72: Realization

"This is a *fine* kettle of fish!" Brad repeated the saying he'd heard from his dad in every adverse situation he could remember. He had eaten and slept in the lodge where he'd been unexpectedly locked by the three Sheepeater men, and now he had no idea what was going on. Would they give him another opportunity to talk with the Chief? Would they leave him locked here indefinitely? Or would they torture or kill him?

God is in control, he reminded himself. *I can trust Him. Yes, I can trust Him, but it sure isn't easy in a situation like this. Why am I here?*

Brad answered his own question. *I'm here to work toward peace with these Native Americans, peace and understanding*." Feeling somewhat calmer once he had spoken his mission and his trust, Brad stood and walked around his present quarters. The lodge had numerous rooms but only one outside door. He peered into each room cautiously. Expecting to find the last room as empty as all the rest, he stuck his head through the doorway and yelped in surprise. There stood his supposedly-deserter guide Duranjaya, just as much a prisoner as himself.

"Well hello, Duranjaya. What are you doing here?"

"I could ask you the same thing."

"Apparently wearing an army uniform and being here qualifies me for the lock-up. And you?"

"As you well know I worked as a scout for the cavalry. The Sheepeaters don't like it. And there's another thing. The Umatilla tribe doesn't much like the Sheepeaters, and they don't like us either. That's why I sneaked away while both you and the Indian were asleep."

"Well thanks for deserting me. I had no idea where I should go."

"I knew he was a Sheepeater. I figured once he woke up and gained his strength he would bring you here, and he did. Right?"

"Yes, you were right, and I did get to talk to the chief. He thanked me for helping the injured man we found, listened to my plea for the Indians to give up, and then he told me I could go without giving me any answer. Here's where they brought me. What will they do to us?"

"They'll consult their spirits, the Sky People, and ask whether we're friend or foe. Then they'll put us through some kind of test where the Great Spirit can answer them. Let's hope it's not a fight to the death of one of us.

Brad remained silent after that. Duranjaya 's words gave him plenty to think about. He walked back to his pallet and lay down, but he didn't sleep. He prayed.

The day dragged on. One of the three Indians brought a simple lunch of berries and a meal biscuit. He ate it, and wished he could share it with Katie. He wished he could write to her and know she would receive his letter, but he had nothing to write with. He smiled. I guess I don't know where the mailman is or when he'll pick it up, either. He had no idea as to where his horse and all his belongings had disappeared.

You'll never get out of here or see her again. He heard the whisper in his mind. His spirit sagged and wilted. He thought about how out-of-control things seemed.

And then Brad remembered scripture he had read many times. *Hope thou in God. Set your mind on things above. In everything give thanks.*

Immediately more cheerful he began to count his blessings. I am well. We travelled safely up the Salmon, avoiding injury and escaping Indian attack. Only You could have planned the events that brought me here. I arrived in the Sheepeater camp and had an opportunity to talk with the Chief. He listened to what I said. I am safe and well right now. You have promised to lead me every day. I'm going to trust You.

His thoughts returned to Katie. I'm so thankful I could be the one to rescue her from Chiddless and help her. I'm thankful that we are growing in our love for one another. I'm thankful I've had this opportunity to regain my status with the army and to escape court martial.

As he counted the many ways he'd been blessed, he thought of additional blessings he would ask: *Help me have another opportunity to talk to the chief, and guide the words that come from my mouth. Guide me safely back to my Katie, and please, do it as soon as you can.* Placing his trust in the True and Living God, he felt peace return to his troubled mind, and he slept.

Chapter 73: Hope

The morning light filtered into Brad's sleeping area and teased him into wakefulness. He rolled from side to side several times before stretching tentatively and rising to a sitting position. He'd slept peacefully in spite of his precarious position and felt confident about the events of the day. He had asked for help and he would receive it.

He heard the wooden bolt scraping across the door and saw the man who'd brought his food. "Eat now," he said, and handed Brad berries and bread with a little water. He accepted the simple meal, thanking the Indian and gratefully lifting his thanks to God.

After he'd eaten, and still feeling stiff, he sat on the floor of the makeshift room and did fifty stomach curls, and then flipping his body over did a group of fifty push-ups, repeating the exercises over and over. *I don't have anything else to do. I'll at the least, get my blood circulating.*

He was glad when his small mid-day meal arrived with the same bearer, and had barely finished eating it when another visitor entered.

Chief Tanmanmo stood before him.

"Please sit." Brad motioned to a place beside him on the mat. "I'm glad to see you Chief."

The chief sat beside him, waited a few seconds, and spoke. "I want to talk more about ending the war. Our families are suffering, losing our homes and possessions constantly, and all because some of our young bucks think killing brings them honor. Some are in our village, some in other places.

"I see. Are you willing and able to collect these young men? Will they follow you?"

"If I bring them to you, will I be allowed to return to my village?"

"I'll do all in my power to see that you can return. The army will also require the release of Duranjaya, their scout. You'd need to deliver the hostile warriors to a specific spot where the army could apprehend them. You and I could choose a specific place on the creek; I could let the army know where it is. We could choose a specific time. Would it be possible for you to bring them? Can you deliver all the troublemakers?"

"I can do it."

Brad continued voicing his plan. "I think they would follow you more readily if I weren't with you, so Duranjaya and I will return to Lieutenant Farrow's troops at the fork of Big Creek, that is, if you'll allow us. I'll inform them that you want to end the war and are bringing the criminals. I'll relay your request to return to your village. They will probably want to question you before they release you. This is a wise choice you are making, Chief. Are you in?"

"I will bring them if I can return to my people afterwards."

"Okay, Chief. What would you say about October 1 as the date for you to deliver them at our agreed upon place on Big Creek? Would 14:00, that is

2:00 P.M., be a suitable time? When can you and I choose the specific location?"

"The arrangement is fine. We will go today. This war can't end too soon."

Chief Tanmanmo pulled a pipe from his clothing, solemnly lit it, smoked it for a few moments, and passed it to Brad. "This is our agreement. It is a promise not to be broken."

Brad received the pipe, puffed it a few times, and handed it back to the chief. "May God make it happen."

***

A few hours later Brad had his possessions back, including his horse. He, the Chief and Duranjaya left the village high on the hill and slid down the steep banks on their horses to the creek. After riding about thirty minutes the Chief stopped at a sandbar. "This is a good fishing place, he said. This will work." Turning and pointing in the opposite direction he said, "You go this way to find the army."

The Chief and he went back the way they had come, the Indian veering off to the right and riding a zigzag course up the hillside to the village. After a ride of several hours Brad and Duranjaya found the army camp. Brad went directly to Lieutenant Farrow's tent.

"Hello Sir;" Brad saluted and stood at attention.

"At ease, Corporal. What can I do for you?"

"I have important information, Sir. General O.O. Howard sent me on a mission. I'm hoping my mission is accomplished."

"Tell me about your mission." Lieutenant Farrow motioned Brad toward a folding chair, and took one opposite his desk.

"General Howard sent me to see if I could negotiate an agreement with the Sheepeaters; get them to turn over the hostiles responsible for all the murders.

I found a chief who was willing to talk, and we made an agreement."

Lieutenant Farrow leaned forward, interest evident on his face. "You have an agreement? Please tell me what you were able to negotiate."

Chief Tanmanmo has a village just a short distance from here. He wants badly to end the war. We agreed that he would bring in the young bucks and any women or children who are responsible for the murders and thievery in return for his freedom to go back to his village."

"Is he one of the guilty ones?"

"I'm sure not. I presented the possibilities of ending the war to him. He locked me up for a day, but he came to me again wanting to talk it over. He wants peace badly enough to take the risk of gathering the hostiles and leading them to a place down on Big Creek where the army can apprehend them. We've chosen the spot and pinpointed the time. He says it's a great fishing site. We didn't talk about how he would convince them to follow him. He knows Indian ways. I'm sure he'll get them here."

"Congratulations Corporal. If this works it could end the war. I'd recommend you for a medal if the plan is carried out successfully."

"Thank you Lieutenant Farrow. Can you have sufficient troops advised of the situation and ready to apprehend the Indians the chief brings?"

"What time and date have you agreed on?"

"October 1 at 1400.

"I'll have Lieutenant W.C. Brown and twenty Umatilla scouts here to help in the final negotiations, and sufficient support troops. We'll question Chief Tanmanmo, and if we believe he's innocent he'll return home. I'll need you here during the apprehension,

Corporal, and then, if this works, you'll be free to return to Fort Boise."

Chapter 74: Return

Corporal Brad Jennings rode toward Boise City with irrepressible joy in his heart. He thought of Katie and the day he would go home to her. He hoped it would happen in the near future. The success he'd experienced with his assignment guaranteed his honorary discharge. The difficulties he'd gone through had been trying, but he'd grown to be a better man through them; he'd stiffened and hardened his faith.

He thought back over the day of the negotiations. He regretted that life on a reservation lay ahead for those fifty one men, women and children who'd been apprehended, but peace in the Salmon River mountains would be the result, and that was good for both the more than two hundred Indians that remained, and the Whites. The army, after examining Chief Tanmanmo, had agreed to let him go back to his village. It would remain unmolested unless the Indians created more unrest by attacking.

His mind leapt back to Katie. *Dear beautiful Katie.* Too long had they been parted. *I can't wait to have her in my arms again and kiss her alluring lips.*

Troubling thoughts assaulted him. *What if she's angry with me again? I wasn't able to write. I didn't tell her where I was going or how long I'd be gone. Maybe she won't want to see me or have anything to do with me. I wouldn't blame her if she never wanted to see me again. This is the second time I've disappointed her.*

Brad realized he'd let his thoughts descend into negativity, and gave himself a good lecture. *I'm borrowing trouble. Most of these kinds of worries are proven a waste of time and energy because they never happen. Pay attention to the path ahead and be careful. That's the most important thing to think about right now.*

Brad's thoughts continued to stray, here and there, back to Katie, ahead to his arrival at Fort Boise, his coming discharge and how he would earn his living from this time forward. *Where will I live? How can I manage to find any work close to Stone House where I will be close enough to court Katie and plan our life together? Or will she have anything to do with me? She's so beautiful she could have any guy she wanted. I haven't been with her enough.* The worry cycle leapt like a lion into his thoughts and he rejected it again.

When he realized what he was doing, how he so easily forgot to lean on God and trust Him, scripture started crowding into his mind; verses about bringing your thoughts into captivity to Christ, about not being anxious, about being sure to walk in the light. Remembering that his future lay in God's hands quieted his spirit. He felt strengthened for whatever lay ahead.

Because he stayed lost in thought the difficult miles melted away. When he finally began to pay attention to his progress he realized that evening approached. The darkening sky told him that time for setting up his sleeping arrangements grew short.

He concentrated on his surroundings now, looking for a spot where he could erect his small tent and build a cooking fire in the morning. The spot found, he hurried through the necessary tasks, dug through his saddlebags for a quick meal, and climbed into his bed-roll.

He was drifting on the edge of sleep when he heard it. A growl. His body tensed at the sound. He lay still, not knowing from whence the sound came. It came again seemingly from close by; almost a roar, accompanied by a tearing of flesh, partly rotted if he could judge by the stink. *It's a bear. He's eating some kind of carcass. I chose a fine place to park tonight, right in the middle of his dining room. Lie still* he told himself, *or you'll become part of his dinner.*

He listened for his horse, but heard nothing. *What a fix I'd be in without a horse. Please Lord, let that bear get plenty to eat before he finds me or the horse.*

The growling, tearing sounds continued for several minutes and then suddenly stopped. Brad stiffened, knowing the bear was moving, but having no idea which direction. He endured the wait until he felt sure the threat was gone, and then he exited his bed-roll to check on the horse. Finding the horse where he'd tied him, he breathed a sigh of relief and headed back to his bed-roll hoping for a night's rest. It took some time before his busy mind would allow even a semblance of sleep, but finally it quieted, and he drifted away in repose.

He made more thorough camping preparations after the bear scare, looking over the surrounding area of any over-night possibility before pitching his tent. Though he had successfully navigated the treacherous Salmon River and its mountains he had yet to pass through many forest filled miles before he reached Boise City, still at least a hundred miles away. The ride would take him at least two days, but more likely three.

He'd never seen so many trees, he thought. He'd be very happy to see the high deserts again; in the deserts you could see where you were going.

Days later when he noticed the trees thinning, he knew he was approaching Boise City and felt deeply thankful to see the long trip ending.

Chapter 75: Reporting

"Glad to see you back, Corporal Jennings. I'm looking forward to hearing your report." General O.O. Howard had sent for Brad immediately when he learned of his return. "Of course I've heard the results of your negotiations; that we have one less war to worry about now."

"Yes Sir, I'm very glad to be back. As you told me before I left on the mission, the travel through those mountains and valleys was incredibly difficult. Of course I appreciated the assistance of Colonel Bernard and his troops through the most difficult parts of the journey. I've seen enough rocks and rivers, enough granite, to last me a life-time."

"I'd like to know one thing. Are you certain we have the trouble-makers in our group of prisoners?"

"The chief that surrendered them to us said the fifty one people were the culprits. He gave his solemn promise to maintain peace among those who were left. I believed him."

"How did you meet this chief, Corporal?"

"He locked me up in his village. I'd taken one of his wounded warriors there."

"Very interesting. The chief offered to surrender right out of the blue?"

"Well no, Sir. I'd been escorted to his lodging right away, and I took the opportunity to talk to him. I prayed a lot first. It was a real surprise when he locked me up."

"It can happen that way sometimes."

"But Sir, He must have thought about what I'd said to him; when he came to me a day later he was ready to make a deal."

"Well, Congratulations, Corporal. However it happened you accomplished your mission. I see no reason you should not be mustered out and go home. I should have the paperwork completed in a couple of days."

"Thank you Sir. That's good news."

"In the next two days while I'm preparing your paperwork you should prepare a detailed report of how your mission went, and specify the terms of the surrender."

"Yes Sir. I can do that. I may need some fresh paper. Brad stood and moved toward the door. "By the way, Sir. I have a question."

"What would you like to know Corporal?"

"I'm wondering what happened to the guy you locked up before I left here. I think his name was Chiddless."

"I let him go after you were well on your way. I gave him a few things to consider before I turned him loose, and told him I didn't want to see him again. I don't think he'll trouble us anymore. At least I hope not.

"He's a real trouble maker. He came by Stone House one day bothering the women about making friends with an Indian. The girls gave him some discomfort, and I gave the reinforcements."

The General smiled and waved Brad out of his office.

Brad found an empty room with a table and sat down. He needed to write that report the General wanted, but he had something he wanted to do first. He wanted to write to Katie.

He dug through his saddlebag and found a tired piece of paper.

Dearest Katie,

I know you're wondering what's happened to me and why I didn't write you. I hope you'll forgive me when you hear what I've been doing.

The General sent me on a mission to give me an opportunity to prove myself. I was supposed to find a way to resolve the Sheepeater War peacefully.

The trip took me into the wild and magnificent Salmon River country of Idaho. Every day as we travelled up those rivers they challenged us; sometimes we wondered if we'd survive the experience. We lived through the adventure, and I'm now at Fort Boise.

The Sheepeater War is over; General Howard has told me he'll give me an honorable discharge. You can't imagine how happy this makes me. The discharge papers will be ready in a couple of days. In the meantime I must write a detailed report of my actions and the terms of the surrender I helped negotiate.

How I've missed you Katie. I wanted to write you, but the travel was difficult and the days were long. I'd pick up a pen, intending to write, and find myself sleeping. Somehow that letter never did get written. If it had been finished I'm not sure how I'd have sent it out. The stagecoach didn't stop by in those mountain river valleys.

I'd like to tell you so many more details of what I learned and what I did, but for now I must get busy on that report. It will be a challenging job, and I want to do it well.

I'm hoping to see you by the end of the week. I can't wait to see your smile and hold you in my arms. Till then I'll see you in my dreams.

I love you, my Katie of Malheur Oregon Country.

Brad J. Jennings

Chapter 76: Time Pressure

The young seamstress at Stone House really wished she could hear from Brad. She found it hard to maintain her positive outlook and her confidence since it had been so long since she'd had a letter. Katie had been trying to keep busy, working regularly on the shirt she was sewing for her absent love. Because of her inexperience with plaid materials she'd consulted with Mrs. McNeill over and over. Then she'd go to the machine and sew a seam or two and have Mene check it over for perfection. She felt proud of the work she'd finished. She'd joined side and shoulder seams and constructed the collar. Mene had shown her a trick to keep the facing seam from turning over and showing the stitching on the right side of the collar, and it looked just the way she wanted it to. Now she needed to join the collar to the shirt.

Katie looked for her pattern guide and read it carefully. She felt a bit confused so she read it again. She matched the notches, pinning right sides together and turning the shirt's front facings back and pinning a 5/8 inch seam along the neckline. Things just didn't look right. Something was missing. She would need Mene's help again. As she was rising to go make her request, she heard the stage pulling in front of Stone House. She ran to the door and greeted the driver.

"Anything for me, Mr. Jamieson? Oh please say yes!"

"Who would send you a letter, Miss Katie? I can't imagine any fella would take time to write you," the stage driver kidded.

Katie, recognizing his banter for what it was, smiled and tried again. Please don't tease me, Mr. Jamieson. Isn't there a letter for me today?"

"Well, Miss Katie, I think maybe I did see something for you." He sorted quickly through the pile of correspondence he'd picked up. "Oh, there it is." He handed the letter to Katie.

Looking at the envelope and seeing it was from Brad, she turned and ran up the steps. "Thank you, thank you Mr. Jamieson. See you next time."

Katie went straight to her bedroom and closed the door. She opened the envelope with trembling fingers, pulled the contents from the envelope, and held the letter close to her heart. *Thank you, Father. He's safe.*

She read the letter slowly, absorbing every word. *Good news, all of it.* And then she realized what he'd said. *"I hope to see you by the end of the week"* She looked at the letter again. The stage probably took two days to get here. That probably leaves me only a day or two to finish his shirt! She ran to the dining table and picked up the shirt; then she ran to Mrs. McNeill's room calling out, "Mene, Mene! Help!"

Mrs. McNeill opened her door. "What's the matter, dear?"

"Oh Mene, I got a letter from Brad. He'll be here in two days or maybe less. I'm not sure how to finish the collar and the buttonholes. Oh Mene, I so wanted to finish his shirt before he gets here."

Katie appears close to tears, Mrs McNeill thought. "Katie, dear. Calm down. We can get the shirt finished, but if we shouldn't, there will be time after he comes. I'll help you put on the collar and do the buttonholes if you wish. I'll teach you how to do the collar on the next shirt you make him. We won't feel the time pressure then."

"Oh thank you, thank you so much. Can we start right now?"

"Yes dear. Let's get started. But try, instead of being anxious about the shirt, to give thanks that Brad is coming home safe. Look forward to his coming, and trust."

"Yes, Mene. That's what I should do. Why do I get so anxious about things?"

"Have you read the verse that says, 'Trust in the Lord with all your heart, and lean not on your own understanding?'"

"Yes, Mene. I've read it, but I don't do a great job of living it. My own understanding fails me over and over. There are more verses in Ephesians that tell me what to think about. They talk about all the good things, the things we have to be thankful for. I don't do a very good job of practicing thanksgiving either."

The two women took the shirt and returned to the Singer sewing machine. Mrs. McNeill sat down to sew, Katie observed closely. She'd missed a pattern piece, the neckband. She watched and learned as the experienced seamstress demonstrated.

Chapter 77: Last Rites

Brad turned in his report to General O.O. Howard early on October 20th. It had taken all of two days for him to finish it.

Thank you Corporal. I'd like you to attend a farewell dinner tonight here at the Fort. I'll give you your release papers then. You're free to pursue your own interests till 1700. Please be here by then. Tomorrow you'll be on your way home, wherever that might be.

"I'm going to Stone House to see my girl. What comes after that is still undecided."

Brad left the Fort on his horse and headed toward Boise City. He wanted to find a special gift for Katie; something that would show her how much he loved her; a reunion gift; or did he dare to hope it could be an engagement gift? The trip consumed several hours. He went to the first supply store he saw and inquired about where he could find jewelry items.

"Sorry, we don't have jewelry here," the clerk told him. "The best suggestion I have for you is that Mrs. Goldstein living just a few miles from here has a collection of old pieces, and sells to people she likes from time to time. Perhaps you could find something there. I'm telling you in advance, the jewelry will come dearly." The clerk gave Brad directions and Brad thanked him before mounting and riding in the direction indicated. He found Mrs. Goldstein's cabin and hitched his horse in front.

Mrs. Goldstein answered his knock.

"Good afternoon, Ma'am. My name is Brad Jennings. I've been told you might have jewelry for sale."

"I see you're wearing a cavalry uniform. I might consider selling to you. Tell me more about why you want the jewelry."

"Mrs. Goldstein, I've been in the cavalry for years. I'm finally mustering out. I've known the girl I love for most of those years, but we haven't been together a whole lot. She's waited patiently through my unexplained and prolonged absences, not knowing if I'd dropped off the face of the earth. I want to find something special for her. She loves me."

"Come in young man. I'll show you what I have. Mrs. Goldstein led Brad to a room that looked like a library and began opening small drawers in what looked like a specially designed chest. "Come close where you can see."

As Brad looked at the beautiful pieces, mostly brooches to pin on a coat or dress, Mrs. Goldstein explained their source and value. He didn't see what he wanted until the lady opened another drawer. It was filled with hair ornaments. He saw it immediately. A corrugated swirling silver mounting set with pearl and diamonds, combined to form a barrette meant to hold a heavy strand of hair. He imagined seeing it in Katie's beautiful long rusty-red locks. He envisioned her smile and her shining eyes when she first saw it and knew he'd bought it just for her.

"I'll take it," he said immediately. Whatever it cost he had to buy it for Katie.

Brad swallowed hard when he heard the price: he knew he would spend almost a third of his severance pay, and would have to scrimp for a long time, but it would be worth it. He watched as Mrs. Goldstein put the barrette in its box. "Is there a chance you could wrap it, fix it so it's pretty when I hand it to her?"

Mrs. Goldstein dug around in a drawer and found a small shiny piece of fabric, wrapped it around the box, stuck a small bauble to the box and waited for Brad to pay. "Thank you Mrs. Goldstein. It's beautiful."

Brad counted out the sum she asked; she re-counted it before she handed the box to him. He looked at his timepiece and noted that he would have to travel fast to get back to Fort Boise by 1700.

"Thank you so much Ma'am," he said, and rushed out the door.

He kicked his horse to a gallop and rode hard for thirty minutes, slowed the horse to a trot to let it rest a bit, and resumed the galloping pace. Brad made it to Fort Boise just a few moments before the appointed time.

He found a fairly large group of officers and enlisted men gathered in the dining room of the fort.

"Come in, Corporal Jennings, and be seated," General O.O. Howard invited. He turned and addressed the group. "May I present Corporal Brad Jennings? Corporal Jennings, along with Lieutenant Farrow, negotiated the end of the Sheepeaters' War. Lieutenant Farrow, will you rise and address the listeners?"

"Yes General. We had been following the Indians all over the Salmon River country without making progress. Corporal Jennings managed to make contact with Chief Tanmanmo by helping a wounded warrior and returning him to their village. His words and actions convinced the chief to gather the troublemakers and surrender them to us. I'd like to recommend Corporal Jennings for the Badge of Honor. His actions saved many lives."

"Thank you, Lieutenant Farrow. Your recommendations have been taken under advisement and approved. Corporal Jennings, please stand and receive your award."

Brad stood, and General Howard attached the Medal of Honor to Brad's uniform. "Corporal, we are proud of the work you have done. Even during your period Away without Leave, we find you were fulfilling the basic role we had assigned you, that of building peace between white men and Indian. We are erasing your Away without Leave record and crediting you with service under orders status. You will receive today your Honorable Discharge as well as your promotion to Sergeant. You are free to go home." The General handed a stack of papers to Brad. "God bless your life," the General said quietly to Brad as he received his release from service.

The General offered thanks and servers brought plates of food to the participants. A happy time of eating and visiting followed.

Now I can go home to Katie. Brad ate hungrily and received congratulations from the troops and commanders, overwhelmed that all past issues had been resolved. A thankful private citizen retired to his private room, and crawled under his covers on the hard cot.

Chapter 78: Homecoming

Mrs. McNeill completed the buttonholes on Brad's shirt, and handed it to Katie. "You finish the hem," she said.

Katie sat in the chair Mene had vacated and pinned the shirt hem in place. She stitched the seam to hold the folded fabric, removed the pins, and snipped off all the excess threads. "It's finished."

"Heat up the iron and press it carefully. Then put it on a hanger. It looks nice already, but the final pressing, done with love, will make it all the more special."

The shirt was beautifully done, thanks to Mene's help. Every plaid matched perfectly, down the shirt-front, on the front pockets, and down the side seams. Katie's heart overflowed with love as she thought of Brad wearing the shirt on which she had worked so hard. She felt sorry she hadn't been able to do the work alone, but there would be time in the future to learn the assembly process better. And that she also had the warm stocking cap and scarf she had knitted all by herself increased her anticipation. She was glad her gift would be ready when Brad returned. There would be more shirts in the future.

Katie was finishing the pressing job when she thought she heard a horse outside. She ran to the door wondering if it could be Brad. There he was, dismounting a strange horse. He looked exhausted and excited, all at the same time.

"Brad, she screamed, "O Brad, you're here!" She ran to him and wrapped her arms around him in a hug.

He finished securing the horse, and then turned her to face him, pulling her close. "Oh Katie, my dearest Katie, It seems like you're about as glad to see me as I am to see you." He pulled her closer, looked deeply into her eyes, and then kissed her tenderly. "I love you, Miss Katie Erickson, more than you will ever know. Then he turned away from her, removed a box from his saddlebag, and gave it to her. "This is a symbol of my forever love for you, Katie."

Katie opened the box and gasped. "It's so beautiful, Brad."

"They're diamonds and pearls, Katie, precious as my love for you. The jewels will be so lovely in your hair." Brad turned her around and released her hair. He ran his fingers through it and gathered it at the back of her head with the gorgeous hairpiece, turned her to face him, and said, "Do you think you could marry me someday, My Katie of Malheur Oregon Country?"

"Oh yes, Brad. I'll marry you, and love you forever too. I'm so glad you're home, you will stay now, won't you?"

"If Amanda and Lewis will have me, I'll stay. I'm hoping I can find a good job somewhere close. But if I can't find that job here, I'm taking you with me next time I leave."

"Come in the house, Brad. I have a gift for you. I made it; well almost. Mene helped me finish some of the hardest parts when you wrote and said you would be here so soon."

Katie led Brad into the house and headed straight for the dining room where the shirt hung on a hanger and the hanger on a hook. I made you a shirt Brad; the first of many I will make for you when I'm your wife. When you wear it, you will have my love to keep you warm."

"It means the world to me that you did all that work for me, Katie. I'll wear it every day because I'll always want to be warm in your love. Come here, my Katie of Malheur Oregon Country. And he kissed her again.

He loves me. Katie of Malheur Oregon Country he calls me. When did I become Katie of Malheur Oregon Country? It happened slowly, I guess. I've been here nearly seven years now.

Suddenly Katie realized that she'd become comfortable in this country. She knew the hills and valleys, the willow-lined rivers and streams. She loved the mist that covered Rinehart Butte in the early morning, the fragrance of sage in the sunshine, the multi-colored sunsets, and the star-filled skies at night.

She loved the variety of experience she'd had at Stone House, the occasional passing through of the army, the emigrants from the East who often stopped in for a meal, even the farmers' visits during the Bannock War when Stone House became their refuge. She'd met so many nice people who were following their dreams to the Northwest.

She'd loved the experiences with Tah-Mano, trying to teach her English and giving her the knowledge of the True God, learning about Indian ways, sharing things that would help her friend.

Most of all she loved the family she'd found. Her mom and dad were gone, along with her life at Tule

Lake. She'd loved them and the place she called home, and probably not appreciated her blessings enough. She would try to give a more mature love to her new family, Amanda and Lewis, Mrs. McNeill, Les and Al, but most of all to Brad. Somehow he'd become her family too, here in Malheur Oregon Country.

The End

Epilogue: Katie of Malheur

Though this book includes many historical events it is not to be considered a history, but if you know the history of Oregon you will recognize many historical names which are included in this story.

Amanda and Lewis Rinehart were real people who built Stone house in 1872 and lived in it during many of the years included in this book. I am not including any of their children in this story since I found the information on them too late for my work on this book.

Amanda and Lewis birthed three children: Carrie May, born in 1871 lived to be only four years old. Arthur, born in 1875 lived 77 years, and James, born in 1877, lived to be only eleven years old. The years Amanda and Lewis lived in Stone House must have been incredibly difficult. Amanda's parents lived in Summerville, Union County; Carrie Mae was born in Summerville the year before the construction of Stone House. Arthur was born in Idaho; Ancestry.com does not list a town. As I understand it, Amanda's parents operated the ferry at Glenns Ferry, Idaho for a time. I am guessing that Arthur was born at their home during their residence there. James was born in Vale very close to the time of the Bannock uprising.

The Army officers I have mentioned participated in the Bannock and Sheepeater wars or in some way in 'disciplining' the Indians for their depredations. Sarah Winnemucca's contributions to the Army are well documented in her book, Life Among the Piutes and Gae Whitney Canfield's *Sarah Winnemucca of the Northern Paiutes.*

Unfortunately the names and doubtful character traits of the Indian agents portrayed in this story are well-documented in history.

The main characters, Katie Erickson and Brad J. Jennings are fictional, as is Katie's membership in the Rinehart family. Tah Mano and her father, Chief Numaga, Bright Star, and Wovoka are fictional. (There was an Indian character named Wovoka who was significant in Indian history. I borrowed his name for the dream sequences in my story.)

Les and Al Vaughne are fictional characters based on two guys I know very well. Mrs. McNeill is based on a family friend of my childhood, the wonderful lady who made my wedding dress using a magazine picture as a pattern. I believe she actually lived in Stone House during my elementary and high-school years.

The villains in this book, Chiddless and his friends, are complete imaginations, I suppose, based on my knowledge that too many of our own race actually sold arms to the Indians and in general incited unrest between settlers and Native Americans.

The peddler who sorely tempted Katie to leave Malheur County is fictional, but many such characters brought pots and pans, fabrics, medicines, and such to outlying communities and found willing buyers.

The Indian education and feeding program I have included may have happened, but I found nothing to substantiate it. There were always people who had the Native people's welfare at heart, so I have included the program in my story.

You're probably wondering what happened to the Indians who were forced to leave their home country and make the hazardous journey to Yakima. They were detained in Yakima for five miserable years during which many of them died of starvation or the constant cold and lack of blankets. Those who were determined to return to their native country in Malheur County left after receiving permission from the Interior Department in late 1881. The Malheur Reservation had been closed but they were given permission to use food supplies that might be left on the premises. Sarah Winnemucca was appointed to oversee this operation. This information is taken from letters in Sarah Winnemucca's Life Among the Piutes.

I hope you enjoyed reading this book and that you know a bit more about the history that inspired it, as well as settlers' lives in the late 19th century.

Author Biography

Marjorie Vaughn Eldred spent the first twenty years of her life with a Vale, Oregon address. Her parents owned a dairy farm west of Vale and struggled to stretch the income it generated. She remembers well her years at Vale Elementary and Vale Union High School, and though now living in Washington State has enjoyed two reunions with her 1955 classmates.

Marjorie currently enjoys the *You Really Know You're from Vale Oregon when* group on Facebook, and would encourage those from Vale to join the group. Wonderful conversations about the past and numerous very interesting pictures and people are to be found there.

Marjorie is the author of three previous books: *Seizing the Treasure* which includes many of her experiences on the farm in Vale; *Journey from Addiction to Freedom: A Family's Prison Experience*; and *Blooms, Blunders and Blessings: Garden Stories I Just Had to Tell.*

Marjorie currently serves as Recorder for the Plateau Area Writer's Association. in Enumclaw, Washington.

She lives with her husband Clio near Buckley, Washington; when the "mountain is out" they enjoy Mt. Rainier's beauty each time they leave their community.

Other Books by Marjorie Eldred

Seizing the Treasure: 101 Nuggets to Warm Your Heart

Warm, fuzzy snippets of wonderful memories and heartbreaking suffering bound together in a multigenerational collection of cherished memories.

Journey from Addiction to Freedom: A Family's Prison Experience

Experience the heartbreak, regret, and courage of an imprisoned young woman as she persistently battles her way to a better life.

Blooms, Blunders, and Blessings: Garden Stories I Just Had to Tell

A celebration in poetry and prose of the joys to be found in nature's colors, shapes, and moods, intermingled with the woes of living near a woodland and unwittingly feeding your hard-earned blooms to the wildlife.

Links for personal Bible Study

http://www.wvbs.org/

https://www.worldbibleschool.org/

If you've read and enjoyed this book I'd appreciate it if you'd go to Amazon and review it. Or if you have other comments you'd like to make they would be appreciated also. Readers use reviews to help them in their buying decisions. Your experience with Katie of Malheur Oregon Country is also very important to me.

Thank you again,
Marjorie

33940786R00202

Made in the USA
San Bernardino, CA
14 May 2016